Tammy Robinson is a novelist from New Zealand. After the tragic deaths of her mother and a close friend, she sat down in 2011 to write a book and hasn't stopped since. She now has eight novels to her name and is working on the ninth. She lives with her husband and three young children on a small farm in rural Waikato.

By Tammy Robinson

Differently Normal
Photos of You
Back to You
Everything I Have

Everything I Have

tammy robinson

PIATKUS

PIATKUS

First published in Great Britain in 2023 by Piatkus

1 3 5 7 9 10 8 6 4 2

A CIP catalogue record for this book
is available from the British Library.

ISBN: 978-0-349-42531-3

Typeset in Garamond by M Rules

Printed and bound in Great Britain by
Clays Ltd, Elcograf S.p.A.

Papers used by Piatkus are from well-managed forests
and other responsible sources.

Piatkus
An imprint of
Little, Brown Book Group
Carmelite House
50 Victoria Embankment
London EC4Y 0DZ

An Hachette UK Company
www.hachette.co.uk

www.littlebrown.co.uk

To Bonnie and Deb,
the best Best Friends a girl could have ever had.

Ellie

This time she's dead for sure.

I rattle the door handle, being careful not to squish the contents of the brown paper bag I'm holding in one hand, and rap my knuckles on the glass. Louder, more insistent. It's a hard one to balance, getting enough volume to attract the attention of an eighty-two-year-old woman who refuses to accept her hearing isn't as sharp as it once was, while also trying to listen intently for any noises coming from within the house.

'Nan?'

Knock knock.

I try to peer through the lacy net curtains she insists on having because they help keep the flies out, but the whole point of them is to block prying eyes, so all I can make out is the outline of the couch against the pale wall behind it, and the window of the dining room.

'Nan!'

Finally, some movement. The hall door swings open and I watch as her figure potters into the lounge and towards the sliding door. While she fiddles with the dicky lock, I close my eyes and take a deep breath to slow my heart rate down. She's going to be the death of *me* one of these days, I'm not even kidding.

'Steady on,' she says, sliding the door open and pulling aside the nets. 'Where's the fire?'

Alfie pushes past her and starts sniffing the air around me enthusiastically. I drop a hand to his silky head and lift the paper bag out of his reach.

I blink at her nonchalant manner. 'Why was the door locked? And why did it take you so long to answer the door? I was worried you'd had another heart attack.'

'I was in the bath.'

For the first time I notice she's in her dressing gown. 'So? Since when do you lock the door when you're having a bath? You don't even normally shut the *bathroom* door, let alone shut up the house.'

She sniffs. 'Since that poor unsuspecting man copped an eyeful.'

I squeeze my eyes closed for a second, not sure I want to hear the answer to the question I'm about to ask. 'What have you done now?'

'Me? I've done nothing. Just been relaxing in the privacy of my own home. *He* was the one who came wandering up the wrong driveway. Certainly got more than he bargained on, that's for sure.' She chuckles. 'It's *his* heart you should be worried about. Never seen someone go so pale.'

'What man?'

She waves a hand dismissively. 'I don't know, some kind of salesman.'

Alfie's cold, damp nose snuffles its way into my hand as he inhales the delicious smells of my day. Nan, bored with the conversation already, turns and heads towards the kitchen.

I follow her inside, making sure to wipe my feet properly on the welcome mat first. My grandmother is as house-proud as they come. She decorated this place herself half a century ago, and despite the interior-design crazes that have come and gone since, she hasn't felt the urge to update the look. Everything is peach or pastel pink, sometimes both together, and made out of embroidered lace and satin. Even the artificial flowers in the vase on the sideboard are colours not usually seen in nature. Alfie trails after us, or more specifically, the paper bag. I place it on the bench and he sniffs at the air longingly.

'What was he selling?' I ask, pulling out one of the bar stools and perching on top.

'Who?'

'The salesman.'

'No idea. I couldn't understand a word he was saying.'

'Why, was he speaking another language?'

'No.'

I lift the paper bag up while she wipes underneath it, even though the Formica benchtop is as shiny and clean as the day it was installed. 'Then how do you not know what he was selling?'

She lines the sponge back up in its place beside the sink, and sighs exasperatedly. 'He was going on about nets, and fibres and cables. I think he might have been . . .' her nose scrunches up, 'a *knitting* salesman?'

It takes about four seconds for me to connect the dots, and when I do, I have to suppress a smile. 'Do you think, maybe, that he might possibly have been from a company that sells internet services? Like an internet service provider?'

'How should I know? He should say so if that's the case.'

'I suspect he tried.'

'Well, whatever he was selling, I told him I wasn't interested, and off he went.'

'Probably to the nearest bar to have a stiff whisky if he really did see you in the nude.'

She points a shaky finger at me. 'I'll have you know I was quite the looker in my time.'

'Yes, *your* time . . . which was a long time ago.'

'Oh ha ha. You can laugh. Time and gravity catches up with us all. You might have a gorgeous little figure now – which you have *me* to thank for, by the way – but one day you'll be scaring salesmen away too,' she warns.

'No I won't, because I'm not going to be walking around my house *naked* when I'm eighty-two.'

'It's my house. If I want to air out my bits, I'll do so. It's good for them.'

'Eww, Nan.'

'Speaking of bits . . .' Her tone shifts. 'He was quite nice-looking, for a salesman. Nice eyes. Kind smile.'

I cringe. 'Please tell me you didn't.'

She blinks innocently. 'Didn't want?'

'Set me up on a blind date with a stranger.'

'Of course I didn't.'

My shoulders sag with relief. 'Thank God.'

'Only because he was already married.'

'Nan!'

'Well excuse me for looking out for my granddaughter's happiness,' she says. 'You've been on what, four dates this summer? Home by eleven every time, and not one of them came back with you.'

'Have you been spying on me?'

'Of course,' she replies, completely unabashed.

'That is wrong on so many levels. Anyway, it was three dates, and I can't help if I wasn't attracted to any of them.'

'You're too fussy, that's your problem.'

'I'm not fussy, I'm just not going to settle for someone who doesn't do it for me.'

'Ellie, they'd all have done *it* for you if you'd given them half a chance.'

'We are not having another conversation about sex.'

'Why not? You think your mother was immaculately conceived?'

'La-la-la-la-la, not listening.' I stick my fingers in my ears until she stops talking. 'Anyway, I'm perfectly happy with you and Alfie.' At the mention of his name, his ears prick up hopefully. His eyes have barely left the paper bag.

'An octogenarian and a dog who spends most of the day licking his own arse.' She arches her eyebrows. 'Aren't you the lucky one.'

5

'I'm happy.'

'You could be happier.'

'Yes, I could, if you stop trying to set me up with any man who crosses your path.'

'What's wrong with that mechanic guy you used to go out with? Oh, what's his name?'

I feel my stomach tighten. 'Logan.'

'That's the one. You two were love's young dream once. The whole town thought you'd end up married with a family.'

'Yeah, well, the whole town was wrong. It was a teenage crush that fizzled out like most teenage crushes do. We're ancient history,' I say brusquely, in an attempt to shut the conversation down. It fails. When it comes to my love life, Nan is relentless.

'Doesn't have to be,' she says. 'I saw the way he was watching you at Chloe's engagement party.'

'The way he watches me,' I point out, 'is inappropriate. He has a girlfriend.'

'Girlfriend or not, he still has feelings for you. It's as obvious as the nose on my face.'

'Any feelings he might have are not reciprocated,' I say, hopping off the stool and pushing it back underneath the bench. 'Logan and I were over a long, *long* time ago, OK? So, and I mean this in the nicest possible way, keep your obvious nose to yourself. Oh, and stop molesting perfect strangers to see if they'll date me. It's humiliating.'

She sighs. 'It's not that I don't love having you back here,' she says. 'You know I do. But I can't help feeling guilty about everything you've given up. Whatever you say, I know how much you loved your job and the glamorous lifestyle that came with it.'

'You didn't ask me to give up my job,' I remind her. 'It was my choice and I did it willingly. You're more important to me than any job. Besides, don't believe everything you see on the TV. It's not as glamorous as it looks.'

I feel a pang, though, even as I say it. I mean every word: my grandmother *is* more important to me than anything. But she's right. I did love my job as head chef on a superyacht, and I worked bloody hard to get as far as I did. Starting as a lowly steward on a smaller yacht in the Mediterranean, I worked long hours for little pay for eight months before a French chef named Christophe took a chance on my burgeoning interest in learning to cook. A no-nonsense kind of guy, he was impressed by my work ethic and the fact that I stayed out of the typical onboard drama: the excess drinking and crew jumping from one bed to another. In my time off, I'd hang around his galley, watching and learning, and after a few months of that, he hired me as his assistant and we moved to a bigger yacht sailing out of the Caribbean.

I spent the next two years learning the intricacies of five-star cuisine from him, before he retired. On his recommendation, the yacht's owners promoted me to be his replacement. It was a huge responsibility; after all, clients paid upwards of $140,000 to hire the yacht for just one week, so they expected, and deserved, the best. I quickly earned industry respect and was headhunted twice for higher-paid jobs on even more expensive superyachts, but when Nan's health took a turn for the worse and she ended up in hospital, I knew it was time to come home. It wasn't easy leaving that life behind, but I've never regretted the decision. Not once. My grandmother is the only family I have left. Nothing's as important as that. *Nothing.*

'Anyway,' she carries on, waving a hand in the air, 'you don't need to worry about me any more. I'm as good as I was before the heart attack, maybe even better thanks to all the "lifestyle changes" the doctor had me make.' She mutters the two words darkly.

'Those changes are keeping you alive.'

'Go back to the boats, I'll be fine.'

'No. I'm staying right here. And I'm getting tired of having this same conversation over and over.'

She changes tack. 'I just want you to be happy.'

'I told you, I *am* happy.'

'Settled down, then. Married, with children. This town is too small, you're not going to meet anyone here. Not anyone decent, anyway.'

'If it's meant to happen, it will. I'm not in any rush.'

'Fine.' She throws her hands up in defeat. 'Ignore my dying wish.'

'You're not dying any time soon,' I say, fervently hoping I'm right.

Her face softens. 'I'm not planning on it, no. But you know no one has control over these things. When I *do* die, I want to go knowing that you're OK.'

'There's more to life than finding a husband.'

'You know what I mean.'

Leaning over, I give her a kiss on the cheek, and her skin rustles like paper. 'I'm staying right here with you. No arguments. Now, do you need me to do anything before I take Alfie for a run?'

She eyes the paper bag hopefully. 'Is that for me?'

'It's Wednesday, isn't it?' I slide it halfway towards her. She pulls it the rest of the way and picks it up cautiously, like we're doing a drug deal. Unrolling the top, she peers inside.

She has a wicked sweet tooth, my nan, and before I came back, she'd think nothing of having a cup of tea and a large slice of cake with buttercream icing for her dinner. No point cooking a proper meal for one, she protested when I discovered just how bad things had gotten. Not a single vegetable in the fridge, but seven kinds of cheeses, four processed meat products, and far too many biscuits, chocolate or otherwise. Out it went, all of it, and now I make sure she eats the foods the doctors recommend. Green leafy vegetables. Fruit smoothies. Wholegrain crackers and bread. Low-fat cheese, margarine and milk. I *do* allow her the occasional treat, though, every Wednesday, otherwise I'd never hear the end of it. And because I happen to agree with her when she says there has to be some enjoyment in life.

'Ooh,' she coos when she clocks the cream-filled jam doughnut inside the bag. 'Jackpot. Thanks, love.'

'Savour it,' I say, reaching for Alfie's leash, which hangs on a hook with various old keys and a cap that used to belong to my grandfather. 'Because if you try and set me up with a stranger again, I'll completely cut off the supply.'

9

'You wouldn't.'

'Try me.'

I head out to the back yard, where my home is. Some people might consider living in an old railway carriage in your grandmother's yard at the ripe old age of twenty-nine to be a bit . . . tragic. Once upon a time I'd probably have thought the same. When I was five, my mother and I moved here after my parents' divorce left her with no money and nowhere else to go. She hated returning to the small town in which she grew up. Hated it with a passion. Saw it as a sign of her failure in life. Divorced. A single mother. It ate away at her, and though I can't be sure it caused the cancer that grew in her bowel, it probably didn't help. She died when I was eight, and I barely remember her. Afterwards, my father made a token offer for me to come and live with him and his new family, but Nan's house was where I felt most at home, where I belonged. Besides, I didn't want to leave her alone after the death of her only daughter.

I bought and renovated the carriage myself when I moved back two years ago, because as much as I adore my grandmother, I knew that the two of us living under the same roof was a recipe for disaster. We are both independent, stubborn women, and we both need our own space. When I saw the carriage come up in an online auction, I fell in love with it straight away and knew I had to have it, despite the fact that it was run-down, leaking and full of spiders and dead birds. It took me almost eight months to get it to a liveable standard, doing some of the work myself but also relying on friends and the odd tradesman. We stripped it right back and then rebuilt it into the snug, waterproof home it is today. My bedroom, complete with a tiny en suite, is down one end, the kitchen sits in the middle, and a living area fills the other end. It even has a small fireplace to keep the place warm in winter. It's small and cosy, but I've lived in ship's cabins and slept in bunk beds that were *much* smaller, so to me the space feels luxurious. Every time I step inside, I feel instantly calm.

Sam

The potholes on the road leading over to the peninsula are even bigger than I remember, and I wince as the car hits a particularly deep one. I check the rear-view mirror in case the blow has knocked something off the undercarriage of the car, but there's nothing left sitting in the road behind, thank God, and I exhale gratefully. The car's a rental, and the insurance excess that the guy behind the counter rattled off disinterestedly as he brushed over the contract was eye-watering. The old me would have challenged it, demanded a cheaper rate, but the new me knows there are far more important things in life to worry about. Besides, that mere three-hour nap I had on an eleven-hour flight will catch up with me before too long, and I'd rather have my head on a pillow when it does.

There's also the fact that I've been dreading this moment for the past four months, ever since I made the decision to pack up my life and come back here. Now that I'm close to my final destination, I have an overwhelming urge to just hurry up and *get there*. Get it over with quickly, like ripping off a Band-Aid. I come around a bend and there it is. Seclusion Bay. Picturesque, with its white sand beach and blue waters. The town itself is small, four blocks of trendy little shops, surrounded by residential suburbs. It's expanded quite a bit since I was last here, I notice as I drive through, my stomach a ball of mixed feelings.

Jesus. I was expecting my grandfather's place to look neglected – as far as I'm aware, no one has been out here for a couple of years at least, since his death – but still, I'm taken aback as I pull into the driveway and the full state of it is revealed. It's unkempt. The garden's overrun with weeds, the trees are taller, the bushes . . . bushier. As for the lawn . . . well. I'm not even sure a normal lawnmower will be up to *this* task. It's my fault, I should have organised someone to look after it, but it was a case of out-of-sight, out-of-mind. I cast my mind back to how it looked when my grandparents lived here and feel ashamed. Someone else I've let down, even though they're not alive to see it.

Turning the engine off, I'm tempted to stay in the car and close my eyes – the jet lag and months of sleepless nights have taken their toll – but I know I'd merely be prolonging the inevitable. Being back here after all this time is hard enough, for many reasons. I don't want to think about what I've left behind, or how I've uprooted my life as I've known it for the last six years. It still doesn't feel real, but then again, not much has these past couple of years.

The air is warm and sticky when I climb out of the car and

13

stretch my back, hearing a *pop* of protest. I swear to God, airline seats have shrunk in size since I first travelled overseas, years ago. Either that or the human race has doubled in size, which is entirely possible. I've certainly grown. I left a young man, fresh out of university, eager to explore the world. I've returned older, jaded, weary. Not fat, though. Any excess weight I might have been carrying has peeled off since the funeral. My appetite just isn't the same when faced with cooking for only one.

I become aware of a low hum and realise the twilight cricket chorus is warming up. Soon they'll fill the night air with their song, at once both soothing and deeply annoying. From experience, I know that in a few nights I'll barely even notice them any more. Their sound will become part of the background, just as the sound of the waves rushing the beach will, and the sound of twenty-four-hour traffic did back in the city I have just left behind. When I first moved there, I thought I'd never be able to sleep again. But I got used to it.

I haven't been here in ten years, and yet the smell of salt in the air is at once familiar. I'd recognise the scent of this beach anywhere in the world. Something stirs in my stomach, reminding me that as much as I don't want to be back here, I once loved this place.

I get my bags out of the back seat of the car and close the door. The alarm chirrups when I push the button. I just need to get inside. Blow off the cobwebs. Pop the cap off one of the beers I purchased at the superette, and sleep. After that . . . I have no idea.

The house is still a shrine to my grandmother and her minimalist Scandinavian tastes. My grandfather's were more eclectic, thanks to his travels, but he adored my grandmother to the bones, so whatever made her happy made him happy. Consequently, everything is either white or wooden, with occasional pops of grey. It always felt a bit sterile to me, though sandy tracks across floorboards never bothered my grandmother and her broom. I head for the one room I always felt at home in, pausing with my hand on the door handle to mutter a silent plea that nothing has been changed since his death.

Nothing *has* changed. It's messier, definitely, but after my grandmother died of breast cancer, there was no one left to prompt my grandfather into keeping anything tidy. Stacks of books teeter on the desk, and on the little side table beside the old yellow couch. Its seat is still sunken from the weight of him and the many hours he spent there. I can almost make out the imprint of his behind. Everything is coated with a thin layer of dust, or sand. A mixture of both, probably. Even though the house has been locked up tight, the beach has a habit of finding its way in through cracks under doorways and loose window panes, the same way it has a habit of finding its way into your soul.

I trail a finger along the edge of his desk, disturbing the dust, and picture him there, with the light of the little brass lamp pooling on the large map of the world that covers the surface. It sits under a glass layer, to preserve it from time and the grubby fingerprints of grandchildren.

He would call me in and we'd huddle together on the

oversized black chair while he pointed out all the beaches in all the countries around the world where he had surfed when he was younger. Like a pirate, he'd fill my head with tales of lands far away, of people made of sand and salt, of nights around campfires, rum-soaked songs lifted on balmy air to the starry heavens. Of waves as tall as skyscrapers and water every shade of blue and green you could possibly imagine. It wasn't all magical, though. He'd also ghoulishly describe all the gory injuries he'd seen. A calf muscle sliced to the bone by a wayward fin. Skin peeled away by coral, nerves exposed, agonising screams. Bones snapped by angry waves. One friend left paralysed after being dumped on his head. Another friend, Neil, shot in the chest by robbers somewhere in South America.

He was thirty-one when he travelled to Hoddevik in Norway to surf and met my grandmother in a bar in Oslo. Before she even finished pouring his drink he was in love, or so he would tell the story. He couldn't explain how he knew, other than it was simply a certainty that he felt in his head and in his heart. He *knew* he'd met the woman he would marry. And he did.

To a young boy, it all sounded tremendously exciting, and I yearned to follow in his adventurous footsteps. It seems a preposterous idea now, that kind of life, but years ago, clutching my freshly printed structural-engineer qualification, I boarded a plane to Hong Kong, determined to carve out my own adventure. I never made it any further. Six months after I arrived, I fell in love with a woman named Mei, and two years after that, we were married. It was a good marriage. A happy marriage. We lived a pleasant life, and had begun making plans for the future.

Almost two years ago, she was crossing the road when she was hit by a car driven by an elderly man who should never have been behind the wheel. Confused, he accelerated when he should have braked. My wife died on a street corner, her hand held by a stranger. I never got to say goodbye.

Ellie

The sun is a fuzzy peach bobbing on the horizon as I head back around the last little jutting headland and onto the main beach, pulling the AirPods from my ears and tucking them into my shorts pocket as I slow my pace down. I touch my smartwatch to turn off the music, and am pleased to see that my time for the four and a half kilometres was a little faster than usual, probably because I was in a hurry thanks to the late start.

There are still a few people around, although barely any compared to a few weeks ago, when the summer influx of crowds was here for New Year. Seclusion Bay lives up to its name for ten months of the year, but December and January it *heaves* under an invasion of out-of-towners, here for the beautiful beaches and a nostalgic slice of small-town life.

Visually, Seclusion Bay appears part of an island, although technically it's not really an island, not by the dictionary definition. A sliver of land called an isthmus connects us to the mainland. It's narrow, no more than fifty metres wide. The road along it is flanked by the sea on both sides, and in summer, when traffic is particularly heavy, it bottlenecks as four lanes on the mainland taper off to the two older ones that run across to our town. It was never designed for that amount of traffic, and it shows. The council keep plugging the potholes that develop every summer, but it's a temporary fix only, and at some point soon they'll have to redo the whole road, with a plan to widen it when they do.

For those two high-summer months, the streets fill with cars and the cafés, bars and shops with people as holidaymakers arrive at the motor camp and the increasing number of new-build holiday homes on our small patch of land. Some local residents even list their properties on Airbnb for the summer and bugger off elsewhere. It's a great way to make a lot of money fast *and* avoid the crowds. In fact, most of the businesses here make the bulk of their yearly earnings over the summer, at least enough to see them through the leaner winter months when barely anyone visits.

For the most part, the people who flock here are well behaved. Because while we may be a fashionable destination, in a niche kind of way, thankfully there's a much hotter place to be up the coast. Only a half-hour drive from here, Whitehaven Beach is longer, sandier and more family-swim-friendly thanks to the gentle slope of the sea floor. The town is also bigger, with more brand-name shops, always popular with the younger crowd.

'Hey, Ellie, nice run?'

I turn to see Keith, one of the ageing hippies who've lived here since the dawn of time, heading into the water, his board tucked underneath his arm. He's the kind of guy who says 'Cowabunga, dude' without a trace of irony. Harmless and completely at peace in his little corner of the world.

'Yeah, it was, thanks,' I reply, reaching down to unclip Alfie from his leash. He quivers in anticipation, and as soon as I release him he's off, galloping towards the water like he was a greyhound in a previous life, ears flapping in the wind, tongue lolling out of the side of his mouth. He hits the water and bounds joyfully through the foamy shallows. It's hands-down his favourite part of our run, and he's earned it.

I tip my head towards the open water. 'Looks like it's starting to go off out there,' I say to Keith. 'Enjoy.'

He winks at me. 'I always do. See you in the morning?'

'You know it. Bright and early, where else would I be?'

I watch Keith paddle out for a few minutes, keeping one eye on Alfie, who has bounded over to a group of kids. One of them picks up a bit of driftwood and hurls it for him to fetch. If he's hoping Alfie will bring it back to him, he's going to be disappointed. Giving back balls/sticks/anything-he's-not-supposed-to-have-in-his-mouth is one trick Alfie has never quite mastered. Instead, he'll make you chase *him* and attempt to prise the object from his clenched jaws. Sure enough, he dives on the stick and streaks off down the beach, howling children chasing him. I'm not worried. He'll come back eventually. He always does.

I watch Keith carving up a wave offshore, his white track like a vein through a slab of deep green marble. The water looks enticing. Inviting. I figure, why not? Taking off my shoes and socks, I tuck my watch and AirPods into the toe of a shoe and stuff a sock on top.

The sand underfoot is warm from the sun, the water as refreshing as always. I walk out, jumping through the waves. When I'm deep enough, I dive underneath the water, trailing my hand through the soft sand on the seabed. Filtered sunlight scatters down from the surface, as if beamed through a prism. A small school of tiny fish dart away, over to my right. Surfacing, I flip onto my back and float on top of the water for a few moments, loving the feeling of weightlessness. A wave swells underneath me on its way to shore, and I bob over it like a cork. Heavy breathing alerts me to Alfie's presence at my side, stick still in his mouth, his eyes alight with pure unadulterated joy. He's a sea creature, same as me, and not for the first time I thank my lucky stars that I grew up in this place.

Feeling revived after our swim, Alfie and I head out of the water and I claim my shoes. Putting wet feet back into socks is an impossible task, as I've learned from experience, but the roads towards home have gentle, dry grass verges, so I hold a shoe in each hand and head towards the access track. As I do, something, a sixth sense perhaps, makes me turn my head and look towards a house a few hundred metres away.

A man is standing at the bottom of the lawn, where the grass bleeds into beach tussock. He is too far away for me to make out his features, but there's something oddly familiar about him. I watch as he whirls around and heads back into the house, closing the door behind him. A light comes on inside and then a curtain is drawn, dimming it. I'm so shocked that I just stand there for a minute or two. It happened so quickly that I could almost believe I'd imagined it, but the light around the curtain is proof that I didn't.

It can't be . . . can it?

Sam

My first night back in Seclusion Bay is a restless one. I'd hoped that jet lag and the sea air might do the trick and knock me out, but no. I still toss and turn into the early hours, watching the light from the moon outside slink across a ceiling that is both achingly familiar and completely strange.

What am I doing back here? Apart from the obvious answer, which is that I have nowhere else to go. I am a man without a home. A husband without a wife.

Hong Kong felt . . . wrong after her death. Still, I stayed as long as I could, because it was the only place in the world that she and I had known together. Our home, her favourite shops, our regular restaurant. These places were all painful reminders of her, and yet reminders were what I craved the most. Not in a sadistic, poke-at-the-wound kind of way. I found that being places she had also been brought a small measure of comfort. A temporary antidote to the pain of my loss.

In the months after her death, I *needed* to feel that pain; in fact I deliberately sought it out. There's no rulebook, as I discovered, for the grief of losing a spouse. No measure of control over how you feel, or how you react. The first time I realised that I hadn't thought of her in an hour, I hated myself. Was I forgetting her already? It seemed so disloyal to her memory. And the first time I woke up to find I had encroached onto her side of the bed, I was angry. It was *her* side. Even if she'd never lie there again.

In the end, my hand was forced by world events. Sure, my homecoming would have happened eventually, but it was only when it became untenable to stay that I knew it was time to leave. Time to head home with my tail between my legs, an adventure abandoned, having never really got off the ground. The relief I felt, though, as I sat at the gate in the airport waiting to leave, was proof that actually I did want – need – to leave Hong Kong. For my own mental health.

When I pull back the curtains in the lounge, the brilliant morning sun falls on the unopened six-pack of beers where I left them on the kitchen island. I didn't feel like one in the end, after my tour of the house – and the past – the night before. It culminated in a barefoot walk across the overgrown lawn to drink in the sight of the beach. There were very few people around, which was good. I felt like a failure coming back here, after I'd been so adamant all those years ago that I'd never return. But all of that seemed so trivial now.

Just as I turned to come back inside, a flicker of blonde hair caught my eye, further up the beach towards town. A woman emerging from the ocean, reaching up to free her hair from the constraints of a ponytail as the shallow water swirled around her legs as if begging her to stay. Hair freed, she flicked her head a few times, the long, wet tendrils slapping around her neck, falling down her back.

I knew a woman with hair that colour once. A girl. This wasn't her, I was sure. She'd be long gone by now. But the reminder took my breath away for a moment, and I was almost tempted to get back in the car and leave this town and all those memories behind. But where would I go?

Ellie

'Here you are, Keith, latte to go.'

'Thanks, Ellie,' he says, taking his reusable cup from me. 'Mahalo.'

His hair is already wet from his morning surf. His wetsuit peeled down to his waist, the empty arms dripping seawater onto the concrete floor. He turns to leave, but then lingers by the cabinet instead. I wait. It's a game we play every day.

'Something else I can get you?' I ask.

He scratches his ribs absent-mindedly. 'Oh just looking at all this food. You sure make it tempting, don't you.'

I reach for the tongs and a paper bag and slide open the door on the back of the cabinet. 'Let me guess, neenish tart?'

'Yeah, go on,' he sighs. 'And a sausage roll, too. I'll call it an early lunch.'

'I'll put it on your tab.' I smile, handing him the bags. He thanks me again and heads outside to where his board is leaning against one of the outside tables.

'That's the breakfast rush over,' Kelly comments from over near the window, where she's wiping down a recently vacated table.

'Mm,' I agree. 'Looks like it.'

It's a tough one. I need the money that the hectic Christmas and New Year crowds bring in, of course, but I'm still not used to the noise and chaos that comes with them. On the yachts, I worked behind the scenes, but here I'm very much front of house too, and it's been a big adjustment. I prefer these tail-end-of-summer mornings, when most of the holiday crowd have left, bar a few stragglers, and it's back to the usual local crowd. The pace is easier on all of us: Kelly taking orders, making the coffees, waiting on and clearing the tables; Maxine and Luke out back, preparing the meals and washing the dishes. I float between the two worlds where needed, but prefer the sanctuary of the kitchen.

Maxine is my full-time, year-round chef. She's been working here almost fifteen years, long before I owned the place, and is so much a part of the furniture that when I bought the business, the previous owner wrote her into the contract as one of the chattels. Luke joins us over the summer break from university, where he's studying medicine. He plans on being an emergency doctor in a few years' time, but for now he's happy loading the industrial dishwasher and assisting Maxine and me when needed. He's a diligent worker, never late, and saves every penny he earns towards his living costs for the rest of the year. I pay him generously, far more than any of the other cafés would, but I know what it's like to be out in the world on your own, and after working with all sorts of flaky people on the yachts, I'm impressed by his work ethic. Kelly is a local girl, late teens, not long out of school, still trying to figure out what it is she wants to do with her life. When I hired her four months ago, I could only guarantee her a job over the summer, so the departure of the crowds isn't quite as welcome to her as it is to me.

Buying the café was one of those fortuitous moments that occasionally the universe drops into your lap. I used to work here while still at high school, a summer weekend job. So I already knew the owner, Bev. When I first came back, I wasn't sure what I was going to do or even how long I'd be back for, just that I needed to be here for Nan. A conversation with Bev one day while she was making my coffee order led to phone conversations with lawyers, contracts being drawn up and signatures scrawled. Turned out she'd been looking to retire, but only if she knew the business was going to someone who'd love it the way she had. And I do, but it was terrifying at first, knowing that people were now depending on me. Maxine and her husband, Trevor, have a disabled adult child in their care. Trevor can't work because of an old back injury, so they rely on her income. I bought the café knowing I had to make sure it remained a success. And touch wood, so far I have.

'I guess you won't be needing me for much longer,' Kelly says, coming back behind the counter and tucking the spray bottle and cloth on the shelf underneath the till. 'Caleb said the campground has almost emptied out; just a few tents and vans left.'

'Yeah, I'm really sorry. I wish I could keep you on, but . . .' I shrug.

'It's fine,' she says. 'I totally understand. The supermarket was advertising for cashiers again the other week, I'll hit Jacob up for a job there. He's, like, trainee manager or something.'

'Jacob?'

'That guy I hooked up with on New Year's Eve, remember? I told you about him.'

'Ah, yes. That's right. That guy.'

She grins at me. 'Yeah, *that* guy. The one with the *really* big—'

Seeing a shadow fall near the door as someone slows down outside to enter, I cut her off quickly. 'I remember.'

'Like, proper massive.' She smirks. I love Kelly, she's a sweetheart, she really is. But she has a habit of oversharing every little detail of her personal life, even the ones that really shouldn't be shared. Then again, maybe it's just what young women do nowadays and I'm out of touch.

Sensing the customer approach the counter, I turn, my smile at the ready. 'Good mor—'

The words die a silent death in my throat, the syllables swallowed, unsaid. He's older, no doubt about it, but it's unmistakably him.

Sam

By the time I see her, I'm too far inside the café to flee without it being obvious. But oh God, I wasn't prepared for this, not at all, and judging by her shell-shocked look, having my face loom in front of her was the last thing she was expecting this morning too.

My whole body goes rigid, in a state of shock, and I stumble, even though the floor is smooth concrete beneath my feet. It's her, Ellie. The girl who was once my best friend in the entire world. The girl I would have done anything for. The first girl to break my heart.

Now, though, she's all woman. My eyes drink in the sight of her, as if they've been parched for too long. She's wearing a sleeveless black T-shirt, and her shoulders are tanned and athletic. Her long hair is tied back in a loose ponytail, but it's the same colour as I remember, a golden blonde like the sand on the beach, streaked with lighter shades bleached by the sun.

30

I realise it *was* her on the beach last night, and my lips curl involuntarily at the memory of her emerging from the water, her second home.

Every cell inside me urges me to step forward, to touch her, check that she's real and not some figment of my imagination brought on by being back in this town. But there's no mistaking it. She says my name, and I know she's real. Her chest and shoulders rise and fall with each breath she takes, and I wonder if she always breathes so fast or whether it's because of me. There is a light sheen on her bare arms. Sunscreen, probably. She always was fastidiously SunSmart. Without thinking, I sniff the air, searching for the familiar smell of Hawaiian tropic that I associate with her; a heady mix of coconut and exotic fruit. But all I can smell is coffee and food.

'Sam?' she says again, as if she can't quite believe what her eyes are telling her.

'Ellie,' I say. My heart is racing, but I force a casualness I don't feel. 'Hi. You look ... well.' I flick a glance up at the menu board, trying to gather my thoughts. 'Can I get a double espresso to go, please.'

She doesn't move, doesn't answer, just stares at me as if I'm a ghost, which I am. A ghost from her past who has just walked in and ordered a drink from her as if the last ten years have been nothing but the blink of an eye.

'Sure.' A girl standing next to her jumps into action. I hadn't even noticed her until then. 'Did you bring a cup with you?'

'No, I'm sorry, I didn't realise I needed to.' I frown. She's younger than Ellie, in her late teens perhaps.

'You don't *need* to,' she says. 'It's just that we give you fifty cents off if you bring in your own. Reusable ones only, though, none of that Styrofoam crap.'

'Ah, I see. I'm happy to pay the full price,' I tell her. I'll pay anything if it gets me out of here faster.

'OK.' She looks curiously between Ellie and me as if she has sensed the tension. 'We do sell reusable, recyclable cups. Would you like to see them?'

'No,' I say, acutely aware that Ellie hasn't stopped staring at me. It takes all my willpower not to look at her. I know that if I do, I'll crumble. For the past ten years I've thought about the possibility of this moment happening, but imagining it was not the same as actually seeing her. 'I'm in a bit of a rush, so if you could just . . .' I gesture to the machine, aware that I sound rude but too flustered to worry about that right now.

She shrugs. 'Sure thing.'

Ellie finally speaks again. 'When did you get back?'

'Yesterday.'

'Why?'

'It's . . . personal.'

Her eyes widen, and I know why. Once upon a time, there were no secrets between us. We were as close as two people can be. An image creeps into my mind, twelve-year-old Ellie, lanky and lean, her nose freckled from the sun. The two of us lying on our backs in the dunes, hidden from beachgoers by long blades of tussock. Hours passing as we talked about everything and nothing. Ellie rolling over to nestle beside me, her face on my chest, her long hair tickling my chin. Asking me to promise that we'd always be best friends, for ever. The reply slipping effortlessly from my lips, emphatic.

Of course. I promise.

With great effort, I focus on the girl's movements as she bangs the grinder on the machine and starts preparing my coffee. In my head, I will her to work faster. I need to get out of here. It's too much. I can't deal with this right now, not on top of everything else. The last time I saw Ellie, she was crying as I walked away from her, both of us having said horrible things, things that couldn't be taken back. What the hell is she still doing here?

'Here you go.' The girl finally plonks a cup on the counter in front of me, pressing down to make sure the lid is on properly. Steam rises out of the little sip hole, as well as the tantalising scent of coffee that makes my nostrils flare and my stomach growl with anticipation. 'That'll be four dollars fifty.'

I pull my wallet out of my back pocket, tapping my card on the screen when the amount flashes up, conscious the whole time of Ellie's eyes on me. Without waiting for the transaction to complete, I pick up the cup. 'Thanks,' I say to the girl. I tilt my head to Ellie and give a tight smile as I turn to leave.

'Sam, wait,' she says, but I ignore her and keep walking, hoping she won't follow.

Ellie

I watch him walk away, feeling utterly confused. That's it? After all this time, *that's* how our reunion goes? Not once, in all the scenarios I have imagined since I last saw this man a decade ago, did I imagine it would happen like this. Not even close. Because just like that, he's gone, leaving me standing there blinking at the space that mere seconds ago was filled by him.

Oh hell no.

'Hold the fort,' I tell Kelly, untying the little black apron from my waist and throwing it on the counter. 'I'll be back soon.'

'No worries,' she replies. 'Hey, who *was* that guy?'

'An old friend,' I say, heading for the door.

He's moving surprisingly fast and is already standing on the kerb, checking for traffic and preparing to cross. He's obviously forgotten the slower pace life tends to move at in this town.

I hear Kelly call out, 'Wait, a friend? Or a *friend* friend?' But I ignore her.

Sam steps onto the tarmac and hurries off.

'Sam!'

I break into a jog, catching up with him just as he reaches the pavement on the other side of the road, outside the entrance to the hardware shop. I touch his elbow, and he reacts as if I've just poked him with a cattle prod, whipping his arm away, spilling his coffee in the process.

'Dammit,' he mutters, shaking the hand that's just been splashed by the scalding liquid.

'Sorry,' I say, ignoring the small part of me that isn't sorry at all. 'Didn't you hear me calling you?'

'Obviously not.' He wipes his hand on his T-shirt, frowning.

I give him a sceptical look. 'I was pretty loud.'

Finally he looks up. 'What do you want, Ellie?'

'I don't know . . .' I trail off, still trying to believe it's actually him. That he's standing right here in front of me, large and real. He's so close I can see the flecks of indigo in his blue eyes. I remember now how up close they look like the surface of a turbulent ocean. His hair is a little darker than it used to be, not quite as blonde, and his skin is pale, like he hasn't been in the sun for a very long time. I remember the deep tan he used to have, the scattering of freckles across his shoulders.

'Look,' he says, 'I'm just here to sell my grandfather's house and then I'll be gone again. So how about we just pretend we didn't see each other.'

'Is that really what you want?'

He nods. 'I think it's for the best.'

'Well *I* think it's just weird, and that you're being silly.'

35

He looks amused briefly. 'Silly.'

'Yes. Silly. I know things kind of went a bit horrible back then . . .'

He snorts. 'Understatement.'

' . . . but,' I continue, glaring at him, 'we're both adults now. Surely we can act like it.'

'Put it this way, if I had known you were still working at the café, I wouldn't have come in.'

I wince. 'Wow. Ouch.'

'Now that I *do* know you work there, I'll find somewhere else to get coffee next time. OK?'

'Oh yeah? Well, good luck with that,' I retort, stinging from his condescending tone. 'I have the best damn coffee in town.'

He shrugs.

I cross my arms over my chest. 'I'm not going to spit in your drink, if that's what you're worried about.'

A small smirk tugs at the corner of his lips before they straighten back into a line. 'I should hope not. That would be disgusting, and also detrimental to business.'

'Look, regardless of . . . everything,' I say stiffly, 'I just wanted to say that I'm sorry about your grandfather. I know how much he meant to you.'

His expression becomes unreadable. 'Thank you.'

'He was such a character. I thought of him when I was surfing on the Lofoten Islands.'

He looks briefly stunned. 'You went to Norway?'

'I did. I mean, I know we always planned on going there

together one day, but after you took off the way you did, I decided to go on my own. Have you made it there yet?'

'No.'

'Shame.' I feel a dart of satisfaction that I've done something I know meant a lot to him. 'Anyway, I went to his funeral. It was . . .' I lift my shoulders as I try to think of the right word, or at least one that won't offend him, 'nice. Small, but nice.'

His eyes narrow, as if my words are a direct dig at him. 'I would have been here, but I couldn't get back. Travel restrictions.'

'Of course. That must have been hard.'

'Obviously.'

'Wow, you turned out really nice, so lovely,' I drawl sarcastically. 'We're incredibly blessed that you've come back to grace us with your presence. I can't wait to tell everyone.'

'At least I'm not still living here in this . . .' he looks around, his tone derisive, and I feel my hackles rise, 'tiny backwater town, *still* working in the café. I bet you even still live with your grandmother.'

An angry flush blooms on my cheeks, and he snorts when he realises he's right.

'Bingo,' he says, looking at me with something akin to pity. It pisses me off.

'For your information,' I inform him, jabbing my finger towards his chest, 'I *own* the café now. And although I *technically* live with my grandmother, it's . . . Wait, no, you know what? I don't have to justify *anything* to you. I mean, how did surfing your way around the world work out for you, huh?

Because I've got to be honest,' I look him up and down, 'you don't exactly look like a man who's been living the dream.'

'I'm sorry that my appearance is unacceptable to you. Please, tell me, how *is* a man who has buried his wife supposed to look?'

Buried his . . . ? Oh shit. My eyes immediately flash to his hand, where a plain silver band adorns his ring finger. 'Oh.'

'Yes. Oh.'

'I'm sorry, Sam. I had no idea.'

'It's fine,' he sighs. 'It's been almost two years, and I'm . . . doing OK.'

'I knew you were married, but not that she . . . ' I can't quite bring myself to say the word.

'Yeah, well.' He shrugs. 'It's not like I've kept in touch with anyone here apart from my grandfather, so how could you have known.'

'You're not friends with anyone from school on social media?' I've searched his name occasionally over the years, usually when I've had a few drinks and am feeling melancholic. But I've never been able to find a trace of him anywhere.

'I'm not on social media.'

I have to admit, it feels kind of good to know that the reason I haven't been able to find him is because he's not on there, and not because he's blocked me.

'Why not?' I ask, curious despite myself.

'It's just not my thing. Posting selfies, and photographs of your dinner.'

'There's a little more to it than that.'

He shrugs. 'Are *you* still friends with any of them?'

'Most of them, yeah.'

'Why does that not surprise me.'

'It *shouldn't* surprise you,' I retort. 'Because unlike some people, I'm not in the habit of cutting friends out of my life for no good reason.'

'Ah. I do believe that dig is aimed at me.'

'No kidding, Captain Obvious.'

'Ellie, believe what you want. You always did.'

I take a step away from him, unable to reconcile the cold, angry man in front of me with my best friend of so many years.

'I really wish I hadn't bothered coming after you now,' I say.

'Well, that makes two of us.'

I lift my chin. 'Good luck with the house sale. I hope it all comes together quickly for you.'

He looks around the street. 'I'll make sure it does. The sooner I get out of this place, the better.'

Sam

You think the world will grind to a halt when someone you love dies, but it doesn't. The numbers on the clock keep moving forward, the sun rises, then sets. Seasons change. People are born, others die. Life keeps soldiering on.

Mei and I lived in a high-rise apartment, with floor-to-ceiling windows in the open-plan lounge/dining area. After she died, I'd stand there, my hands pressed against the glass. Watching a city that never slept, wondering how on earth all those people could keep going when even the thought of life without her seemed impossible.

My grandfather only met Mei once, when he came to Hong Kong for our wedding. A skilled reader of people, he took her hand in his and I held my breath until he smiled. She'd been approved.

'She's a beauty,' he whispered in my ear as we waited by the luggage carousel. 'And a gentle soul. Genuine. I can see why you fell in love with her.'

I wasn't even sure if he'd make the long flight. He was in his seventies by then, and the scourge of age and a physical life had crept up on him. He walked with a stick; nothing fancy, a plain brown piece of wood with a black rubber tip on the end that gripped the floor so he wouldn't slip over. I remember standing in the arrival hall at Hong Kong International Airport and watching him come through the automatic doors, flanked by my parents. None of my other relatives could make it – flights too expensive, couldn't get time off work, one of the kids fell off the trampoline and broke his arm; the excuses were many – but I really didn't mind at all. As long as my grandfather was there, that was all I cared about.

I'd always intended on bringing Mei back to New Zealand to introduce her to the rest of my family eventually. But for various reasons we kept putting it off, and in the end it never happened. She worked for a media production company. Long hours, demanding employers. Time off together was a rarity, and to be treasured. We had a raft of things we would get to 'one day'. Like the trip home, and buying a house with a garden. Having a baby, that was the big one.

One day.

After my run-in with Ellie, I skip the hardware store, where I'd intended on enquiring about local outdoor labourers, heading instead for the supermarket. I fill a trolley without much thought, then drive straight home. Seeing her again after all this time has stirred up thoughts of the past and the friendship we once shared, and I don't like it. I don't want to be reminded of that time in my life, or of the girl I thought

41

would always be a part of my life but who hurt and betrayed me so deeply.

I start unpacking the groceries, but once the cold stuff is away, I abandon the rest, leaving the bags on the benchtop. Taking a beer from the fridge, I twist off the top and throw it into the sink, hearing it clink off the metal. Then I head outside, onto the deck, and take a seat, lifting the bottle to my mouth as I stare out to sea and finally let my thoughts roam to *her*, and the last time I saw her.

Ellie was my first friend here in Seclusion Bay. The first person to even really acknowledge my existence. My grandparents moved here when I was four, and we started coming to stay with them for a few weeks over the summers. I was eight the first time I properly met her, although I'd noticed her before. The other local kids usually ignored me, or whispered about me behind their hands, cracking up with laughter at whatever witty insult they'd managed to come up with. I wasn't special; they treated all the summer kids the same. But even though Ellie hung out with them, you could tell she was different. She smiled at you, for one thing.

When I moved to the bay permanently to live with my grandparents and started at the local school, Ellie was the only one to extend the hand of friendship. The only one to invite me to her birthday. To sit with me at lunchtime, or choose me to be her partner on school assignments. It didn't take long before the two of us were thick as thieves, spending all our free time together, either at her house or mine, or at the beach. I taught her to surf; she taught me to drive. When she got her first period, she decided I was marginally less embarrassing than her grandmother, so it was me she called, and me who bought her very first tampons.

I held back her hair the first time she got drunk and threw up and thought she was dying. And the second, and the third . . .

She would jump up and down on the beach, screaming my name, at every single surf competition I ever entered. Sneak into my room late at night to help me study when I was failing English. She'd fall asleep on my bed, textbook in hand, and I'd look at her and know I was the luckiest guy in the world to have her as my friend. We argued over so many things. Whether chicken nuggets were better than chips, our very different taste in music (I liked rock, she preferred nineties grunge), and whether October was too soon to start talking about Christmas. But nothing ever came between us until Logan Wheeler did.

He'd never liked me, and he liked me even less when he started dating Ellie. The feeling was mutual. I couldn't stand him. The way he'd sling his arm around her possessively and glare at any guy who even looked at her. It was like she was his trophy, and I hated it. Couldn't understand what she saw in him. It was the only thing that ever caused tension between us. One day, that tension exploded. And I told her I never wanted to see her again.

Ellie

'Are you OK?' Kelly asks, as I hurry back inside the sanctuary of the café and head behind the counter to where my small office is.

'Yeah, I'm fine,' I tell her, waving a hand as I brush past her, hoping she won't see the tears in my eyes. 'I just need to . . . I'll be back in a minute. Sing out if it gets busy.'

As I close the door behind me and lean against it, I can't decide if the tears that spill over are sad or angry ones. Probably a mixture of both, I think as I wipe them with the back of my hand. If only I'd had some kind of heads-up that he was back in town, instead of being taken completely by surprise at the sight of him like that. Turns out time hasn't mellowed him out at all; he's *still* so angry, and I, typically, reacted to his anger with my own. I close my eyes, remembering the last time I saw him. I don't have to think too hard, it's all there in my mind. After all, losing the best friend you ever had is not something you easily forget.

A group of us had headed to the beach around lunchtime that day, nursing hangovers from the big party after the national surf competition the day before. It was the first time it had been held in our town, and we'd gone a tad overboard from the excitement of it all. I hadn't spoken to Sam yet that morning, which was unusual for us, but I knew he was out for a celebratory breakfast with his grandfather and I didn't want to intrude. He'd come first in his division, beating Logan to the title in the process. I could still feel the pride that had warmed my heart as I'd watched Sam carving up the waves, but also the guilt I felt trying to hide it from Logan. I didn't want to risk upsetting him again. We'd had a massive argument the night before when he'd accused me of paying Sam more attention than him, but he'd turned up that morning on my doorstep with flowers and a sheepish apology and I'd forgiven him. He might have had a point, after all. But Sam was my best friend, had been for years. I was still trying to figure out how to balance spending time with both of them, but no matter what I did, one of them inevitably always felt left out.

Once we'd staked out our patch of sand with towels and bags, most of us went for a swim in the ocean to cool off from the heat of the sun. I remember we were just hanging out in the waves, chatting, laughing, completely carefree. I had no idea that my life was about to change for ever. Chloe's puzzled expression was the first sign that something was wrong. I turned to see what she was looking at, and spotted Sam climbing out of the back of a police car. He was too far away for me to make out his expression clearly, but I could tell from his angry gestures as he pointed to us that he was agitated and upset, and I had an uneasy feeling in my stomach as I paddled back to shore.

'Of course it was them,' he was saying as I walked up the beach and scooped up my towel to dry myself. 'Logan and his mates. No doubt about it.'

'What's going on?' I asked him, wrapping the towel around my waist and knotting it. If he heard me, he made no sign of it.

'Well go on, arrest him,' he urged the officer. 'Arrest all of them.'

'You need to take a step back and try to calm down,' the cop told him. 'I'll have a chat to the guys.'

'Hey.' I moved to stand in front of Sam. 'What's going on?'

'I'll tell you in a minute,' he said quietly, his jaw tense.

Our friends had all started to trickle out of the water and were slowly joining us. I looked up and saw Sam's eyes narrow at someone over my shoulder.

'It was him,' he said, raising his arm. 'I know it was.'

I turned around and realised he was pointing straight at Logan, who picked up his towel and starting drying his chest with it. He ignored Sam and smiled at the cop.

'Hey, Pete,' he said. 'How's the engine on the Valiant running now?'

'Mate, she's smooth as since you worked your magic on her. The missus and I took her up the coast last weekend for a long cruise. No problems at all.'

'Glad to hear it.'

'Are you kidding me?' Sam snorted. 'I should have known you guys would know each other.'

Pete shrugged. 'I know everyone in this town, and not just because of the job. I grew up here. Logan's father and I have been mates since we were kids. I was even best man at his wedding.'

'So you must know what he's like then,' Sam replied.

'What's that supposed to mean?' Logan said, dropping his towel to the sand and standing up straight, his arms rigid at his sides.

'You know *exactly* what I mean,' Sam retorted. 'You stole my car last night. Don't even try to deny it.'

I heard a few shocked gasps and whispers from our friends. I was reeling from the revelation myself, trying to make sense of it. Someone stole Sam's car? And he thought it was Logan?

Logan frowned. 'Mate, I've got no idea what you're talking about.'

'I'm not your *mate*,' Sam hissed. 'And you're full of shit.'

'I'm not,' Logan protested. 'It's the first I've heard of it. I mean, what's this town coming to, eh? Hang on, are you sure you didn't just park it somewhere and forget? My grandmother does that a lot.'

'You think you're so clever,' Sam said coldly. 'But you're not going to get away with it.'

Logan held up both hands in a peace gesture. 'I'm sorry. I was just trying to lighten the mood.'

'OK, enough.' Pete turned to him. 'Did you take his car?'

'No.' Logan shook his head. 'Why would I?'

Pete shrugged. 'Fair enough.' He looked at Sam. 'Unless you've got any proof . . .'

'You want me to do your job for you?' Sam said incredulously. 'There must be fingerprints or DNA or something.'

'I'm afraid the fire would have destroyed any evidence.'

'Fire? What fire?' I asked. 'Can someone please tell me what's going on here?'

Sam looked at me, his face softening. I could see pain as well as anger in his eyes. 'You know I left the car at the surf club last night because I'd had a few drinks.'

I nodded. It was right after my fight with Logan, who had taken off with his friends into the night. Sam had wiped away my tears and walked me home before heading to his own place. Before I started going out with Logan, we'd think nothing of sleeping over at each other's house, but now that I had a boyfriend, it felt . . . different. Wrong. I missed it, though.

'Well,' he continued, 'this morning I went out for breakfast with my grandfather, then afterwards I walked to the club to pick it up, but it wasn't there. I checked everywhere, then I went straight to the police station to report it stolen.'

'The car had already been found by then,' Pete interjected, taking over the story. 'A guy out for an early surf spotted it in a ditch around five this morning. Still smouldering.'

'Where?' I asked, horrified by what I was hearing.

'Couple miles down the coast, on a beach access road. We're damn lucky the bush around it didn't burn as well.'

There was a feeling of dread in my gut. 'So the car is . . . ?'

'Completely destroyed,' Pete confirmed.

'Along with all my gear,' Sam said bitterly. 'Including my surfboard.'

My heart plummeted to my feet. In all the years I'd known Sam, I'd never seen him lose his composure like this. Never seen him snap at anyone the way he kept snapping at Pete. It just wasn't him. But now I knew why.

Logan whistled through his teeth. 'That sucks. I'm sorry to hear it. But it's got nothing to do with me.'

Sam stepped away from me, towards Logan. Out of the corner of my eye, I saw Pete tense up, ready to intervene as they squared up to each other. Logan was slightly bigger, but Sam was stronger. It would be a pretty even fight, and one that had been brewing for a long time.

'That board belonged to my grandfather for years before he gave it to me,' Sam told Logan through gritted teeth. 'He'd had it since he was my age, and it's been all around the world with him. Do you have any idea how devastated he's going to be when he finds out it's been destroyed?'

Logan pulled a face. 'Fairly devastated, I would say.'

'You're not even sorry, are you?'

'I've got nothing to be sorry for. I didn't do anything. And you can't just go around saying I did. In fact, if you don't shut up, I could sue you for defamation, right, Pete?'

'I don't think there's any need for that. You both just need to calm down,' Pete said. 'Where were you last night, Logan?'

Logan's eyes swivelled to the cop. 'Seriously?'

'I have to ask.'

'I have my own car; why the hell would I want to steal his crappy old one?' Logan retorted. 'It doesn't even make any sense.'

'Humour me. Answer the question.'

He crossed his arms over his chest. 'I was at the clubrooms, along with half the town.'

'And after that?'

'After that . . . ' His eyes flickered to me briefly, and I knew he was remembering our fight. 'After the club closed, the guys and I hung out on the beach for a while. Played some touch rugby. Had a few more drinks. Then we all crashed out at Trent's place. Right, guys?'

I watched our friends, boys I'd known almost my entire life, nod and agree with him. They looked just as bewildered by what was going on as I was.

Pete looked at Trent. 'Is that what happened?'

Trent nodded. 'It was.'

'Your parents can vouch that you guys were there last night?'

'Well, yeah. I mean, my room is a sleepout attached to the garage, but they probably heard us when we came home. The security light usually wakes my dad. And mum cooked us breakfast this morning.'

Pete nodded. 'OK. Sounds legit to me.'

'Wait, seriously?' Sam reeled. 'You're just going to take their word for it?'

'Listen.' Pete stepped towards him and put a hand on his shoulder in what was meant to be a comforting gesture. 'I know you're upset. It's understandable. But you can't just go around accusing people of crimes without any proof.'

Sam shrugged his hand off. 'I don't believe this.'

'You've got no reason to think these guys had anything to

do with it, other than the fact you don't like each other. I'm sorry, Sam, but I've known them for a long time. If they say they didn't do it, I believe them.'

'So they get away with it?'

'If anything changes, we'll give you a call. But honestly, this kind of thing happens more often than you'd think. Opportunists. The best thing for you to do now is to get on to your insurance company and just move on.'

'Money can't replace everything,' Sam told him, his voice anguished. 'How the hell am I going to tell my grandad?'

'Come on.' I reached out and wrapped my fingers around his arm, giving him a gentle tug. 'I'll drive you home and we'll do it together.'

He stared over my shoulder. 'I know it was you, Logan.'

'Listen, we both know I don't like you,' Logan replied darkly, stepping forward, his eyes on my hand. I took it off Sam quickly. 'Never have, and never will, especially after this. But I didn't steal your car. So quit with the accusations, before I get my father to call his lawyer.'

'Go.' I pushed Sam gently in the direction of my car. 'Start walking, I'll be there in a sec.'

I bent down and picked up my bag, stuffing my towel in as I slipped my feet into my sandals. I needed to get Sam away from the situation. As I went to follow him, I felt someone touch me on the shoulder. 'Ellie, wait. You believe me, right?'

I looked up at Logan, feeling torn. I knew he didn't like Sam, but to do something like this? In all the years I'd known him, he'd never been one to break the law. He was

51

the smart-ass in class. The cheeky guy who frequently pushed boundaries. But I didn't think he was a criminal. I scanned his face. He seemed sincere.

'You were so angry last night,' I said in a low voice.

'Can you blame me,' he protested. 'The guy hauled you up on stage in front of everyone and acted like you were *his* girlfriend. You have no idea how that made me feel in front of my family. All our friends. But even though I was mad, it was mostly at myself. Because I hate feeling jealous, and I'm working on it, I promise. I didn't do this, Ellie, I swear.'

I nodded. 'It's fine. I believe you. Don't worry, I'll sort it out. But right now I need to help Sam, OK?'

'Sure.' Then he smirked at someone behind me, and I turned, realising Sam hadn't gone far at all. He was still standing close enough to have heard everything, and the look on his face was one I'd never seen before. It was as if a door had just slammed shut between us.

Sam

I never want to see you again.

That was what I said to her that day. Up until Mei died, that moment on the beach, the moment that I realised Ellie was more loyal to Logan than she was to me, *that* was the worst moment of my life. It wasn't even about the car, or the surfboard. It was the fact that she didn't believe me. Because my gut, my instincts, everything told me it had been Logan.

'But how do you know it was him?' she asked, following me up the beach path as I walked quickly away from her. 'You heard Pete, there's no proof or anything to suggest he did it. Sam, wait. We need to talk about this.'

I whirled on her. 'What's there to talk about? You've already made up your mind.'

'OK.' She held her hands up in an effort to calm the situation. 'This is crazy. I know how much that surfboard means to you, but—'

'It means a hell of a lot more to my grandfather.'

'I know, but what happened wasn't your fault. Like Pete said, this kind of thing happens all the time. Your grandad is not going to blame you.'

'Of course he won't, but that doesn't make me feel any better. He's still going to be upset. Anyway, it's not about the surfboard. Not any more.'

She dropped her bag to the ground and took a step towards me, reaching out her hands. I took a step backwards and watched them fall back down to her sides, her eyes sad. My emotions were all over the place, torn. She was my best friend, she meant everything to me. But I couldn't get her words to Logan out of my head. She was supposed to be on *my* side. Always. And up until that point, I'd believed she was.

'How can you believe *him*, Ellie?' I asked, my voice trembling with my sense of betrayal.

'It's not a case of believing him and not you, Sam.'

'That's *exactly* what it is.'

'It's just . . . there's no proof,' she said helplessly.

'I don't need proof. I saw the way he looked at me yesterday, when I beat him to the title. He was pissed.'

'I know, but enough to do something like this? I mean, he can be an idiot, yeah, but I've never known him — or any of those guys for that matter — to do something as dumb as steal a car. Why would he risk a criminal record just because you beat him in a competition? It doesn't make any sense.'

'He hates me, Ellie. You heard him. And not just because I beat him, but because of you.'

54

She pulled a face. 'Come on, that's an even dumber motive.'

'He hates our friendship.'

'He does,' she admitted. 'But he knows we're just friends. And he's working on his jealousy issues.'

I snorted. 'You're an idiot if you really believe that.'

Her eyes widened. 'Did you seriously just call me an idiot?'

'I guess I did.'

'Wow, Sam. Just . . . wow.'

I stared at her intensely, as if memorising her face, unable to shake the feeling that everything we had was slipping away. I was unable to stop myself from saying horrible, hurtful things. Hearing what she'd said to Logan on the beach, and seeing his smug smile when he knew she was on his side, had cut right through me, so now I was lashing out at her.

'If I mean anything to you,' I told her in a low voice, 'anything at all, then you'll believe *me*. Not him.'

'That's not fair, Sam. Why do I have to pick a side?' she retorted angrily. 'I could say the same thing to you: if *you* really care about me, you won't ask me to choose between you and my boyfriend. There's no proof. No evidence that he's done anything wrong. And he seems sincere. I've got no reason *not* to believe him. I'm sorry, I am. But you're being completely unreasonable.'

I exhaled slowly and straightened my shoulders, determined not to show her how much she'd hurt me. 'You know what? You should probably go back to your *boyfriend*.'

She nodded. 'You're right. A bit of space is what we need right now. You go home, and I'll call you later.'

'No. Don't bother.'

She stared at me, uncomprehending. 'What are you saying?'

'I think we're done, Ellie.'

Her expression turned incredulous. 'What do you mean, we're done?'

'I can't be friends with someone I can't trust. Someone who doesn't have my back.'

'You're kidding, right?'

I shook my head. 'Lately it's felt like you care more about him than you do about me. Today has proved it.'

'You ... *asshole*,' she blurted. 'I can't believe this. I ... I really can't. I have *always* been here for you. When no one else in this town would even speak to you, who welcomed you? Who has always been your biggest cheerleader, your staunchest supporter? Me, Sam. *Me*. You're my best friend.'

'Not any more,' I said. 'Seems like Logan has your loyalty now.'

She picked up her bag and slung it over her shoulder. 'You know what? If that's how you feel, fine.' Her eyes were glassy with unshed tears that I could see she was trying so hard not to release.

My resolve started to weaken at the sight of her pain. I hated hurting her. But then Logan appeared over the sand dune. He walked up the path and stopped beside her, frowning.

'Hey, what is it, baby? What's wrong?' he asked, placing an arm around her shoulders protectively.

'This is between us,' I told him, my anger returning quickly. 'Nothing to do with you.'

'Anything that hurts my girl has *everything* to do with me,' he retorted, his eyes flashing. 'And anyone who dares to hurt her should remember that.'

'Is that a threat?'

He pushed her behind him and took a step towards me. 'It's a promise.'

I tilted my head to stare at Ellie. 'You see what I mean? He has anger issues, Ellie. Serious ones. How can you believe anything this guy says?'

'I . . .' She lifted her shoulders, wiping the tears from her cheeks.

'Come on,' Logan said, tugging her hand. 'I'll take you back to Chloe and the others. Your *real* friends.'

'If you go with him, Ellie,' I said, 'that's it for us.'

She wiped her face with one hand and gave me the saddest look I'd ever seen. 'Seems like you've already made that choice, Sam,' she said.

Then the two of them walked away from me, but not before Logan flashed me a look of triumph.

'I mean it, Ellie,' I called after her. 'There's no coming back from this. I never want to see you again.'

But she didn't reply. She just kept walking, until they disappeared from view, and that was the last time I saw her, until today.

To distract myself, and feeling sick with old anger and regret, I find some gardening tools in the garden shed and spend most of the day hacking away at trees and bushes. I have no plan in mind other than to reduce their size and tire myself

57

out enough to hopefully get a proper night's sleep. Around 4 p.m., I decide to knock off, satisfied with the amount I've managed to get done. The rest can wait for another day.

The beers have been in the fridge, chilling. After a quick shower, the first one goes down quickly. I take the second out to the deck and survey my handiwork. It's not great. In fact, I've probably done lasting damage to some of the trees, but hey, at least I can see further up the beach now, which will let the sun into the house earlier in the morning. Back when my grandmother was alive, the place had a well-manicured air about it, but if I can just get it looking tidy enough for a quick sale, I'll be happy.

Growing up, I lived for the holidays, when I'd be allowed to come and stay here with my grandparents. Not because I didn't get on with my parents. I did. They were fine as far as parents go. Showed the right amount of interest when needed, and I can't remember either of them ever raising their voice to me. It was just that I had more in common with my grandfather. A deep love of the ocean for one thing, and an abiding thirst for adventure.

My father is an accountant and makes a very respectable living from it. He and my mother still live in the house I grew up in, four bedrooms, two bathrooms. Palatial by the standards of the day, but it echoed horribly with just the three of us. I had an older sister, Olivia. *Have*, I should say, because she's still my sister, even though I only know what she looks like courtesy of photographs in an old red album. She was two when she died from meningitis, I was barely a month old.

Growing up, my parents talked about her, but never her death. I know that it happened quickly, from information pieced together over the years from neighbours, family friends and cousins. She went to bed a little grizzly, and in the morning she was gone. My frantic mother carried her tiny, cold little body out to the front lawn to wait for the ambulance and woke the entire neighbourhood. Mrs Bottomley at number 9 never forgot the sound of her screams.

Olivia's presence lingered everywhere in the house, and at every family occasion. Every milestone I met, I sensed their sadness that she never had the same chances as I did. They never really got over her loss. No one would have blamed them if they'd become overprotective of me because of what had happened, but they didn't. Instead, they encouraged me to try new experiences. They pushed me to make the most of life, and gave me the freedom to explore and find the thing that became my passion.

It was my grandfather who taught me to surf. By the time I was eleven, I'd earned the respect of the older surfers in town. Not the younger guys, though. Not Ellie's friends. I had a natural talent in the water, and they didn't like it. When I was fourteen, I begged to stay with my grandparents permanently so that I could practise surfing any time I wasn't at school. I had dreams of becoming the next Kelly Slater, touring the world as a professional surfer. My parents allowed it, because they knew how much it meant to me.

With the second beer almost finished, I turn on the television and flick through the channels, hoping the noise will help drown out the rising sense of loneliness I feel. A familiar harbour appears onscreen, one that was the backdrop of my life in Hong Kong. The presenter is talking to someone about preparations for Chinese New Year, due to start in a couple of weeks. With a pang, I remember how excited Mei would get at this time of year, so proud of her traditional heritage. Memories assail me. A city of red lanterns, mandarin trees adorning doorways. The smell of frankincense and dumplings. Every year she would buy a small kumquat tree and bring it home to sit by the door of our apartment, ostensibly to attract good luck. She told me how, growing up, her parents would take her to the Lam Tsuen Wishing Trees every Chinese New Year. They'd write a wish, tie it to a mandarin and toss it into the tree. If it caught and stayed, the wish would come true. She loved it, even though she lamented the fact that nothing she wished for ever turned up.

I put the beer on the coffee table and get up, flicking the TV off again. There is a desk in an alcove in the corner of the lounge, and after a bit of rummaging, I find a pad of paper. The first two pens I try don't work – the ink has dried out – but I strike lucky on the third. As soon as the nib touches the paper, the words pour out, one after another, like they've been building up inside me just waiting for an outlet. I write so fast my hand cramps up, and it's only then that I stop, blinking at the page now covered in words. I don't even remember most of what I've written, nor do I reread it. Instead, I fold the page up and search the drawers until I find some string, which I tie around it. Then I head outdoors and down towards the beach, knowing what I need to do.

Ellie

It's hard to put into words exactly how I feel after seeing him again, but my best friend, Chloe, insists I try. A real-estate agent at the town's sole agency, most days she swings by the café around lunchtime for a catch-up and a free coffee. We've been friends since we were seven, and it takes her about 0.03 seconds to realise that something is up when she sees my face. I tell her everything.

'Sam,' she says, sitting at the table nearest the counter, using a fingernail to unpick the cellotape from the top of her plastic sushi container. I don't usually let people bring food from other establishments into my business, unless they have a genuine medical condition that I can't cater for, like coeliac disease. I do offer gluten-free food, but can't guarantee there's no cross-contamination because of the amount of flour we use in the kitchen. Chloe, however, is a law unto herself, and does what she pleases, when she pleases. I don't mind, because it means we get to hang out every day for an hour or so.

'Yes,' I reply.

'Sam Emerson.'

'Yes.'

'*The* Sam Emerson, the one who—'

'Yes.' I cut her off, aware that Kelly is loitering by the kitchen door, listening. 'That one.'

'Wow.'

'I know.'

She twists the cap off a little soy-sauce fish and squirts it onto the top of each sushi roll. 'How long has it been?'

'Ten years.'

'Shit. Seriously?'

'About that.'

'Man, we're getting old. So, he said he was married? But that she died?'

I nod, remembering the way his voice trembled when he mentioned her.

'That's really sad.'

'I know.'

'How does he look?' She uses the tail of the fish to smear wasabi.

'He looks . . .' I bring the scene on the street to mind, 'older. Paler. Kind of weary.'

'Still hot, though?'

'Chloe.'

'What? I know you guys were just friends, but even you have to admit he was cute. I had a major crush on him for, like, six months when we were fourteen, remember?'

I nod. 'You made me steal a photo of him from his house and you slept with it under your pillow. I felt so guilty about that.'

'Didn't matter anyway.' She shrugs. 'He only ever had eyes for you.'

'As a friend.'

'Oh Ellie, still as blind as you always were. You loved him. You were devastated when he left.'

'Of course I was. I did love him,' I agree. *As a friend*. He was a massive part of my life, for a long time.'

I thought that eventually he'd cool off, but he didn't. He was a stubborn, fiery Scorpio, but then so was I. After a week of waiting for him to call and apologise, I started to think maybe he'd actually meant it when he said he never wanted to see me again. Then I ran into his grandfather in the street, and he told me Sam had left town. Moved back home to live with his folks for the rest of the summer holidays, with plans to attend university in the South Island in the new year. It was about as far away from me as he could get, and that was when the bottom dropped out of my world. I was beyond devastated, but also so, *so* angry. As far as I was concerned, I'd done nothing wrong, so there was no way in hell I was going to call and beg him not to give up on our friendship. Because if he could let it go over something like that, I obviously never meant as much to him as I thought I did.

Logan and I broke up not long after Sam left. He couldn't handle how devastated I was over losing my best friend, and kept accusing me of having more than just platonic feelings. It wasn't enough for him that I'd lost Sam because I'd stuck up for *him*, and in the end, his jealousy drove me nuts and I finished things.

I never stopped truly missing Sam, or hoping that he'd realise how totally unfair he'd been and make contact. I couldn't deal with the idea of him just being gone for ever, so I kept that small slice of hope tucked away in my heart. Then my grandmother heard the news from one of her bowling friends, who happened to be Sam's grandfather's neighbour. She delivered it so casually, unaware that with every word she spoke, my heart felt like it was being stomped on.

Such an exotic place for a wedding, she told me over the dinner table. *Hong Kong.*

Stomp.

Lindsey's seen the photos, reckons they make a lovely couple. Said she's very beautiful, Sam's wife.

Stomp.

His grandfather says he's never seen Sam so happy.

It was then that I realised our friendship was really over. I hadn't even known he was in Hong Kong, let alone getting married. He'd gone on to live a life I knew nothing about, and now we were little more than strangers. If something as major as that didn't see him extending an olive branch, nothing would. The friendship I'd honestly thought I'd have for life was gone.

Now here he is, back in town, and apparently I still care about him, because I swear to God, I felt like I couldn't breathe when he first looked at me.

'Do you think it's possible to both hate and love someone at the same time?' I ask Chloe.

She shoves a teriyaki sushi roll into her mouth and chews, watching me stack the freshly cleaned and still steaming-hot coffee cups beside the machine. Her eyebrows shoot up when the cups clatter noisily against each other because my hands are shaking so much.

'I don't know. Wait, what do you mean . . . you love him?'

A couple approach the counter with the food they've selected from the cabinet. I ring up their purchases and process the payment. After they head for a table by the window, I pull out the seat opposite Chloe and collapse down onto it, elbows on the table, my chin in the palms of my hands.

'Of course I love him. Like I love you. Well, I mean I *loved* him. Once. Before he turned into such a giant jerk.'

'You guys never resolved things, did you?'

'How could we? He didn't give us a chance, just left town. Literally overnight.'

'Well, maybe that's what you should keep reminding yourself. He was in the wrong, not you. Accusing Logan like that? Not cool.'

'Yeah. Although . . .'

Her eyes narrow. 'Although what?'

'I don't know. Sometimes I wonder, what if he was right?'

She shrugs. 'I think if that was the case the truth would have worked its way out of the woodwork by now. It always does.'

'I guess. Anyway,' I attempt to change the subject, 'your wedding is only a few weeks away. What's still left to organise?'

'Nuh-uh, nice try.' She licks some errant wasabi off her finger and puts the empty plastic container back inside its brown paper bag, sliding it across the table towards me to dispose of. 'While obviously *not* as important as my wedding, Sam coming back is still a pretty big deal. This is me you're talking to, I know how much he meant to you. I also remember how devastated you were when he left. What are you going to do?'

'Nothing.'

'I think you should talk to him.'

I gape at her. 'Um, putting aside the fact that he made it blatantly obvious that he has zero interest in catching up, why would I want to do that? There's no point in dredging any of it back up. It was painful enough the first time.'

'Ellie, you know I love you, right?'

I narrowed my eyes at her, wondering where exactly this was going. 'Yes . . . Why do I sense there's a "but" coming?'

'There's no but. I love you unconditionally.'

'OK.'

'But . . .'

'There it is.'

'You are terrible at relationships. And I don't just mean terrible, I mean *fucking* terrible.'

'Don't hold back.'

'You admit it yourself. No guy is ever good enough, you find something wrong with them every single time.'

'So?'

'So I'm no shrink, but I think this might all stem from the trauma of what happened with Sam.'

'I wouldn't exactly call it trauma.'

'Well, I would. And I think that until you get some kind of closure over what happened with him, no guy is ever going to make you happy. You're always looking for a way out, right from the start. It's like you expect every guy you meet to hurt and abandon you like he did.'

'I do not expect that,' I protest too loudly.

'Think about it. Your last few "relationships" . . . ' she does quote symbols in the air, 'you broke up with all of them before they had the chance to break up with you, admit it.'

'That's not true.'

'Isn't it?'

I stare at her, poised to deny it again, but something stops me. A fear, really, that if I analysed my dating history with her accusation in mind, she might . . . *might* have a point.

'Exactly,' she says, satisfied with her diagnosis.

'Even if that's true, and I'm not admitting it is,' I tell her, 'why would talking to Sam change anything?'

'I don't know,' she admits. 'But it's worth a try. If you could just make peace with what happened, it might help you to ditch the trust issues you so clearly have.'

'Can you blame me? I mean, this is an ambush right here.'

She rolls her eyes. 'Dramatic, much?'

'It doesn't matter anyway. He made it *very* clear that he doesn't want to talk.'

'So? Why should he get to call all the shots?'

I feel myself bristle. 'Actually, that's a good point. Why should he?'

'Thatta girl. Confront him, make him listen to *you* this

time. He needs to hear how much of an arse he was for treating you the way he did. Who knows, maybe he'll even say sorry.'

'Maybe,' I reply doubtfully, feeling some of my earlier bravado desert me. 'But … then again, his wife has just died. I mean, that's got to really mess someone up. Maybe I should do as he asks and just leave him alone.'

She pushes her chair back and gets to her feet. 'No disrespect to his wife, but she's dead, and he doesn't get to use that as an excuse to avoid reality. The fact of the matter is, he *owes* you an apology for the way he treated you, Ellie. This is your chance to make him see that he put you in an impossible position and then completely threw his toys out of the cot like a spoiled toddler when things didn't go his way.'

'You make it sound easy.'

'Oh I know it won't be, believe me. I don't want to see you get hurt again. But you're my best friend, and I want you to be happy. I don't want you to have any regrets, and I think if he leaves town without you telling him how he made you feel, you will regret it. Just promise me you'll think about it.'

'OK. I'll think about it.'

She checks her watch. 'I have to go. I have an appointment on the other side of town in ten minutes. Drinks after work at mine? Hamish has soccer practice so he won't be home till late. We can get a pizza and decide on a plan of action.'

'Not tonight. I need to go for a run.'

'You and I have very different definitions of the word "need",' she sighs. 'Afterwards, then.'

'Can't. It's poker night with Nan and a few of her friends.

You could always come and join us,' I suggest, already knowing her answer. Sure enough, she snorts.

'Your grandmother is a total card shark and I refuse to give her any more of my money.'

'Suit yourself.'

'You're seriously choosing a run and a few card games with some geriatric women over pizza, wine and my company?'

'I'll tell her you said that.'

'Don't you dare.'

'Enjoy your pizza, Chloe.'

She walks backwards away from me, pouting. 'Last chance to change your mind . . .'

'I'll see you tomorrow.'

'Fine. Weirdo.'

I pick up her rubbish. 'That's why you love me.'

Sam

There's a sense of homecoming as I pick my way around the last of the rocks and lay eyes on Sailor's Beach, a tiny bay a couple of kilometres up the coast from town. For the most part the locals have managed to keep it a secret from tourists, although every summer word gets out eventually and some make the trek. Unless they're surfers, though, they don't tend to stay long. The beach looks picturesque, a cute little basin of emerald-green water, but a break in a sandbar offshore throws up dangerous rip currents. After a couple of near-drownings, the council had signs erected to deter swimmers. For surfers, though, a rip current can be a handy way to get out to the waves quickly and without expending a lot of energy.

The small headlands that jut out at each end of the bay are rocky, but the sand in between is white and soft. If you come here after the tide has been in to wash the shore clean of any trace of humanity, it's like you're the first person in the world to discover it. Trees line the hills all around the bay, and a well-trodden but narrow path snakes over the top of each side for those unwilling to risk the tide and clamber around the rocky points.

The gnarly old pohutukawa tree is still there, its roots clinging to the sandy bank, although more have been exposed by erosion since I was last here. Long branches with leafy green plumage extend from the solid trunk. Some dip to the sand, creating seats for children to ride like pretend horses. A tyre swing on a rope dangles from a taller branch. I remember hanging off it when I was a kid, and I'm tempted to give it a whirl for old times' sake, but I'm not sure if it'll hold my weight and I'd hate to be the one to break it after all this time.

There are still crimson flowers on some of the branches. New Zealand's native Christmas tree. I close my eyes and breathe in the salty summer air, and it almost feels like my life in the city was a dream. Like I've never been away. I have, though, of course. I've lived another lifetime in another world, but standing back here, it's like none of it happened, and I have nothing at all to show for it.

The wind rustles the paper in my hand, reminding me why I'm here. My grandfather and I would drape our towels over these branches while we surfed here. If there is any tree in the world that holds sentimental meaning to me, it would be this one. However, there's a problem. I don't want anyone to find my note, and judging by the tyre and the footprints in the sand underneath, this tree is as much in use now as it was back then.

Looking around, I spot a pine or spruce of some sort in

71

amongst the trees down the other end of the bay. Whatever it is, it looks Christmassy, which seems fitting. It's the only tree of its kind that I can see, and for some reason that seems important. I head along the shore, then clamber up the bank, using the undergrowth to pull me up. A tiny amount of bush-whacking and then I'm touching its trunk. My fingers on the bark release the smell of pine into the air. Most people in China don't celebrate Christmas. It's more of a token day, like Valentine's. Mei grew to love it, though, after being married to me. I tie the note to a branch on the front of the tree, facing out over the ocean.

Somewhere across those waters, my wife lies in a hillside grave in an overcrowded cemetery. Leaving Hong Kong and her behind was easy in the end. I'm almost ashamed of the relief I felt when the plane's wheels left the tarmac and I caught my last glimpse of that enormous grey, wintry city, before my whole world became a pillow of delicately coloured clouds, the sun on the horizon like a beacon drawing me home.

I tried for almost two years to stay on there without her. I worked, ate, slept occasionally and socialised with our friends, even though the dynamic had changed and I was now 'the widower' amongst the couples. I went on living, because what other choice did I have? Unlike my wife, my lungs kept breathing in air, and my heart kept pumping blood around my body. The mechanical side of life went on for me; the emotional side of it suffered a death along with her.

I miss her every single day, although I realise it's not with the same intensity of those early days. That kind of grief is all-consuming. Unsustainable. No one would ever recover enough to go on if grief remained that powerful. It's more of an ache now. Always there, but not always strong enough to demand my full attention. Being back here, I realise, is possibly the best thing for me if I'm to move on, which I know I have to. I couldn't do that in Hong Kong. The ties were too strong, the reminders too many. Here, I have no history with Mei. She never existed in this place. Being back here, maybe I can begin to let go.

No one falls in love expecting it to end. But it has. She has gone.

I'm still here.

I jump down from the bank and wander down to the shoreline. Crouching, I dip my hands in the water, swirling them around, then cup my palms and watch them fill. I splash the water over my face and hair, almost like I am reacquainting myself with my surroundings.

Three months ago, back in Hong Kong, I went to a rooftop party thrown by a colleague, John, and his wife, Susannah. Nice couple. One of the few who had stuck around through all the hard stuff after Mei died, when other friendships had fallen by the wayside. There was a woman there, a friend of Susannah's from the UK. She'd been six months into a year-long plan to make her way around Asia when the pandemic hit, and had been stuck in Hong Kong ever since, bored out of her mind, apparently. The stereotypical traveller: tanned skin, hair bleached by the sun, clad in loose clothing that wafted around her like a cloud as she moved. An expressive talker, her wrists jangling with the weight of bracelets haggled from roadside markets. As terrible as it sounds, I don't remember who spoke to who first, or at what point it became obvious the direction in which the evening was headed. I don't even remember her name. I wasn't drunk, but I wasn't sober either. We made out in a dark, concealed corner of the dirty rooftop. It was completely devoid of any connection or affection. She made it very obvious that she was up for sex, but in the end I couldn't go through with it. She was perfectly nice, but it was all . . . wrong.

I woke the next morning in my own bed and cried, though not from shame or regret as I'd anticipated. I cried because it felt like the closing of one door and the opening of another. The technicalities, when I tried to think about it, fried the circuits in my mind. Where did I even fit into this world now? Was I still a husband, only no longer with a wife?

Ellie

I watch from my vantage point on the hill above Sailor's Bay as he emerges from the treeline at the other end of the beach, jumping the last metre off the bank and landing on the sand.

What on earth was he doing up there?

It feels wrong to be spying, but it's not like I followed him here, I remind myself defensively as I watch him walk back along the beach, his bare feet in the lapping water. This is the same route I take every day for my run, and have done for years. I was making good time today, and ironically was thinking about him as I popped over the hill and saw him down on the beach, standing by the tyre swing. I damn near twisted my ankle ducking off the path and into the scrub for cover. Thank God Alfie came straight back when I gave a low whistle, and is now lying in the scrub beside me.

Sam crouches down and dips his hands in the water, staring at his cupped palms for a few moments before lifting them up and tipping the water over his head. He repeats this a few times until his hair is wet; I wonder why he doesn't just strip off and jump in and be done with it. Then he stands up and shakes his head, and I get such a vivid flashback of teenage Sam that it steals the breath from my throat. Without thinking, I sit down heavily on some dry bracken. It crunches, loudly, and he turns to look my way. All I can do is hope there's enough scrub to hide us from view, or that Alfie won't get bored of staying still and give the game away.

Sam scans the hillside, but in a disinterested way, as though his mind is elsewhere. There's a brief moment of panic when it looks like he might be heading in our direction, but thankfully he continues past the trail, towards the rocky path around the headland. I always take the hill path because it gives me that extra bit of cardio. And thank goodness, because otherwise I'd have run straight into him.

After waiting ten minutes to ensure that I've given him plenty of time to leave the bay, I pick my way down the path cautiously. There's no sign of him, and although I tell myself that whatever he was doing in the trees is absolutely none of my business, there's no question I'm going to look. I can't help it. My curiosity has been piqued.

I've just about given up and decided he was merely relieving himself, when a breeze blows in off the sea and ripples through the trees like a wave. I see it then, a piece of paper attached to a branch of a young pine tree. I step forward and untie it before my morals have a chance to catch up and remind me that this is not a good idea. Because it's crystal clear, judging from the off-the-beaten-track place he has chosen to hide it, that he was pretty determined that this paper should never be found. But I'm churned up from seeing him again, and desperate for even a sliver of insight into the man he has become, so I unroll the paper and I read . . .

Dear Mei,

Thank you.

I don't know if I ever said that to you enough. Not out loud, those exact two words. It's just not one of those things you think of saying when you're living together day to day, or at least I didn't. I can't speak for other men. Other husbands. Perhaps I'm the only lousy one. I'm sure I said it to you in a million other little ways, but still, I should have said the actual words.

Thank you.

Because of course it's too late now, and as soon as you died, all I could think about was all the things I should have said but didn't. All the words left unsaid that now have nowhere to go and no one to listen. It's like they're pent up inside me, driving me a little bit mad if I'm honest. Maybe writing this letter will help, maybe not.

For a long time I kept replaying our last conversation over and over in my head. It was nothing extraordinary, the last words we spoke to each other. Unworthy even of remembrance, and the more time that passes, the less I'm sure I remember it accurately. It's all a bit fuzzy now. You were heading out the door to work, running a little late, as usual. I wish it had been for a really good reason, like we'd lingered in bed and made love one last time. But it was the usual story. Snoozed the alarm once too often. Your 'quick' shower turned into a lengthy one, as it always did. Your eye make-up didn't go on as perfectly as you wanted the first time. You were frustrated and panicked. I was sitting at the bench when you left, looking at something on my phone, the news probably. I don't even remember if I looked up when you kissed me on the top of my head. I hope I did. You stole my last piece of toast on your way out the door. We briefly discussed what we'd have for dinner, and whose turn it was to take the rubbish out (mine). It was just all so trivial, our last ever conversation.

I hate that.

It should have been filled with declarations of love, of how much you meant to me. How happy you made me, even when you did things that drove me mad, like insisting on watching those awful reality shows on TV, or never clearing the hair out of the drain in the shower, even though it was all yours. And even though you always made me sort out any utility bill issues, or insurance, or medical, despite the fact that YOU spoke the local language and I didn't.

I was happy. You made me happy. I can only hope that I made you happy too.

I don't know what I believe, if I'm honest. You know I'm not a religious man. But I'm no atheist either. I'm somewhere in the middle — there probably isn't even a word for it. I think that if some people choose to believe that their deceased loved ones are still with them in some way, then good for them. Because hey, whatever makes you feel better at the end of the day. And who am I to judge? Or anyone, for that matter. People get worked up over the stupidest things, and I probably did too, but I try not to do that any more. Life really is too short.

If believing in the afterlife meant it came true, I'd do it for you. But I don't think it works like that, and I'm not sure I could carry it off with any great conviction anyway.

Thank you, Mei, for loving me, and letting me love you. I'm sorry for all the things we missed out on. The plans we'd vaguely made for the future. I'm sorry for continuously putting the 'when will we have kids' conversation off. And for often leaving the toilet seat up, sometimes even on purpose. I'm sorry I wasn't nicer to your mother. Don't get me wrong, she's hard work, but I know it bugged you that she and I didn't get on. I should have tried harder, for your sake. I doubt I'll ever see your family again now that I'm back in New Zealand. That's weird, I suppose. For a while, I was part of your family. Now I'm not.

It's almost Chinese New Year. I remember the stories you told me about the wishing trees. Obviously if I could have just one wish come true, it would be this:

I wish you were still here.

But I'm pretty sure others will have made that wish before, and if it was as easy as that, no one would ever really die.

So instead, I wish for other people not to make the same

mistakes we did and mess up their priorities. I wish that I'd understood while you were still alive the importance of not putting things off for another day. I wish we hadn't put work and the idea of success above our relationship as often as we did. How many times did we put work first? More times than I can count. So many dinner dates cancelled, Saturday morning lie-ins interrupted. That holiday we booked to Thailand last year; the one that had to be postponed after something important came up at your work (I think it was when that scandal broke on the singing show). I remember how stressed out you were trying to sort the PR, how life-and-death it seemed to you at the time. Well, guess what? It wasn't life OR death. It was just work. Those plane tickets are still languishing in a computer system somewhere, unused, waiting for a holiday we'll never take.

And guess what, despite everything, after all the loyalty you showed your employers, they replaced you a week after you died.

One week.

Seven days.

One hundred and sixty-eight hours.

They simply carried on as though you'd never even been there. The void you left filled by another. One falls, another one steps up to take their place.

It's just the way the world works.

I wish I'd known all this back then.

All my love,

S

I finish reading with tears in my eyes. It's obvious that he's in a world of pain. He sounds so lost, and my heart breaks for him and everything he has been through. I stare out to sea and watch a yacht in the distance, its sails white against a dusky pink sky. Despite what happened between us, the thought of him hurting brings me no pleasure. The opposite, in fact. The part of me that once cared for him wants to do something to help, but I'm not sure what. And how can I, when he won't even speak to me?

Realising that he might come back here, I roll the letter up and tie it to the tree branch again, hoping I have the right one, or that he won't remember if I haven't.

As I step back and look at the paper gently rustling in the breeze, I have an idea. Maybe there *is* a way I can communicate with him, without him knowing it's me.

Sam

Another restless night, courtesy of my earlier run-in with Ellie. In hindsight, I probably should have prepared myself mentally for the possibility of seeing her, but I really thought she'd have been long gone by now. The thought of her living and working in the same place for all these years is frankly depressing. I could hazard a guess as to what kept her tied here, though. Her grandmother. Ellie is nothing if not loyal, as I learned the hard way.

The sun is not long up when I admit defeat and roll out of bed. Various twinges and aches remind me of my walk the evening before, the most physical exercise I've done in a while. It seems a bit silly now, in the light of a new day, leaving the letter in the tree. I imagine someone chancing across it, reading my personal thoughts, and feel exposed. Not because they could identify me; they couldn't. I didn't sign it with my name, just an initial. But still. It's not a nice feeling.

I boil the jug and then make myself a coffee using the granules I purchased the day before from the supermarket. It smells OK, I think, giving it a tentative sniff as I carry it out onto the deck. The outdoor furniture is weathered, the paint peeling from the salt air and the harsh winds that often blow in off the ocean, but the bones are good, the chairs sturdy. Made in a time when things were designed to last. One of the table legs is missing a screw and wobbles a bit, and the whole lot could do with a new paint job, which I'd be tempted to do if I was planning on sticking around. I remember meals around this table on warm summer evenings. Stars overhead, fairy lights strung around the spouting of the house, music drifting out through the open doors. Platters of food and jugs of cordial. Laughter, conversations, the ocean a steady constant noise in the background.

A few early surfers are already out on the water, and swimmers are churning up and down the beach doing their laps. I watch them, trying to remember how it felt to ride a wave, but it's been so long. I *know* it was exhilarating, but the exact feeling eludes me.

The coffee is not great. It's not bad, but it's not great either. I manage half a cup before my inner coffee snob decides that's enough. There's a bitter taste in my mouth and a coating on my teeth, or maybe I'm just imagining that. I never used to be like this, obsessed with caffeine, but after Mei died, it was pretty much all that got me to work and enabled me to function, and now I have an unhealthy reliance on it. I swirl my mug and stare at the liquid left in the bottom. Maybe drinking this sludge might actually work in my favour by helping to decrease my dependence. I take another sip and feel my face scrunch up in distaste. Then again, maybe not.

I think about the espresso I bought yesterday from Ellie's café. Even though half of it ended up being spilled, it was still one of the best cups of coffee I'd had in a long time.

Dammit.

Ellie

'I have information,' Chloe announces, early the next morning.

I hold the phone at arm's length and squint at the numbers at the top of the screen. It's just gone 6 a.m. My alarm would have gone off in another fifteen minutes anyway, but still, fifteen minutes' sleep is fifteen minutes' sleep. It all adds up. Especially after I stayed up late last night deciding what to write to Sam. The pile of screwed-up, discarded pages in my rubbish bin is testament to the amount of time I spent trying to get it just right.

'It's six o'clock,' I mumble.

'Two minutes past, actually.'

I touch the speakerphone button and put the phone on the kitchen drawer beside my bed, sitting up to rub my eyes. 'Why are you calling me at six in the morning?'

'I told you, I have information.'

'This *is* Chloe, right?'

'Yes. Duh.'

'Don't duh me. You're *never* up this early.'

'No,' she concedes. 'Not typically. But in case you've forgotten, I'm getting married soon, remember? And I have *so* much still to do, so instead of sleeping, I lay awake plotting seating plans and song lists, and I still can't decide whether to wear my hair up or down, because on the one hand I like the way my neck looks when it's up, but on the other hand, I'm worried that my ears stick out too much.'

'Chloe.'

'Then of course my mother-in-law decided to put her oar in and say that as far as *she's* concerned, only models and influencers get married with their hair loose, though how the *fuck* she even knows what an influencer is, I don't know, because she can barely even manage to turn her phone on. Oh, and guess what my idiot future husband did last night?'

'Uh . . .'

'He only went and sprained his fucking ankle at soccer practice, so I don't even know if he'll be able to do our first dance any more, even though we've taken all those lessons from Steph, for, like, five months now. Seriously, I could throttle—'

'*Chloe.*'

She finally stops talking. 'What?'

'Breathe.'

'I *am* breathing.'

'Sure you are, like you're on the verge of having a heart attack. Take some *slow* breaths. Sloooow.'

'No time for that,' she says dismissively. 'I have to be at the flower vendor's farm at eight to finalise the bouquets, button-holes and tables. That's another dilemma. I've always, my entire life, thought I wanted to carry pale pink Juliet roses down the aisle, but yesterday I was flicking through a bridal magazine in the waiting room and there were these bouquets of, like, gerberas and dahlias and all sorts of different-coloured flowers and they actually looked kind of cool. So now I'm doubting my choice. And if I'm doubting *that* decision, how can I be sure about anything? It's just so much pressure, you know? I mean, how does anyone make these massive decisions?'

'Massive? Really? You don't think you might be going a teensy bit over the—'

'Yes, *massive*. Dammit, El, I only plan on doing this wedding thing once in my life, so I want everything to be fucking perfect. Is that so bad?'

I pull open the drawer underneath my bed and find clean shorts and a T-shirt. 'No, of course not,' I soothe. 'Everything *will* be perfect, and you know how I know? Because you have impeccable taste. The most perfect taste of anyone I know. So no matter what you decide, it will be amazing.'

She sniffs, slightly mollified. 'You really think so?'

'I know so. Now, about this information . . .'

'I don't suppose you could take the morning off, come to the flower place with me? I could really use a second opinion.'

I hesitate before answering, and she misreads the silence.

'What's the point of being the boss if you can't take time off whenever you want?' she snaps. 'Or when your best friend is having an emotional crisis and needs you?'

I slide the note I spent so much time composing in the early hours of the morning across the table towards me. 'It's not that. We've quietened down enough for Kelly and the others to hold the fort.'

'Then what?'

'It's just, I was planning on starting later anyway, because I want to go for a run first.' I wince in anticipation.

'Are you serious?'

'What?'

'You ditched me last night to go for a run, remember? Wait.' Her tone lowers suspiciously. 'Are you secretly seeing someone and all these runs are just an elaborate excuse so you can meet up and fuck?'

I stumble midway through pulling my shorts on and bump my thigh against the edge of the table.

'No,' I protest, rubbing my leg. It's going to leave a bruise for sure. 'Not seeing anyone, and *not* an excuse. I legitimately went for a run.'

'Mm. Pity. It's been a while since you got any.'

'Thanks for the reminder.'

'You're welcome. Hey, maybe you'll get lucky at my wedding. The maid of honour usually cops off with someone, doesn't she? It's, like, practically one of your duties.'

'Not going to happen.'

'It might. You know Logan would be up for it.'

'Putting aside the fact that I'm sure Sarah, his *girlfriend*, wouldn't be too happy, I'm not interested in Logan. At all.'

'I know he was a bit of a dick when you guys broke up, but

it was only because he was madly in love with you. He still is, according to Hamish.'

'Have you heard yourself? He was obsessive. It wasn't healthy, and you shouldn't brush that behaviour off as simply being lovesick.'

She sighs. 'You're right. He's not as bad as you think, though. Hamish wouldn't still be best friends with him if he was.'

'Are we done? I need to get going.'

'I don't know. All this exercise. I swear to God, Ellie, if you look better in my wedding photos than I do, we really will be done. I'll never forgive you.'

'As if that could even be remotely possible.'

I mean it, too. Sure, I'm attractive in a healthy, athletic, surfer-girl kind of way. But Chloe is stunning. Positively ethereal. Delicate features, long, cascading waves of dark hair, pale skin. She even modelled a bit when we were younger. Her appearance gives off an aura of serenity that is one hundred per cent completely at odds with her personality. Chloe is a storm trapped in a dove's body.

'I don't know,' she says forlornly. 'The stress of all these decisions is making me comfort-eat. I polished that whole pizza off by myself last night, then hated myself for it. And you, actually, a little bit. It was your fault for not coming, after all.'

'I'm sorry.'

'You should be. Hey,' she brightens, 'maybe I should come for a run with you ...'

'Uh ...' There's no way I'd be able to do what I plan to do with her tagging along. Not without having to explain about

Sam's letter, and then she'd no doubt want to read it. He'd hate that, I know he would. It's bad enough that *I* read it.

'. . . but not this morning,' she continues. 'I've already eaten and I don't want to get a stitch. Plus I need to get ready for the flower farm. So you'll come? I'll pick you up at quarter to eight? Pretty please?'

I check my watch. It's 6.15. If I leave now and run fast enough, I should have enough time to get to the tree and back and have a quick shower before she gets here. 'OK. Yes, I'll come.'

'Thank you!' she squeals. 'You're the best maid of honour ever.'

I fire off a couple of quick messages to Maxine and Kelly, letting them know I'll be in later, then carefully fold the letter up and tuck it into my back pocket. I can't find string in any of my drawers, but I find a red ribbon from a gift someone gave me last birthday. I tuck that into my pocket too and set off, only remembering as I reach the end of the street that she never told me that information after all.

Sam

'Did you have trouble finding the door?' the girl behind the counter asks with a smirk. She's the same one who made my coffee yesterday. *Kelly*, her name badge says.

'Sorry?'

She jerks her head over my shoulder. 'I've been watching you walk back and forward past the window for, like, five minutes now.'

'Oh, uh, no. I was just . . . looking for . . .'

'Relax. She's not here.'

'Who?'

She tilts her head slightly and gives me a look that says, *Really?*

I drop the act. 'That obvious, huh?'

'To a highly intuitive person such as myself, yes. What's the deal with you and Ellie anyway? Why are you avoiding her?'

'There's no deal.'

'She said you were an old friend.'

I look down at the counter and swallow hard, before replying softly, 'Yes.'

'There's more to the story, though,' she says shrewdly. 'The way you guys looked at—'

I cut her off. 'Just a double espresso to go, please.'

She sighs disappointedly. 'I get it. You don't want to talk about it. Fine. Cup?'

'Yes, please. A cup would be helpful.'

She snorts with laughter. 'I wasn't going to make you drink it out of your hands. I meant, did you bring a reusable cup? Fifty cents off, remember?'

'Ah, yes. I do remember now that you mention it, but no, I haven't got one.'

'Well, today is your lucky day, because as I mentioned yesterday, we happen to sell a fine range here in store. Would you care to see the selection?'

'Uh . . .' I flick a nervous glance behind me.

'Don't worry, she won't be back for a while yet. She's gone shopping for wedding flowers.'

The news that Ellie is getting married hits me like a punch in the stomach, knocking the air out of me. I shouldn't care. I *don't* care. And yet . . . I feel sick at the thought. I swallow hard and try to sound casual. 'Wedding?'

Kelly crouches down and reaches underneath the counter, her voice muffled. 'Yes, been in the works for a while. They got engaged *ages* ago, like, five years. But that's what it's like around here. No one's in a hurry to do anything.'

'Yeah,' I answer softly. 'I remember.'

She stands up again, her hands full of cups, which she places on the counter. 'So, are you from round here?'

'No, not originally. My grandparents lived here, and I came to live with them when I was fourteen.'

'Why? Did something happen to your parents?'

'No,' I reply, surprised by her blunt questions. 'Living here was just a better fit for me back then, with my . . . interests.'

'Interests?'

'Are you this nosy with everyone?'

She shrugs. 'You call it nosy, I call it taking an interest. I think I'm going do an online creative writing course, so I need lots of inspiration for the story assignments.'

'I'd rather you didn't write about me.'

She goes on as if I haven't spoken. 'Where's your grandparents' place?'

'The north end of Main Beach Road.'

'Really? Maybe I know them. Do they come in here?'

'They're both dead now.'

'Oh. I'm sorry to hear that.'

'That's why I'm here. To clean the house up a bit so I can sell it.'

'A property on Main Beach Road, eh?' She whistles air in through her teeth. 'If I had a spare million, I'd take it off your hands.'

'I doubt it's worth that much.'

'You'd be surprised. House prices here jumped massively around six months ago, at least according to Chloe. That's Ellie's friend. She's a real-estate agent who comes in most days.'

'Chloe?' The name rings a bell.

'Dark hair, tiny. Tendency to boss people around. She's been Ellie's best friend since way back.'

Ah yes, Chloe. I remember her, part of the large group of friends Ellie hung out with. I want to tell Kelly that she's wrong. That for the longest time, *I* was Ellie's best friend. But of course I don't.

'Anyway, here are the cups we have. They're eight ninety-nine each, which might sound a lot, but you'll soon make that back in savings on future coffees.'

'Quite the salesperson, aren't you?' I remark, surveying the selection.

'Actually, I'm from a generation that happens to care deeply about the environment,' she retorts, picking up one of the cups. 'Now this one is my personal favourite. We get paintings done by local artists printed on them. We also sell other stuff with the images on, tea towels, tiles, T-shirts, et cetera. But it's the end of summer, so stock's pretty much cleaned out.'

'I'll take it,' I say, without even really looking at it. I know she said that Ellie would be gone for ages, but the more time passes, the more nervous I get. I wasn't very nice to her yesterday, and I'm well aware that grief isn't an excuse for bad behaviour.

'Excellent choice, sir.' She pushes the other cups to the side and moves to the coffee machine. 'Double espresso in a reusable cup coming right up.'

'My name's Sam.'

'Kelly.'

'No, Sam. S . . . A . . . M.'

She looks at me confused for a few seconds, then groans. 'Ugh, dad joke,' she says, rolling her eyes.

'I'm not a dad.'

'You're old enough to be one, though. No offence.'

'I'm not *that* old.' I wonder just how old she thinks I am. I know that grief has aged me. The lack of sleep, not to mention the fact that I've gotten into a bad habit of convenience food since Mei died. Quick, easy, generally tasteless meals. If you can even call them that. Some nights I'll just have a cheese sandwich for dinner. Others, a banana.

She clicks the lid firmly closed on my new cup and slides it across the counter. 'Well, S . . . A . . . M, that will be twelve ninety-nine, thanks. Unless you'd like a cake to go with it? A cream doughnut, maybe?'

'Just the cup and the coffee, thanks.'

'Oh, hang on a sec,' she says as I tap my card. She pulls open a drawer beneath the counter and sifts through its contents. 'I'm sure I saw one in here somewhere,' she mutters. 'Aha.' Nudging the drawer closed again with her hip, she holds something out to me.

'What's that?'

She rolls her eyes. 'Here's an idea, why don't you take it and find out.'

I gingerly hold one corner between my thumb and finger and she releases it. It's a business card. *Chloe Simpson, Realtor.*

'You said you're here to sell your grandparents' place. I thought that might come in handy.'

'Why? Do you get a commission on referrals?'

She shakes her head. 'So cynical. No, S . . . A . . . M, I don't.'

I hold the card back out to her. 'Thanks, but I think I'll find someone else.'

'You could do that.' She nods, accepting it. 'Of course we *do* only have the one agency here in town, and while there are other agents *at* that agency, and I *hate* to admit this because she's a bit of a pain in the ass, it's pretty common knowledge around here that Chloe is the best.'

Dammit. 'Really?'

'Really.'

She offers the card again. This time I take it and tuck it into a pocket.

I'm almost at the door when she calls out again. 'Oh, and S . . . A . . . M?'

'Yes?'

'Ellie goes to the bank every weekday morning around ten and is usually gone for twenty minutes or so.'

I smile ruefully and lift my coffee in salute. 'Thanks.'

'And don't forget your cup next time.'

Ellie

Every time I go for a run, I check the tree. It's like a little ritual. Finish work, head home for a quick change and to look in on Nan, then I'm off. Run along the beach and over the little hill to Sailor's Cove, jog along the beach until I get to the end, check the coast is clear, then climb up the bank. My hopes are dashed every time I see the two pieces of paper still tied to branches near each other. Sam's letter, and mine. Several times I almost lose my nerve and am tempted to rip mine down, but then I remember how sad Sam sounded. I have no idea whether my note will in any way console him, or whether it'll have the opposite effect, but I have to try.

At the flower farm, Chloe told me what she'd found out through internet sleuthing. Sam's wife, Mei, was killed in a horrible accident. Hit by a car on her way to work. She was only twenty-six. Every time I try to imagine how he must have felt hearing the news, I want to cry. It must have been awful for him, losing her so tragically, left on his own to grieve in a foreign country. I mean, I know he would have had colleagues and friends, but still, I wish I could have been there for him. The thought of him going through it all on his own is heartbreaking.

I start to think that he has no intention of going back to the tree. Maybe this was just something he needed to get out of his system. Some people burn letters to lost loved ones. Sam tied his to a tree. Some kind of therapy, I guess.

But when I check again on the evening of the fifth day, both letters are gone.

Sam

Dear S,

I won't do that awful thing people do when they say 'I know how you feel', because I don't, and because I think it completely trivialises what you're going through. I haven't suffered a loss like yours; no one has. You are the only husband in the whole wide world who lost your wife Mei, and as such, you're entitled to feel and grieve however you want. (And yes, anyone who tells you that your deceased loved one is still with you is an idiot. An idiot with good intentions, sure, but an idiot just the same. Whether you believe in the afterlife or not, it's NOT the same thing as having them still here with you. It's just not.)

However, while I might not have suffered your loss, I have lost someone I loved. I know how much it hurts. So much so that sometimes you wonder how you can possibly survive without them.

I know you know this, because you seem like an intelligent kind of guy, but you will survive, and it does get easier. It really does. If you'll allow me the use of a well-worn cliché, time heals the wound. But it leaves behind a scar. And maybe on particularly cold or rainy days, the scar will prickle. Or when it's too hot, or when the wind blows in from the east. My point is, it will still hurt from time to time. But you'll find a way to live with it.

You'll never forget, and you'll never stop loving her. But you do need to find a way to carry on living, and I don't just mean going through the motions. You, more than anyone, understand how quickly it can all be taken away. Obviously I never knew your wife, and yet I can say this with absolute certainty. She would want you to be happy. She wouldn't want you to feel regret or guilt for what was or what might have been. She would want you to embrace this messy, imperfect, complicated ride we call life. Grieve, yes. Always. But make sure you live, too.

DG

I turn the piece of paper over and scan the back for any clues as to the identity of the writer, but it's completely blank. Who is DG? And how the hell did they find my letter?

Ellie

'Is it true?'

I breathe in slowly and deeply, mentally preparing myself before turning. Beads of condensation coat the outside of the wine glass in my hand. I take a sip before swapping it over and wiping my hand on my dress. Even though it's 6.30 in the evening, the air is still muggy and humid. 'Is what true?'

Logan Wheeler stares at me with a tortured expression, one heavily borrowed from James Dean. He's somehow managed to make it look even more wounded than usual, but I know it's just an act, so it doesn't have the same effect on me as it does on other girls. 'I just heard that guy is back in town.'

'If you mean Sam, then yeah. It's true.'

He snorts, triggered. I can't help but bristle at the jealousy that flashes across his face.

'What does he want?' he asks stiffly.

'Nothing to do with me, if that's what you're worried about.

Although you shouldn't be. We're not together any more, remember? We haven't been for a really long time. Speaking of, where *is* Sarah?' I crane my neck to look around Chloe's back yard for Logan's long-suffering girlfriend.

'Cut it out, Ellie,' he says.

'No, *you* cut it out. This possessive act of yours got old a long time ago.'

He looks down at the ground, and uses the sharp toe of his boot to kick out the root of a weed growing in the lawn. I don't think Chloe will appreciate the hole this will leave behind, but I let it go.

'I'm sorry, OK?' he says finally. 'You know I can't help it.'

'That's not true.'

He steps forward and stares into my eyes earnestly. 'I love you, and I always will, because unlike some people,' his tone turns bitter, 'I can't just turn my feelings off.'

'It was a long time ago and we were never that serious.'

'Then why did you kiss me that night? It's because you still have feelings for me too, Ellie. I know you do.'

I cringe at the memory, foggy as it is. I was probably the drunkest and most devastated I'd ever been that night, courtesy of the fact that I'd just learned from my grandmother that Sam was getting married. 'That was a mistake, and I've apologised for it.'

'Nah.' He shakes his head. 'It wasn't a mistake. You just can't admit you still love me.'

I choose my next words deliberately. With Logan, I've learnt it's best just to spell things out. No grey areas, no mixed signals. Just the truth, no matter how much it might hurt him. 'Logan, I cared about you once. But I've never been in love with you.'

The wounded puppy look comes back. 'I don't believe you.'

'It's true.'

'You're just trying to be a bitch so I'll stop loving you. It's not going to work.'

'Oh my God, this conversation is going nowhere.' I step around him, intending to walk away. He grabs my arm, stopping me. 'You've got three seconds to let go,' I say calmly. 'One.'

He holds on for a brief moment, his fingers tightening and his eyes flashing as he tries to figure out whether I'm serious or not. Knowing him, he thinks it's some kind of sick foreplay. Finally he reluctantly lets go. Slowly, though, as if he's letting me know it's on his terms. 'Sorry. *Fuck.*' He kicks the ground again in frustration. 'It's your fault, Ellie. You drive me nuts. You always have, since we were thirteen years old.'

I finally spot Sarah in the crowd, over by the bar Hamish and the guys built a few years ago out of old pallets. As if sensing my gaze on her, she turns, narrowing her eyes as she notices Logan standing far too close to me.

'Your girlfriend's coming,' I tell him.

'Say the word and I'll dump her.'

'Nice, Logan. Real nice.'

He checks to make sure Sarah isn't within earshot yet. Luckily for him, she's been waylaid briefly by Issy, but her eyes remain firmly fixed on us. 'Just promise me one thing, OK?'

'No.'

'Stay away from that guy. He's bad news. Remember what he did.'

'It was complicated, though. I mean, you can understand why he was upset.' I watch as Sarah brushes Issy off and scurries towards us.

'Upset, sure. But to accuse me? Just because he was jealous that I was with you?'

'Funny,' I muse. 'He said the same thing about you.'

His jaw clenches. 'I mean it, Ellie. Stay away from him.'

'Hi, Sarah.' I turn and smile brightly at her as she blows in like a ship under full sail and wraps a proprietorial hand around Logan's upper arm. A thick layer of Angel perfume trails in her wake. It's cloying in the hot, muggy air. 'How's things?'

'Ellie,' she says, slightly nodding her head, ignoring my question.

She hates me, and I don't blame her, although I've never done anything to hurt her. It's not my fault her boyfriend's such a disloyal dick. Growing up, she and I were even friends. Well, not *friend* friends. Acquaintances. It's a small town, with a small school. Everyone knew everyone. Unfortunately, it's common knowledge that Logan still has feelings for me, even though I've done everything I can to discourage him. The kiss, six or seven years ago, was a stupid mistake that I regretted instantly, but it was enough to fan the flames of his affection, to give him false hope.

She rolls her eyes sideways without even moving her head, glaring up at Logan.

104

'I've been looking everywhere for you,' she says, through gritted teeth.

'I've been right here the whole time,' he replies sullenly, taking a swig from his beer and shrugging her arm off in the process.

'I better go and find Chloe, see if she needs any help.' I back away as Sarah starts muttering in a low tone and Logan's face clouds with anger. *This* is why I started avoiding gatherings years ago, because they inevitably ended with Logan glaring at any guy I talked to and ignoring his own girlfriend until they ended up in a blazing row. I hated it. He seems even worse tonight, though. Obviously finding out that Sam is back in town has rekindled his anger.

When Sam moved here full-time at the age of fourteen, he got the usual cold shoulder from most of the local kids. They were a tight-knit bunch, fiercely territorial. It was bad enough putting up with the influx of crowds every summer, taking over our town and beaches, but an outsider who moved in and never left, *and* who could surf better than any of the local boys? Well, that was just insult upon insult. Sam and I had been summer friends since we were ten, but after he moved here we became best friends, always together. They slowly grew to accept him, but never completely, and never Logan.

I wander through the throng, searching for Chloe, and find her inside the house scooping home-made creamy onion dip out of a big bowl into smaller bowls.

'Hey,' she says, licking the spoon before rinsing it under the tap and dropping it in the sink. 'There you are. Has Hamish fired up the BBQ yet?'

'No idea.'

She sniffs the air. 'Smells like it. Help me empty these chips into bowls, would you.' She opens the pantry and starts tossing packets onto the white benchtop.

I love Chloe's kitchen. I love Chloe's *house*. She and Hamish built this place two years ago, in one of the newer subdivisions in town. They were pretty much the first house, surrounded by empty sections. Now, every section has a house on it, most of them eerily similar. But where the rest are a sea of pale brick with double garages and minimal lawns and gardens, Chloe and Hamish opted for a sleek black wooden design with a large back yard designed for entertaining, complete with spa pool. It's very tasteful and stylish, just like her.

I pick up a packet of salt and vinegar and pull open the top, breathing in the tangy smell it releases. A headache has started to make itself known in the back of my skull, probably courtesy of Sarah's perfume.

'Did I see you talking to Logan?' Chloe asks, emptying chips into a large crystal bowl.

'No, you saw me *cornered* by Logan,' I reply resentfully. 'You could have rescued me.'

'Oh no.' She screws up her face. 'You're kidding. Was he up to his old tricks? You guys have been pretty good lately.'

'Yeah, well, that was before he found out Sam is back in town.'

'Ah.' She picks up a chip and nibbles daintily on the end. 'I wondered how he'd feel about that.'

'Wonder no more. He's pissed off, and jealous, *and* issuing demands he has no right to issue.'

'Like what?'

'Like trying to get me to promise I won't have anything to do with Sam. I mean, the cheek of it.' I grab a handful of chips and shove them into my mouth. 'To think he has *any* say over *any* aspect of my life.'

Chloe winces as a shower of crumbs falls from my mouth onto the bench.

'Sorry,' I mumble.

'Maybe try a few less next time,' she replies, fetching a dish cloth and restoring the bench to its pristine state. 'And just ignore Logan. You know he's never got over you.'

'That doesn't excuse his behaviour.'

'Maybe not. But he's harmless.'

'It's borderline harassment.'

She pulls a face. 'OK, so he can be a bit . . . annoying.'

'Are you listening to yourself? Would you be saying any of this if he wasn't Hamish's friend?'

'We grew up together, remember? He's *all* of our friend.'

I don't say anything, just stare at her, waiting for diplomatic Chloe to bugger off and loyal friend Chloe to take her place. Under my stare, it doesn't take long.

'You're right.' She nods. 'Of course you are. He's out of line. I'll ask Hamish to have a word, tell him to back off.'

'I've told him myself.'

'I'm sure you did, but he's more likely to listen to Hamish.' She picks up and carefully balances three bowls of chips. 'Grab the dip and follow me, will you? There's something else I need to tell you.'

'What?' I ask, following her to the bar outside, where a bunch of our friends are gathered for this pre-wedding/end-of-summer-soccer-league get-together. She reaches through them and places the bowls down, then takes the dip off me and plonks that down too. A multitude of hands immediately dive for them. 'What do you need to tell me?'

She heads back towards the kitchen. 'Help me with the salads.'

'Chloe.'

'What?' She opens the fridge and disappears behind the door.

'What did you want to tell me?'

'Oh yes.' A hand holds out a bowl of coleslaw for me to take. 'I had a call from Sam.'

It takes a few moments to sink in. *My* Sam?'

'Can you technically still call him that?' She emerges with an egg, pasta and bacon salad and tilts her head thoughtfully.

'You know what I mean. What did he want?'

'He wants me to go and have a look at his grandad's house. Well, *his* house now. Advise him on what needs to be done to bring it up to sale standard and give him an appraisal value.'

'Are you going to do it?'

'Of course. As long as he understands that I get the listing when he's ready to sell. I'm not doing all the work and then having someone else swoop in and get the commission.'

I make a noise in my throat. 'Weird.'

'Why is that weird? It's called valuing yourself.'

'No, not that. I mean the fact that he called *you*.'

She narrows her eyes at me. 'Why wouldn't he call me? I'm the best agent in town. In the region, actually.'

'Yes, obviously. It's just ... surely he remembers that you and I are friends?'

'So?'

'Well, he made it pretty clear the other day that he wanted nothing to do with me.' I shrug. 'It seems weird, that's all.'

'Ellie, in the nicest possible way, not everything is about you.'

'I know that,' I mutter defensively. 'Anyway, I don't care what he does, or who he does it with. I just thought it was a weird decision, that's all.'

Her face softens. 'Have you thought any more about talking to him?'

I screw up my face. 'I have.'

'And?'

'I'm not sure. Frankly, I'm worried about making things even worse.'

'How can they possibly get worse?'

'I don't know,' I admit.

She picks up a bowl of salad in each hand and starts to head outside, pausing to kiss me on the forehead on her way past. 'Sometimes,' she says, 'you just have to put your big-girl knickers on and go for it.'

Sam

She's been wandering around for at least ten minutes without speaking, poking her head into rooms and cupboards, making 'mm' noises and jotting things down in her black diary. I was right, I recognised her face as soon as I opened the door.

'Well?' I ask, a little too sharply, unable to bear her silence any more. It's hard not to perceive it as judgement on the house.

'I'd forgotten how beautiful this place is,' she says, smiling. 'Your grandmother really did have impeccable taste.'

I frown. 'You've been here before?'

She looks surprised. 'You don't remember?'

I shake my head. 'Should I?'

'You had a party here, I think it was for your seventeenth birthday.'

As soon as she says it, of course, the memory floods back. How could I have forgotten? My grandfather, always keen for me to fit in, let me invite half the senior year. In a small school like ours, that was only supposed to be around fifteen people. Word spread, though, as it does, and before I knew it, there were teenagers everywhere, spilling out of the house and down onto the beach. Even kids from other schools up the coast came.

Considering the amount of underage drinking, I was lucky it never got out of control. If it had, I wouldn't have even been around to stop it. That was the night Ellie got drunk for the first time. I remember the feeling of panic I had when I realised she was missing from the party and no one knew where she was. Thankfully she hadn't managed to get far, and I found her curled up in a ball in the dunes in front of the house. I tried to get her to go back to the party, but as soon as she got to her feet, she started retching. I held her hair out of her face while she threw up, then lay down with her under a star-streaked sky and let her rest her head on my chest as she drifted off to sleep, mumbling about how the world was spinning too fast.

'That was one epic party.' Chloe pulls a face. 'Well, at least until the cops turned up and confiscated the stereo. It fizzled out pretty quickly after that.'

'I'd forgotten about that.'

She smiles. 'I never really thanked you for looking out for Ellie that night.'

'No thanks necessary.'

'No, I mean it. You were a good friend to her.' She turns away, and as she does, she mutters under her breath, 'For the most part, anyway.'

I flush, embarrassed that she is clearly judging me for the way my friendship with Ellie finished. Of course she knows what happened. She was there. But I have no wish to get into it with her, so I change the subject abruptly. 'I know the house has some issues, but is it sellable as is?'

She nods. 'Absolutely.'

I exhale, relieved. 'Great.'

The relief is short-lived.

'*If* you're happy to take a much lower price than it's potentially worth.'

'Ah.'

She consults her diary. 'Don't get me wrong. I can see that you've done some work clearing the outside, and it looks great.'

'But?' I prompt, annoyed by her pause.

'*But* ... for most people, the street appeal doesn't really come into it when they're considering price point. Gardens and trees are an easy fix, after all. It comes down to the land and the structure at the end of the day.'

'OK, so tell me what needs to be done.'

'Well, for a start, most of the wooden joinery on the back of the house, all the sea-facing windows and this door frame' – she taps it with her pen – 'is rotten. That's what you get when it's exposed to the elements for so long and not treated frequently.'

'OK, so I need to treat it.'

She shakes her head. 'Unfortunately, it's too far gone. We're talking full replacement.'

'Every window?'

'Most of them. It depends how much money and time you want to pour into the house to get the best price for it.'

I feel a sinking sensation in my stomach. I didn't intend on

112

spending much time *or* money here, but it doesn't sound like a job that can be completed in a hurry.

'Also,' she points at the far wall, 'that fireplace is no longer compliant and needs to be disabled, and an alternative form of heating installed. And I suspect the insulation is not up to scratch either.' She consults her diary again. 'There *are* some quick, easy fixes as well.'

'Oh.' I smile weakly. 'Good.'

'A few loose cabinet doors, a missing hinge on the master bedroom wardrobe, and the light switch in the upstairs en suite isn't working, so you'll need to get an electrician in to look at that.'

'And that's it?'

'Pretty much. Oh, wait, your spouting is rusted through on the east side of the house, causing that horrible water stain on the paint. I'd repaint that and patch the spouting, if possible.'

'Right,' I say slowly, feeling like all the wind has been knocked out of me. She takes pity on me.

'Look, Sam,' she says. 'Some of my suggestions are purely cosmetic, some are necessary. But at the end of the day, it's all up to you.'

'What do you mean?'

'If you're after a quick sale and you're prepared to accept less than what you could potentially get, then that's your decision. I'm just here to guide you into getting the best price for the place.'

I look around the room, noticing for the first time how much it has aged.

'And to be honest,' she continues, 'there's a high chance that whoever buys the place will knock it down and build from scratch anyway.'

I frown. 'You mean . . . ?'

'Yes. Bulldoze the whole house to the ground.'

I wince. 'Who would do that?'

'Surely you've noticed all the new-builds around here?'

'Maybe,' I lie. Truth is, I haven't paid much attention to my surroundings at all.

'A lot of people from the cities have started buying properties up and down the coast and turning them into their own little havens away from home.' Her face darkens. 'They fled here at the first sign of trouble.'

'Trouble?'

'Lockdowns.'

'Ah.'

'Anyway,' she shakes her shoulders as if brushing the memory away, 'like I said, it's entirely your decision. These are just recommendations.' She gestures with her diary. 'There's a chance you could do all this and it'll be for nothing if they decide to rebuild.'

'There's no way to know in advance, is there?'

'I'm afraid not.' Her phone emits a shrill tone from inside a pocket and she reaches for it. 'I'm sorry, I thought I'd turned it off.'

'It's fine.'

She frowns at the screen. 'Actually, would you mind if I take this?'

'Go for it.'

'Thanks.' She swipes the screen, turns and heads outside onto the front deck. 'Chloe speaking.'

Ellie

'Hi, Chloe,' I say sweetly. 'Just calling to check in and see how my best friend is on this beautiful summer's day.'

'Really?' she replies cynically. 'So the timing of this call has nothing to do with the fact that you know full well I'm at Sam's house right now for our appointment?'

'Oh gosh, is that today? I'd totally forgotten.'

'We talked on the phone two hours ago, Ellie. I mentioned it then.'

'Fine. I *might* have remembered. So?'

'So . . . what?'

'Has he . . . ah, has he mentioned me at all?'

'Ellie, Sam is standing like three metres away from me right now. I told you I'd call you after I left, remember?'

'Yes, but you were taking ages.' I'm aware I sound petulant, but I don't care. 'I mean, how long does it even take to appraise a house?'

'Do I tell you how to do your job?'

'All the time.'

She sighs, taking pity on me. 'He looks like you said he looked. The same guy we used to know but different. Sadder, like he's had a tough time of it. Which he has.'

I feel a twinge of sympathy. 'How's the house?'

'The house looks the same as it did back then too,' she says. 'But like it's been neglected. Kind of like Sam, when you think about it. I don't think his grandfather did much to maintain it after his grandmother died. I really should get back to him, Ellie. He's waiting.'

'OK. If he does happen to ask about me . . .'

'I'm here for business only.'

'I know, but *just in case*, can you maybe, kind of casually drop into conversation how successful I've—'

'*Ellie.*'

'I'd do it for you,' I mutter defensively.

'This is just like when you used to ask me to pass notes to him in class,' she sighs. 'And there was me thinking we were all adults now. Got to go, we'll talk later.'

Sam

While Chloe takes her phone call, I look around the room that holds so many memories. She's right. My grandmother was an adept socialiser, and every summer this was a house filled with laughter and conversation, the chink of cutlery on plates and the sound of wine being poured into glasses. Music filled the air from discreetly hidden speakers. It was a house designed for people. For living. Stories, quarrels, love. Not this sad silence that echoes through the rooms now. The thought of someone knocking this place with all of its history to the ground makes me feel sick.

Chloe comes back into the room. 'I'm sorry about that,' she says, smiling. She's barely taken three steps, though, before her phone starts ringing again.

'You're very popular,' I comment.

She smiles through gritted teeth. 'Yes, it's, ah, a very *persistent* client. I'll just get rid of them.'

'*I said no,*' she growls, heading outside again. Then her tone changes abruptly. 'Oh, sorry. Yes, this is Chloe. I thought you were someone else. I assume you're calling about my email? We really need to lock the catering numbers in and finalise the menu.'

I walk over to the kitchen island and slide open the second drawer. The notepad I hastily stashed in there when she arrived is sitting on top of an array of cutlery, the page half covered in my scrawl. I stare at it. Am I seriously considering writing back to a complete stranger? One who not only invaded my privacy by reading what were clearly very personal thoughts, but also felt it appropriate to reply? My first reaction was naturally anger. I can understand someone seeing a note tied to a tree (although I'm not sure how they could have, to be honest. I checked, twice, and there's no way it was visible from the beach), but as soon as they opened it, they must have realised its private nature. Yet they still read it, *and* replied.

I hear Chloe's voice grow louder, her tone angry. Whoever she's talking to is copping an earful. I can't make out what she's saying, but nor do I want to. It's none of my business.

I read over what I've already written and cringe inside. It's such a vulnerable thing to do, opening up my thoughts to another person, and yet this is quite possibly the best form and manner in which to do so. Completely anonymously.

I tried talking to friends back in Hong Kong, but it was all so horribly awkward. After Mei's funeral, in that first year, it quickly became apparent that people would much rather pretend she had never existed than bring her up in conversation and risk having to hear the actual, honest truth about how I was feeling. When they asked how I was, they didn't really want to know. They were just being polite. I saw it in their eyes. Fear of what I might say. Or that I might dissolve into an inconsolable mess at their feet.

Or worse, that I might react with anger, as I sometimes did. I wasn't angry with them, but with the unjustness of it all. The complete and utter unfairness of what had happened to my wife. My sweet, innocent Mei, who had done absolutely nothing to deserve it. I couldn't get my head around the fact that evil people, the really sick, twisted ones who committed some of the most despicable acts known to man, got to carry on living. Why did *they* deserve to live and not my wife? How was that fair?

About six months after Mei died, I punched a man from work. He was a bit of a prick anyway, but I still shouldn't have done it. I'd overheard him in the lunchroom complaining about how miserable I was, and that I should be over it by now. Like there's a time limit on grief. I didn't punch him because of that, though. I punched him because when he realised that I'd heard, instead of apologising, he doubled down, told me I needed to stop milking my wife's death for sympathy. After all, he argued, at least she'd died quickly. It wasn't a horrible, pro-longed death like Ryan in accounts' wife, who'd died of breast cancer. *That* had been awful, he'd said. The implication being, of course, that Mei's death was somehow less significant. *That* was when I hit him, and although his nose wasn't broken, it was horribly swollen for a week. I was hauled into HR. Word spread. People avoided me even more.

Nobody wanted to hear that I barely slept, or that some days I drank more whisky than water. That I cried when I saw her toothbrush next to mine, or that I'd chased a woman down the street who had looked so much like Mei from behind I was convinced it was her. That I'd scared her by not letting go of her shoulder until a passer-by had made me. They didn't want to know that I'd stood on the corner where she had died and contemplated stepping out into traffic myself.

They didn't want to hear any of that.

'Sorry about that.' Chloe comes back into the room. Immediately I can tell that something is wrong. She appears distracted, her brow furrowed as she flips her phone case shut. She's clearly stressed out about something, but is making a valiant attempt to hide it. 'Where were we?'

'You were saying it's my decision whether or not to fix up the house before I sell it.'

'Right. Yes. You know what, just do whatever the hell you want. Everyone else does.' She collapses onto the couch and buries her face in her hands.

'Uh, OK. Chloe, this might be none of my business, but is everything all right?' I ask cautiously, not really wanting to get involved, but feeling like I should at least show some kindness, given that we have a shared history.

'No,' she mumbles into her hands. 'Nothing is all right. Everything is very much *not* all right.'

'The phone call was bad news, I take it.'

She runs her hands over her hair. 'The worst. That was the events manager from Saltwater.'

I stare at her blankly.

'The very prestigious wedding venue at Whitehaven? Stunning architectural design, right on the beach?'

I shake my head, still none the wiser.

'Well, I was *supposed* to be having my wedding there,' she says. 'But they've just called to say there's been some kind of mix-up, and *somehow* they double-booked my date. Apparently my email was filed in the wrong place by someone who was temporarily covering the manager's position. How does that even happen? I mean, what kind of outfit are they running? Fucking amateurs.'

'Oh.' Something niggles at my brain.

'And because the other couple booked and paid their deposit first, they're going to honour *their* contract. Not mine. Can you believe it?'

'That's . . . not good.'

'Not good? I'm fucked. Completely fucked. They were very apologetic and said they'd refund my money, blah blah blah, but where am I supposed to find another venue at this short notice? I'll sue them for this, I swear to God.'

She's not even really talking to me any more as she mutters away to herself, seemingly on the verge of a full-blown panic attack. I realise what it was that confused me.

'Hang on a second, *your* wedding?'

She stops muttering and looks up at me. 'What?'

'Sorry, it's just . . . Are you and Ellie both getting married?'

'Ellie? No.' She frowns. 'Ellie's not getting married. Why would you think that?'

I ignore the relief that floods through me. 'Something that someone said.'

'Well, you must have misheard. I'm the bride. Ellie is my maid of honour.'

'Right. Well, congratulations.'

'Thanks,' she replies, her voice wobbling. I notice that her eyes are suspiciously glassy, as if tears have welled up in them. 'I'm sorry, I'm usually more professional than this.'

I shuffle my feet, hoping that the tears won't spill over. I haven't had to comfort a crying woman in a long time. I'm not sure I even remember how. 'It's fine, honestly.'

'This wedding is just really stressing me out, you know?'

I nod, even though I don't know. My wedding in Hong Kong was organised entirely by Mei and her family. All I had to do was show up, and pay for it, as is tradition for the groom's family over there.

'There's just so much to organise and so many decisions, and when I finally start to relax and think everything is sorted, this happens!' Her voice quivers. 'What am I going to do? It's too late to find anywhere decent now. All the beachside venues book out years in advance.' She sniffs, and the dam holding back the tears finally breaks.

Shit.

I don't have any tissues, but remember seeing a roll of old paper towels in the pantry. I fetch one and pass it to her. She takes it and blows her nose noisily.

'I'm sorry,' she says, her voice muffled through the paper.

'Don't be.'

122

'What am I going to do?' she repeats, wailing.

I look over her shoulder at the large open-plan living room with its bifold doors that open out onto the deck. Her earlier words flutter through my head.

Your grandmother really did have impeccable taste.

There's a high chance that whoever buys the place will knock it down and build from scratch anyway.

Why not give the house one last, spectacular hurrah?

'I suppose you could always have your wedding ... here,' I say, without really stopping to consider what I'm offering.

She lowers the paper towel and looks at me like I've suddenly grown two heads.

'I mean,' I add quickly, 'I know this place probably isn't anywhere near as fancy as the one you had your heart set on, and like you said, it's falling to pieces. But it *is* right on the beach, and as you can see, there's plenty of room.'

She stares at me, her mouth opening and closing a few times, but she doesn't speak, and I realise she's probably trying to think of a way to say no without hurting my feelings.

'You know what, forget it.' I hastily backtrack. 'It was a stupid idea. Ignore me.'

'You'd seriously do that?' she says finally. 'Let me have *my* wedding in *your* house?'

'It was just an idea. But of course you wouldn't want ...'

'I'd love to.'

' ... to have it in an old place like ... Wait, really?'

She claps her hands in front of her face and squeals. 'Yes! Sam, that would be amazing!'

Before I realise what's happening, she has jumped up and thrown her arms around my neck, giving me a grateful hug. I stiffen, unaccustomed to touch as I am now.

'You're a lifesaver,' she says, releasing me and stepping away. 'I don't know how I'll ever repay you for this.'

'Oh, no need for that. It'll be nice for the place to have a bit of life in it one last time before it sells. Are you sure it will do, though? I mean, your list of things that are wrong with it was pretty extensive.'

She looks around the room, her eyes narrowing determinedly. 'You just leave all that to me.'

Ellie

'I'm sorry, he what now?'

'You heard me.'

'Maybe, but my ears are struggling to make sense of it.'

Chloe replaces the lid on her raspberry and lemonade kombucha drink, the one she's just helped herself to out of the café fridge. 'He offered me his place.'

'That's what I thought you said. For your wedding.'

'Yes. For my wedding.'

'He does know there will be people *from this town* at the wedding, right?'

'He's widowed, Ellie, not dumb.'

'Are you going to pay for that drink?'

'Put it on my tab.'

'You don't have a tab.'

'Then put it on *your* tab.'

I cast a look around the café, checking one last time to

make sure everything is clean and ready for the morning, then flick the lights off. 'He seemed so determined to be left alone, though, that's what I don't get.'

'Maybe he just wanted to be left alone by you,' she says without thinking, then immediately looks apologetic.

I flick her a hurt look as I pull the doors shut, turn the key and give them a rattle to make sure they're locked properly. 'Ouch.'

'Sorry. Ugh, blame this last-minute shred diet, it's making me cranky.'

'Didn't you eat a whole pizza the other night?'

'I did. Then I hated myself, so I went on a diet. Keep up.'

'I don't even know why you're bothering. You look amazing and you know it. All ready for your wedding. The one you're thinking of having at Sam's house.'

'Look, I'm not going to question his offer. All I know is that he's an absolute lifesaver.'

'Yeah, but it's not exactly the wedding you dreamed of, is it? Are you sure you wouldn't rather postpone until you can make it work with Saltwater?'

'Are you kidding me? That place can burn to the ground for all I care,' she mutters darkly as we walk to the side street where I've parked my car. 'I will be slagging them off to anyone and everyone until my dying breath.'

'I don't doubt that for a second.'

'And so what if the wedding won't be *exactly* as I planned,' she says. 'Honestly, trying to plan it all perfectly was just stressing me out anyway. Maybe this is the universe's way of telling me to relax and go with the flow.'

'Go with the flow?'

'Yes.'

We've reached the car. I fish my keys out of my back pocket and press the button that unlocks the doors. 'You're just ... not exactly a "go with the flow" kind of girl.'

She breathes in deeply and exhales slowly. 'People change, Ellie. Namaste. I've been listening to some podcasts on mediation and mindfulness. I'm working on being more Zen.'

'Zen?'

'*Yes*,' she says grumpily. 'Zen.'

'Careful, your Zen is slipping.' I open the driver's door and put all the windows down to let the stifling heat of the day out. It's just gone five and the temperature is still up there. I have to bite my bottom lip to keep from smirking, because the last thing I want to do is upset her. It's most likely just another phase she's going through, like when she dabbled in Buddhism, and crystals, and – briefly, thank God – scientology. But hey, anything that helps to keep her calm before the wedding can only be a good thing.

'You're smirking.'

'I'm not,' I protest. 'Am I dropping you off?'

'No.' She checks her watch. 'I'm meeting a client back in the office at six to go over a contract. I'd better get back and check it, make sure that incompetent receptionist hasn't fucked up the figures like last time. I swear to God, she's as pointless as decaf coffee.'

'Hey, I happen to sell a fair bit of decaf coffee, thank you.'

'Yes, but what's the point of it?'

'It tastes just as good.'

'Yes, but it doesn't *do* anything.'

I climb into the car and reach for my seat belt. 'As much as I'd love to stay and have my livelihood slagged off by you, I'm running out of daylight hours.'

She closes the door for me and steps back. 'Let me guess, you're going for another run.'

'Maybe.'

'You have an unhealthy obsession.'

'Says the goddess of Zen.'

'Lunch? Tomorrow? We need to come up with a new plan now that the wedding location has shifted. There's so much to be done, and I'm going to need everyone's help if we're going to pull this off.'

'Fine. You know where I'll be.'

She blows me a kiss as I drive away, heading for the beach. To save time, I changed into my shorts and sports top at the café, so I don't need to head home first. I could have walked to the beach – it's only two blocks away – but I park down the far end today, away from town. Lately I've been starting my run from here, even though it cuts a fair bit off my usual route. I wasn't lying to Chloe. *Technically* I'm going for a run, but also it's a run with a mission.

I'm not really expecting to see anything in the tree – after all, my hopes have been well and truly dashed every other day – so when I climb up the bank and see something white fluttering in the breeze, it feels like my heart jumps up into my throat. *Oh my God.* He wrote back.

I untie it with trembling fingers and jump back down onto the beach, where I peel off my shoes and socks and wade out into the water until I'm knee-deep. Delaying tactics, really. Stalling. I'm honestly scared to open it and see what he's written. What if he's angry? What if this is basically a note telling me I'm a terrible person for reading his private letter?

DG,

You probably won't ever see this, because why would you return to the scene of your crime, but just in case you do, I have a couple of questions. The first, obviously, is how did you find my letter? You couldn't have seen it from the beach ... I checked. So?

The second question, also fairly obvious I imagine in this situation, is who are you?

I'm embarrassed that you read it, and I'll admit, I was annoyed too. That letter was supposed to be private. But I've given it some thought, and I realise that by putting it in a public place (even though I was quite sure it was well hidden), it's partly my fault.

So, on the off chance that you do see this, I wanted to say thank you. Your words got me thinking. I'm not quite sure why I'm opening up to you, a stranger, but you were right. Mei wouldn't be happy with the way the things have been. The opposite, in fact. I've been selfish, and not the easiest person to be around, either. I alienated most of our friends back in Hong Kong. Although if I'm honest, I think they were

129

always more her friends than mine. I was more of a friend by association. Or maybe that's just how it felt.

Anyway. Thanks for responding. It helped.

S

PS I'm sorry you lost someone too.

Sam

I'm sound asleep when a pounding on the front door jolts me awake. It takes me a few moments to register where I am. Whoever it is, they're hammering like there's either a tsunami bearing down or my house is on fire. Those are the only two reasons I can think why they'd want to break my door down at – I peer at my watch – *ten past eight on a Saturday morning.* Christ.

'What?' I snap gruffly, throwing the door open.

'Morning, Sam,' someone says brightly. I squint against the light and realise that Chloe is standing on my doorstep, and she's not alone. My driveway is filled with various cars, vans and work trucks, not to mention people. They've been milling around, but now they all turn to stare at me, and it's *then* that I realise I'm standing there in only a T-shirt and my underwear.

'Sorry,' Chloe says, her eyes dropping to my crotch and snapping quickly back up to my face. She's clearly trying hard not to smile, and failing. 'I did text to warn you that we were coming.'

I drop my hands in a vain attempt to cover myself. 'When?'

'About an hour ago.'

I look around blankly. 'I don't know where my phone is.'

She frowns. 'It's not by your bed?'

'No.'

'Then . . . how do you check your socials when you wake up?'

'He's not on social media,' someone says drily, and as soon as I hear her voice, I close my eyes and fervently hope there really *is* a tsunami on the way.

'Not . . . on social media?' Chloe asks, seeming bewildered at the very thought.

'No, it's beneath him, apparently. Hi, Sam.'

I open my eyes. 'I never said that, Ellie.'

'Something along those lines. Nice underwear.'

'Thanks. Though I'm not sure it's the first impression I wanted to give half the town.'

'As traumatic as seeing you in your underwear is, I think they'll live.'

She smirks, and a dimple I'd forgotten she had curves in her cheek, just above and to the right of her mouth. I stare at it for a second too long. Her hair is twisted up messily on the top of her head, and she's wearing a white T-shirt and a cute pair of faded cut-off jeans. My eyes sweep down the length of her legs before I even realise what I'm doing. There's no doubt about it, my best friend is all grown up, and not only that, she's absolutely stunning. Surprisingly, I feel the first stirrings

132

of an erection, and close the door so that only my head and shoulders are poking out. *What the hell?*

'Is there a reason you've brought half the town into my front garden at this ridiculous hour on a Saturday morning?' I ask Chloe gruffly.

'Um, yes. Is the offer of using this place for my wedding still open?'

'Of course.'

She sighs with relief. 'Great. Thanks, you're a literal lifesaver.'

'Well, not *literal* . . .' Ellie mumbles. Chloe ignores her and carries on talking.

'Remember how I said I'd take care of tidying the place up a bit?'

I nod. 'Yes.'

'Ta-da.' She throws her hands up. 'I've assembled the gang for a working bee. They're all here to pitch in and help out.' She nibbles her lower lip, fretting. 'We've only got a couple of weekends to get the place up to scratch, so I thought an early start was best.'

I peer over her shoulder, deliberately not looking at Ellie. I recognise some of the faces, including some I'd hoped never to see again. Particularly Logan Wheeler. He's leaning against a truck with his arms folded across his chest, as if he'd rather be anywhere but here. I feel my spine prickle at the sight of him, and I'm tempted to make his wish come true by marching across the lawn and shoving him off my property. Maybe not in my underwear, though. His old friends Hamish, Trent, Malcolm and another one whose name I can't recall are also here. Taller, minus a bit of hair and with a few extra kilos in front. Some women and the odd child are standing around – girlfriends and wives, I assume.

'All these people have offered to help you?' I ask.

'*Well* . . .' says Chloe.

'Offered or were ordered,' Ellie pipes up, balancing her hands like they're a set of scales. 'It's kind of the same thing, I guess.'

'But if this is a bad time . . .' Chloe trails off, looking vulnerable again. I remember her tears the other day and have no desire to see a repeat.

'It's fine. Just give me five minutes to get some clothes on.' As I close the door, I hear Ellie mutter something that sounds like 'You owe me for this, Chloe,' but I can't be sure.

Ellie

Chloe spins on her heel. 'Owe you for what?'

'Uh, hello? Making me come here. Now I get to spend the whole day being glared at. Not exactly what I thought I'd be doing on my day off.'

She smiles sweetly. 'You're most welcome.'

'I don't think you understand—'

'No, I do. But this is your chance, see? To have that chat with Sam that we talked about.'

'In front of everyone? I don't think so.'

'Obviously not when the others are around, no. But I'm sure an opportunity will come up.'

'Still, I'd rather be—'

'You're my maid of honour, Ellie. I need you here. Please?' She opens her eyes wide in a puppy-dog expression that she knows I can never resist.

'Ugh,' I sigh. 'Fine. That's the only reason I'm even here at stupid o'clock in the morning.'

'You're up earlier than this every other day for work, a surf or a run, so don't start.'

'That's different, I actually enjoy doing those things.'

'Ellie, this is important to me. I don't have a plan B for the wedding. I need you to promise me that you won't piss him off.'

'Well, I mean I wasn't planning on it.'

'He's the only chance I have of saving my big day.'

'That's not true. I'm sure we would come up with another plan if we had to.'

'*This* is a good plan, right here.'

'OK. Relax, I won't do anything to muck this up for you, I promise.'

'Thank you.'

While we were talking, Hamish had wandered up to stand by Chloe's side. 'What's the hold-up?' he asks. 'Some of the guys are making noises about leaving.'

'Let me guess.' Chloe pulls a face. 'Logan.'

'I'm surprised you even got him here in the first place, to be honest,' I say. 'He *hates* Sam.'

'He does,' Hamish agrees. 'But he's also our friend, and he wants to see us happy.'

'Yeah, I'm not buying that.'

Hamish laughs. 'Fine. The truth is, he's scared that if he doesn't help, Chloe will fire him from being my best man and then he'll miss out on the free food and booze.'

'If he thinks our wedding is just an excuse for a big piss-up,

I've got news for him,' Chloe replies darkly. 'And you can tell him from me that if he doesn't help today, he's not only out of the wedding party, he's also uninvited from the wedding. Oh, and he won't be welcome at our house ever again either.'

Hamish backs away. 'OK, I'll tell him.'

I elbow her when I see the front door reopening. 'He's back.'

She slaps on the kind of megawatt smile that she normally reserves for her clients. 'All sorted?'

Sam opens the door wide. He's had a quick shower, I realise, noticing that his hair is wet. 'Knock yourself out.'

She turns and puts two fingers in her mouth, emitting a piercing whistle that I've been fiercely jealous of since we were kids. No matter how much I practise, all I can muster is a weak whooshing sound.

'Listen up!' she hollers. 'I want all the plants, paint, timber, potting mix bags and tools unloaded onto the lawn around the back of the house, and then everyone meet on the deck and I'll run through the plan and assign tasks.'

I step to the side and plaster myself to the wall, out of the way, as she and Hamish head inside, followed by a steady trickle of our friends. Logan glares at me as he walks past, carrying a bag of potting mix on each shoulder. If this feat of strength is meant to impress me, it fails.

'Wow, if looks could kill,' a voice comments drily.

I stiffen, realising Sam has slipped outside and is standing beside me.

'If they could, we'd both have been dead a long time ago,' I reply.

'I know he hates me,' Sam says. 'And believe me, the feeling is completely mutual. But what did you ever do to make him look at you like that?'

'It's . . . complicated.'

Chloe's head pops around the door frame. 'Don't just stand there, chop chop. Come on, people, time is money.' Then she disappears again.

Sam snorts. 'Time is money?'

'She's firmly in bride mode,' I admit. 'You soon get used to it.'

He shakes his head. 'Uh, listen, I wanted to say sorry about the other day. Seeing you again . . .' he runs one hand through his damp hair, 'it took me by surprise.'

'You and me both.'

'That's no excuse for being rude, though.'

'I wasn't *rude*,' I retort, bristling. 'But even if I was, can you blame me? You—'

'Ellie, I meant me. *I* was rude.'

'Oh.' My anger deflates. 'Right.'

'After all, we're both adults now.'

My eyes involuntarily drop to his broad shoulders before I force them back up to look at his face again.

'That's right,' I agree, hoping my cheeks haven't coloured. 'We are.'

'So I'm happy to call a truce this weekend, if you are,' he says. 'For Chloe's sake.'

I stare at him cautiously, mixed feelings churning in my stomach. I'm still so *angry* with him. But . . . he's right. We *are* adults now, no longer angst-ridden teenagers. Standing this close, I can see the golden stubble on his chin, maybe even a light scattering of grey. I'm not sure if it's that, or just really blond. His lips are as full as I remember, his nose just on the side of large, but suited to his face. There are wrinkles at the corner of his eyes that are new. I remember everything he has been through, and my anger softens.

'A truce.' I nod, holding out my hand. 'For Chloe.'

He looks down, slightly amused, but takes it. 'For Chloe.'

His eyes search mine and I feel my ribs suck in sharply at the familiarity of it. I can smell him, the tangy citrus scent of his body wash, mingled with the earthy scent that is purely him.

'There you are.'

Chloe reappears and shoots me a questioning look. I realise Sam and I are still holding hands, though no longer shaking. I drop his quickly, as if it's scorched me.

'You OK?' she asks.

'I'm fine.'

She turns to smile sweetly at Sam. 'Is it all right if I steal my maid of honour away? She's supposed to be helping me, but she has a tendency to get sidetracked.'

'I do not,' I mutter defensively.

'I remember,' Sam says softly, and something inside me goes *kerplunk*.

'So?' she asks, whirling on me when we're out of his earshot. 'How did it go?'

'How did what go?'

'The talk.'

'Chloe, we were only outside for about a minute. We didn't have time to talk.'

'Oh.' She looks disappointed. 'Then why were you holding hands? I thought it meant you'd made peace and forgiven each other, or something like that.'

'We agreed on a truce, actually.'

'A truce?'

'Yeah, to be civil to each other for your sake.'

She pulls a face. 'Well, I guess that's something.'

Sam

Beer tastes even better when you've earned it after a hard day of physical work. I'm not the only one to think so, judging by the satisfied sighs and smacking of lips from around the deck. The sun is low in the sky. I have no idea what time it is, but it's the first time I've really stopped since Chloe assigned her list of jobs this morning. There was a brief break allowed for lunch, which was platters of club sandwiches prepared by her mother and aunt, but most of us ate on the run, chomping down with a hammer or paintbrush still in hand. She didn't say it outright, but Chloe's demeanour made it obvious that slackers would not be tolerated.

I thought I'd done a fairly decent job of tidying up the grounds, but it was nothing compared to what they look like now after Chloe's had us trimming, mowing, edging, pruning, removing and digging all day. It's like the grounds of a show home, more like it looked back when my grandmother was alive.

'There's still so much to do,' she frets from where she's seated on one of the long built-in wooden bench seats that run around two sides of the deck.

'Yeah, and plenty of time to do it. Look how much we've accomplished already,' Hamish points out. 'Focus on the glass half full, baby, not the glass half empty.'

She rolls her eyes. 'You know where you can shove that glass, right?'

Ellie laughs. 'What happened to Zen Chloe?'

'I don't think my DNA was designed for Zen,' Chloe admits. 'I appear to be permanently wired in the fight-or-flight mode. Always on alert.'

Hamish passes her another beer. 'This'll help calm you down.'

'I haven't finished the first one yet.'

'Well there's your problem then.'

I observe them discreetly from my seat on the top step, feeling a pang inside. They all have such an easy relationship with each other, just as they did when we were at high school. And just like then, I feel like an outsider. I never really fitted in, not even when I was with Ellie.

Logan and most of the other guys left an hour ago. Chloe finally agreed we could down tools, but only because her husband-to-be jokingly threatened to call the wedding off if she didn't. You can tell just by looking at him that he'd never do that, though. Their love is blindingly obvious in the way they look at each other, their shared smiles, the way they touch hands for a brief moment, like they're re-anchoring themselves.

It hasn't been easy having them all here in my grandfather's house. If I'd known the other day that Hamish was Chloe's fiancé, and that he was still very much friends with Logan, I doubt I'd have offered her the house as a venue. Hamish and the others, from the little time I spent with them, seem to have grown into normal, decent guys. But the same can't be said for Logan. Several times I caught him glaring at me with an angry look on his face. Worse, I saw him staring at Ellie in a way I didn't like at all. It was proprietorial, as if she belonged to him. My fingers tighten around the beer bottle at the very thought. *Never.*

'Thanks for doing this.'

I feel someone sit down in the space beside me, and the breeze must be coming from just the right direction, because I smell it then. Her signature scent. Sunscreen. Fruity and coconutty, it fills my nostrils and hits like a punch in the guts. I managed to avoid her most of the day, but now she's right there beside me, and I can feel the warmth of her skin as she lifts a bottle to her mouth, her arm almost brushing up against mine.

I clear my throat. 'What are you thanking me for exactly?'

'For doing this for Chloe and Hamish. It's very generous of you to open up your home to a bunch of strangers.'

I take a swig of beer and stare straight ahead. 'Hardly strangers,' I reply. 'I recognised quite a few faces today, some I could have done without seeing.'

I finally turn my head to look at her, and when I do, I wish I hadn't. She's staring up at me, and I feel myself sucked into the whirlpool of her eyes, still the most expressive of anyone I've ever met. They are the colour of faded green sea glass, framed by long black lashes.

'Logan,' she says. 'I'm surprised you let him on the property, to be honest.'

'I almost didn't, believe me. I only did it for Chloe.' I pull a face. 'Did anyone actually leave this town after high school? Because it sure seems like the whole gang's still here. You guys do know there's a big wide world out there, right?'

Her expression turns hard. 'Ah, you're back to that, are you?'

'Back to what?'

'Judging us.'

'I'm not judging.'

'What would you call it then?'

I take another swig of beer and shrug. 'Merely an observation.'

She snorts. 'Yeah, that's exactly what a judgemental person would say.' She stands to leave and I look up at her in surprise. 'Anyway, I just wanted to say thanks.'

She's genuinely upset, I realise. Before I think about what I'm doing, I reach out and encircle her wrist with my fingers, then wonder if she felt the same jolt I just did.

'I'm sorry,' I say quietly. 'You're right. I'm being unkind. Please, sit down again.'

Her eyes are pinned to where I am touching her, and realising this, I let her go quickly. There's a long pause, and then she nods stiffly and sinks back down.

'At least you agree that you're being a dick,' she says.

'Uh, I believe I used the word "unkind".'

144

She takes a drink, then wipes her upper lip. 'I know. I just translated it into local speak. You know how hick we are around here. We like to call a spade a spade.'

My eyebrows shoot up. 'You're calling me a spade?'

'Well, you always did have kind of a square head,' she retorts, grinning.

It comes back to me now, the easy banter we used to toss back and forth. The way she was never afraid to call me out when she thought I was being a prat.

'I'm sorry if I made you feel judged the other day,' I tell her. 'I was surprised to see you still here, that's all.'

Her eyes are curious. 'Where exactly did you think I'd have gone?'

'That's a good question. I'm not sure, to be honest. Anywhere but here.'

She looks straight ahead to where the sun is dipping below the horizon. 'I did leave, actually, for quite a few years. Worked on yachts, mostly in the Mediterranean. I'm a fully qualified chef.'

'You're a chef?'

She nods.

'Wow. I'd never have picked it.'

'Why not?'

'Remember those biscuits and cakes you'd bake sometimes after school? Only you couldn't be bothered to follow a recipe, so you'd just bung a whole lot of stuff into a bowl and hope for the best.'

She laughs. 'Hey, it worked out sometimes.'

I grimace. 'Sure. And sometimes the end result would be hard little moon rocks that'd almost break our teeth.'

She shoves me lightly with her shoulder. 'You still ate them.'

'Only because I didn't want to hurt your feelings.'

'And because you were a starving teenage boy who ate anything and everything.'

I hold up a finger. 'Except for your ...'

' ... grandmother's cooking.'

We both finish the sentence at the same time and laugh.

'How is she?' I ask.

'She's ... OK.'

I can tell immediately that there's something she's not telling me. 'But?'

'She had a heart attack a couple of years ago.'

'Oh Ellie, I'm sorry to hear that.' I'm immediately ashamed that I haven't asked after her grandmother before now. She was a huge part of my life growing up. 'How is she now?

'She's pretty much the same as she was before. But then she seemed OK before it happened too, and that's what worries me.'

'Is that why you came back here? Because of her?'

She tilts her head in confirmation.

'How old is she now?'

'Eighty-two.' She looks at me, and I can see that there's something she's unsure about saying. Her lips form the first word but then close again.

'What?' I prompt her.

'It's just, she'd love to see you. She always had a soft spot for you.'

'I have one for her too,' I admit. 'Have you told her I'm back?'

'No.' She shakes her head. 'No way.'

'Why not?'

'Nan has ...' She pauses while she tries to think of the right words. 'How do I put this? Uh, she has an unhealthy preoccupation with my love life.'

'Ah.' I flush and stare out to sea, where the sun has completely disappeared now. The surface of the water, so brilliantly on fire a few minutes ago, has darkened. The voices of the others behind us seem muffled, even though they're only a few metres away. It's like the rest of the world has faded out while I'm talking to Ellie. I cough to clear my throat, then force a casual tone. 'And that has ... what to do with me?'

'Nothing, of course,' she says swiftly. 'But you remember what she was like. Always adamant that you and I would one day end up as more than just friends.'

'I remember,' I say softly, as the words land gently on my heart. 'So how *is* your love life?'

'Non-existent,' she admits.

'I'm sorry to hear that,' I say, though for some reason, I'm not sorry at all. We stare at each other for a moment, neither of us saying anything. Her expression is unreadable, which surprises me. There was a time when I only had to glance at her to know what she was thinking. My eyes linger on her lips and I startle, realising that I'm imagining how easy it would be to lean over and kiss her. I wonder what she'd do if I did. Whether she'd kiss me back, or whether she'd slap me across the face. Shocked by my thoughts, I tear my eyes away.

'We're heading off now, Ellie,' Chloe says loudly.

'I'll come with you,' Ellie says, getting to her feet, and I instantly worry that I've made her feel uncomfortable. 'I'm knackered after all the work you made us do today. Remind me never to get a job working for you.'

'Pfft, today was nothing,' Chloe retorts. 'The hard work's still to come, so toughen up.'

Ellie and Hamish groan.

'In that case,' Ellie says, rubbing her eyes wearily. 'I *definitely* need a long soak in the bath and then my bed.'

'Come on, Cinderella,' Chloe coaxes her, one hand on her back. 'Let's get you home before you turn into a pumpkin.'

'That's not quite how the fairy tale goes,' Ellie laughs.

I start clearing the table, anything to distract myself from the image of Ellie in a bathtub that just popped into my head. She stops in her tracks, reaching for an empty chip packet.

'We should help Sam clean up first,' she says, scrunching it into a ball.

'Of course,' Chloe agrees.

'It's fine, leave it,' I say curtly, annoyed with myself for the direction my thoughts have taken and for letting myself get lulled into nostalgic longings. It's because I'm back here in this place. Being around Ellie all day has been . . . comfortably familiar. Like all those years we've been apart have passed in the blink of an eye, and even though so much has happened, we've fallen straight back into our old rhythm. She's as easy to be around as I remember, still the same clever, funny girl I used to know . . . only now she's a mature, sexy, even more vivacious version. And *that* has been causing funny feelings inside my chest all afternoon.

'We don't mind,' Ellie says, reaching for an empty glass.

'I said *leave it*,' I snap, immediately regretting my tone when she looks at me like I've just slapped her. Chloe and Hamish exchange a shocked look. 'I'm sorry,' I say stiffly, well aware that I've completely overreacted. 'It's been a long day. But I really do appreciate all the work you've done on the house.'

'It's the least we can do to thank you for coming to our rescue at the last minute,' Hamish replies, holding out his hand for me to shake. I do so reluctantly. I'm fairly sure that, as Logan's friend, he would have been in on what happened all those years ago, but as I said to Ellie earlier, we're all adults now. I'll never forgive Logan, but Hamish seems to have at least grown into a half-decent man. Surely Chloe wouldn't be marrying him if he hadn't.

'It's not a problem,' I tell him. 'Honestly. But I do insist on paying, so if you could give me the invoices for everything, I'll make sure to take care of them.'

'No way.' Chloe shakes her head. 'This is on us. The other venue – *whose name I won't mention* – have refunded our deposit. It's more than enough to get this place up to scratch.' She nudges her fiancé. 'Tell him, Hamish.'

Hamish shrugs ruefully. 'Sorry, mate, you're not going to win this one.'

'It's true,' Ellie adds. 'She's incredibly stubborn. You may as well give up now.'

'I can't do that,' I say, feeling myself smile involuntarily. 'But I will drop the subject, for now.'

'Good idea,' Chloe says cheerfully. 'We'll see you in the morning. Maybe you'll even be dressed this time.'

I blink at her. 'You're coming back tomorrow?'

'I did say it was a working bee *weekend*, didn't I?'

'Right.'

'We'll be back next weekend too. I told you, there's still so much to be done. We can't paint the house until we've replaced the windows, which I've measured today. Trent is in charge of sourcing those this week – he knows people who know people – so they'll do a rush job on them for us and we should be able to install them next weekend. Then we can crack on with the painting. Tomorrow we'll do all the prep work. Sand the wood and get it ready. I've assigned Luke, Casey and a couple of others to water-blast and stain this whole outdoor dining area. Oh, and we need to prep the walls for paint inside as well.' She sighs. 'So much to do, but we'll get there.'

'I had no idea you were going to do that much,' I say, shaking my head.

'Wait until you see what colour she's painting the inside walls,' Ellie says, her eyes flashing mischievously. She cocks her head at Chloe. 'What's it called again? Fuchsia?' She looks back at me. 'It's like a bright pink. Think of a flamingo.'

I stare at her, feeling my face blanch. 'Oh.'

'Don't be cruel, Ellie,' Chloe laughs. 'Relax, Sam, I won't do anything outrageous. I was thinking a nautical white, pretty much what you have already, but freshened up. I'll bring the colour charts with me tomorrow for you to look over, because ultimately it's your house, your decision.'

'She *says* that,' Ellie muses. 'But she means as long as you pick something she likes.'

Chloe doesn't deny it. 'I've drawn little stars beside the ones I think would suit the place. But see what *you* think tomorrow.'

Ellie

'I think that bit of wall is done, Ellie,' Chloe says drily, startling me. 'I mean, you've been working on it for quite a while now.'

'Just making sure I do it properly,' I reply primly, scrubbing at an imaginary spot on the wood by the large lounge windows. When I'm satisfied that it's gone – even though there was nothing there in the first place – I turn to smile at her. 'I know you have ridiculously high standards.'

'Uh-huh. Really. So it's got nothing to do with the fact that Sam is working just out there then?' She points over my shoulder.

'Is he?' I do my best to look like I'm not bothered. 'I hadn't noticed.'

She rolls her eyes. 'I'm not *stupid*, Ellie.'

'Well, you have your moments.'

Her eyes narrow. 'I saw you guys last night. What's going on?'

'Nothing.'

'It didn't look like nothing.'

'Chloe, in case you've forgotten, we can barely stand each other, remember? This is just a temporary truce. For your sake.'

Her expression makes it clear she's not convinced. 'Looked to me like you guys took a beautiful trip down memory lane, perhaps remembered just how much you once meant to each other.'

'Don't be silly,' I scoff. 'I mean, do I still care about him in some way? Sure, I guess. I feel sorry for him because of what he's been through. It's so tragic. But I'm not going to just forget about how much he hurt me.'

'I'm not saying you should. But holding a grudge won't do you any favours either.' She checks to make sure no one is close enough to hear what we're saying. 'Remember when Hamish and I had been together for, like, six months, and he got drunk and kissed his ex at that party?'

I nod.

'That almost killed me. Some of our friends, my mother, they were all in my ear, telling me, "once a cheater, always a cheater". Meanwhile, he was totally beside himself and begging me for a second chance.'

'I remember. The florist had never had so much business.'

'I could have walked away then. Not forgiven him. It would have been so easy.'

'It's hardly the same thing as what happened between me and Sam, though.'

'Isn't it? I mean, you felt betrayed by him too.'

'I guess.'

'I'm just trying to remind you that people make mistakes. All the time. It's one of the joys of being human. We can't control what other people do; all we can control is our reaction to it.'

'When did you get so wise?'

She nudges me with her elbow. 'Told you I'm not stupid.'

I pull her in for a hug. 'You're definitely not stupid.'

She steps away, but holds onto my upper arms, peering earnestly into my eyes. 'At the end of the day, I just want you to be happy, and to not regret not making peace with him while you have the chance.'

'Fine.' I roll my eyes exaggeratedly. 'I'll talk to him.'

'Good girl. Now,' she points over my shoulder to where our friend Caitlin is sanding the staircase banister, 'why don't you go and help Caitlin.'

'Why is she doing the staircase? I thought we were just doing this room and the outside.'

'Because,' she says, her eyes sparkling, 'I had *the* best idea last night. I spoke to Sam about it this morning, and he's agreed that we can get ready here on the big day.'

I gulp. 'Here?'

She nods. 'Yep. Right here. It makes perfect sense. This way, I don't have to worry about messing up my dress or make-up in the car, or stress about the time. I can be right here, on the spot. He's going to let us use the master bedroom and en suite.'

My heart skips a beat. We're going to be getting dressed here in Sam's house?

'I can make my grand entrance down the staircase,' she continues. 'We'll have an aisle of chairs, leading down to the archway that'll be set up on the edge of the lawn for the vow ceremony. I want *that* view behind me.' She points out to sea. 'The photos will be stunning, don't you think?'

'So stunning,' I agree weakly, still trying to get my head around the fact that I'll be getting dressed in the same house as Sam.

'Chloe.'

'Hey, Sam, what's up?' Chloe asks, turning.

I take a moment longer to compose myself, but as soon as I turn, all that composure falls away. As does my jaw. He's shirtless. As in . . . *he's wearing no shirt*. The last time I saw him like this, he was still a boy, on the cusp of becoming a man. His chest was concave more than anything, his limbs long and gangly and his ribs prominent, no matter how much he ate.

Not any more. Now, he has crevices and ridges and little dips and solid plateaus in all the right places. And at the bottom, where his stomach disappears into his low-riding shorts, he has lines on either side that make a V shape, pointing down towards his . . . With a mammoth effort I force my eyes upwards, over his ribs, his sternum, along his collarbones, up his neck to rest on his jaw, hoping the flush on my cheeks isn't as visibly obvious as it feels.

'I thought maybe we could go over those paint colour charts now,' he says.

'Um . . . I'll just head over to the staircase,' I stammer, annoyed at myself for my reaction.

'Yes,' Chloe says, clearly a bit transfixed by the sight of him herself, which makes me feel marginally better. 'The staircase. It's . . . ah . . . it's over there.'

'I know where it is, Chloe.'

She tears her eyes away from Sam and arches her eyebrows at me. 'Sorry. I thought you might have been too distracted to remember.'

I give Sam a wide berth, then turn and poke my tongue out at her.

Sam

It's the weirdest thing. I could have sworn something was up with Ellie yesterday when I went over to talk to Chloe about paint samples. The way she blushed and suddenly could only look everywhere but at me, well, I'm rusty and out of practice, but if I didn't know better, I'd say she was checking me out, then got embarrassed about doing so. She completely avoided me after that, and left the same time as Chloe and the others did.

I decide to head to Sailor's Bay after breakfast. The whole way there, I tell myself it's not because I want to see if the mysterious DG found my reply. I'm not bothered either way. But when I get there, there *is* a new letter in the tree, and the way my pulse quickens when I see it tells me that I do care after all.

Dear S,

The scene of my crime? Wow. Harsh, considering you freely admit in your letter that my words helped you. However, I am nothing if not reasonable, so I'll admit to a misdemeanour, a MINOR wrongdoing on my part. I sincerely hope that you will take into consideration my previous good behaviour and this apology when you're considering my punishment.

I am sorry for reading your letter. (Sort of.)

As for your questions, I did notice the letter from the beach. You mustn't have checked properly. And I told you who I am. It's right there on the bottom of my letter.

DG

PS Jokes aside, I'm glad my words helped. There's a fine line between offering comfort and being a patronising jerk. I'm glad I managed the first one.

Ellie

Dear DG,

Apology accepted, even though you somehow managed to both apologise and insult me at the same time. Are you implying that I didn't look properly because I'm a man? I'm assuming, from your tired use of this well-worn cliché, that you must be a woman. Correct me if I'm wrong. I checked again. It is impossible to spot a letter in the tree from the beach. Unless maybe you're ten feet tall and can see above the scrub in front. ARE you ten feet tall? Does DG stand for Doreen the Giraffe? It does, doesn't it. I'm on to you.

Your letter was helpful, yes, and not patronising at all. It's not even like you said anything new. In the last two years I've heard all the platitudes that exist about grief, believe me. I think your words connected because you're the first person who never knew Mei to say them. Somehow, strangely, that makes what you have to say more believable. Having been through loss yourself, you seem to understand. I appreciate the fact that you acknowledged my entitlement to my grief, instead of pointing out, as so many others have, that everyone loses someone at some point and that therefore what I'm feeling is no more special or different to what others around the world go through every single day.

So thank you. I know I already said that, but I'm trying to make the effort to say those kinds of things more often.

S

PS Do you want to know what I'm really scared of? That eventually the world will forget Mei was even here. I know I'm not the only one who loved her, but I worry that once her family are gone, and I'm gone too, no one will remember her.

Sam

Dear S,

You got me. Yes, I'm a giraffe, living in the hills above Sailor's Bay. Haven't you heard of me? I'm quite famous in these parts. My name is NOT Doreen, however. No offence to Doreens the world over, but it's a very ... plain sort of name, don't you think? I like to believe I'm more exotic than that, maybe a ... Dakota. Or a Delilah. I suspect I'm more of a Daisy, though.

I'm happy you feel you can open up to me, especially about your fears. I need to be upfront, though. I'm no grief expert. If we're to continue this correspondence (which I hope we are), and you're expecting some kind of free therapy, I can't guarantee I won't say the wrong thing. In fact, I can almost guarantee that at some point I will. It's kind of an unwanted talent I have. So, having established that, here is my unprofessional, non-expert opinion ...

I think you need to give yourself, and your wife, more credit. On any given day, more people than you know are thinking of her. After all, she had a life before you, and one outside of you. Best friends, her first boyfriend, favourite teachers, fun colleagues, family, that guy she shared a brief connection with on a bus once. Along the way she will have touched many lives, and I guarantee you that all of those people remember her. They might not think of her every single day, but they do think of her.

It's like surf waves. When you're watching them from shore, you think they're moving towards you. But in actual fact, the particles of energy inside each wave are moving perpendicularly. And as they move up and down inside the wave, they bump into each other on their journey, transferring energy to each other in the process. In other words, those water particles are a part of the wave, yes, but they are NOT the wave. They are not even travelling in the same direction.

Life is like that. We're not always on the same journey or travelling in the same direction as the people we meet. But when we bump into each other along the way, we transfer energy whenever we make an impression. Whether it's good or bad, for a lifetime or only a brief moment. That energy, those ripples, will always be here. Long after we're gone.

DG

PS Thank you for accepting my (partial) apology for reading your letter. Someone told me we should say those words more often.

Ellie

Dear DG,

Wow. Just, wow.

You're wrong, you know. Because you do seem to know exactly the right thing to say. I don't think anything has ever made more sense.

Maybe you SHOULD become a therapist.

S

PS Are you a giraffe who surfs? How do you know all that stuff about waves?

Sam

The new windows are in. I was worried, I'll be honest, that the white aluminium joinery Chloe ordered wouldn't suit the timber look of the house. But they blend in fine, just like they were always there. I know it shouldn't worry me – the new owners will do whatever the hell they want with it anyway – but I feel obligated, as if for as long as it's in my family's hands I should respect my grandmother's design.

I can't believe how much we've achieved in just two weekends. The whole inside of the downstairs area has been repainted, as has the staircase and half of the outside of the house. The rusted piece of spouting has been replaced, along with all the windows that face out to sea. The lawns and gardens have been completely transformed, and Chloe has also had her friends, dust, vacuum and mop the whole house. Everything now sparkles and smells like lemon. My grandmother would have *definitely* approved of that.

'You'll notice a massive difference in the temperature inside when winter hits,' Chloe says as she wipes our mucky fingerprints off the window panes with a rag. 'That old framing was just letting the wind blow right in.'

'Yes, I'm sure the new owners will appreciate the aluminium joinery.'

'Oh,' she says. 'That's right. You probably won't be here for winter, will you.'

'I was hoping not to be. But I guess that will depend on how long it takes the place to sell.'

She glances sideways to where Ellie is using newspaper to clean the glass in the new front door. I know she's wondering whether Ellie heard our exchange. Given the fact that she's standing less than two metres away from us, I'd say she did, even though she makes no sign of it. She probably can't wait for me to sell up and move on.

Ellie

He's avoided me pretty much all weekend, but that suits me just fine. I can't look him in the eye without feeling guilty that *I* know it's him I'm writing letters to, but he has absolutely no idea that it's me. I know I should confess, but I like the fact that he feels he can open up to me. There are glimpses of the fun and camaraderie we used to share in the old days, and it's only now that I realise how desperately I have missed it. Chloe is an amazing friend, the best. But it's not the same as what I had with Sam. There was an instant connection between us, even when we were kids. He got me, and I got him. People used to roll their eyes at our little jokes, the ones that were only funny to the two of us.

Hearing him tell Chloe he hopes to be gone before winter doesn't actually bring me any joy. If anything, the thought of him disappearing from my life again makes me sad.

Someone grabs my messy topknot and shakes it. Yelping

in protest, I attempt to duck and twist to see who it is. Trent grins at me.

'You missed a bit, squirt,' he says.

I try to kick him on his way past, but he's already out of reach.

'Too slow,' he crows. 'As usual.'

Most of the others are heading off too, leaving only Hamish, Chloe, Sam and me behind.

'Squirt?' Sam asks after they've all gone. He doesn't look at me when he speaks.

'He's always called me that. They treat me a bit like a little sister, as you probably remember. Oh *shit*.'

In my enthusiasm to clean the windows, I've leaned on the recently painted outside of the house a little too hard, and the paint wasn't *quite* as dry as I'd thought.

'Problem?' Chloe materialises beside me.

'Nope.' I dart quickly to stand in front of the mess I've made and fix a bright smile to my face. 'Nope. No problem here.'

Her eyes narrow. 'Step aside, Ellie.'

'I don't want to.'

'Don't make me physically move you,' she says. 'You know I'm stronger than I look.'

She's right. I move. She emits the kind of noise a jet engine makes when it's throttling up on the runway. I wince.

'Ellie!'

'It was an accident!'

'I don't have time for accidents! We have less than two weeks until the wedding to get everything finished.'

'Pfft,' I scoff. 'That's *plenty* of time.'

'Ellie.'

'Yes, Chloe?'

'You will fix this.'

'Of course.'

'You will fix this *now*.'

I look around. 'As soon as I find out where they put the leftover paint.'

'I can show you where it is,' Sam says.

I glance at him dubiously, searching for an ulterior motive. He looks nothing but helpful. 'Thanks.'

Chloe hasn't finished. 'You need to sand that bit first and *then* repaint. Don't just slap new paint over it.'

'As if I'd do that.'

She stares at me, unblinking.

'As if I'd do that to *you*,' I clarify.

'I'll make sure it's done properly,' Sam reassures her.

She nods at him. 'Thank you.'

He jerks his head at me. 'I think they put the rest of the paint in the shed.'

'Thanks for saving me,' I whisper reluctantly, as we head down the steps and across the lawn.

'You're welcome. She takes things a bit seriously sometimes, doesn't she.'

I shrug. 'It's her wedding. She's been looking forward to this day for a long time. You can't blame her for wanting everything to be perfect.'

'I know you're her best friend, but even you have to admit she can be scary.'

'She's not scary. Have you seen her? She's, like, four-foot-nothing.'

He arches one eyebrow at me.

'OK, she's a *little* bit scary,' I admit. 'But don't tell her I said that.'

We've reached the big old wooden shed that sits on the far west side of the property, thankfully out of sight from the back lawn where the wedding will be held, otherwise Chloe would have probably insisted it be torn down. It's an eyesore, to say the least.

'I told Malcolm to put the rest of the paint in here,' Sam says. He flicks the rusty latch over and then tugs at one of the sliding doors. 'I'm assuming he did.'

The first door opens relatively easily. The second requires a bit more effort. I stand back and pretend I'm not watching the way the muscles in his arms become perfectly defined with his exertion. He's started to get a bit of colour on his skin, I realise. A light tan. Maybe it's all those morning walks to the tree. At the thought of the letters, I flush guiltily.

'You OK?' he asks, looking at me curiously.

'Never better,' I declare, stepping forward and peering into the shed. It's dark in there. I don't wait for my eyes to adjust before I take a quick step backwards again. 'I can't see the paint.'

'You didn't exactly look very hard.'

'I don't really know what I'm looking for anyway. It's probably better if you . . . ' I gesture feebly.

He stares at me, confused. 'You don't know what a paint tin

looks like?' Then an expression of understanding flashes across his face. 'Ah,' he says.

'*Ah* what?'

'Nothing. Don't worry, I'll find it.' He steps forward, but I put a hand on his arm to stop him going any further.

'No,' I say. 'You meant *ah* something.'

'It's just . . . you know. I remember.'

'Remember what?'

'Your fear.'

'My . . . fear?' I pull a face. 'I have no idea what you're talking about.'

'You don't have to pretend with me, Ellie.'

'I'm not pretending anything.'

He regards me for a few moments, then steps to one side. 'OK then. After you.'

I gulp. 'OK. Sure.'

I take a tentative step towards the black, cavernous inside of the shed that to my mind looks like something out of an Indiana Jones movie. My vivid imagination is conjuring up visions of cobwebs. Lots and lots of cobwebs. I take another cautious step, then another.

'You really don't have to do this,' he says mildly, his voice startlingly close to my ear. I shudder involuntarily, and I'm surprised to feel goosebumps spring up on my skin, as if he's just run his fingers lightly up my arm. *Sweet Mother of God.* I squeeze my eyes shut, thinking that if his *voice* can have that effect, imagine what his actual touch might do to me.

'Yes I do,' I mutter, grateful that the shed is dark

enough that he probably hasn't noticed the flush colouring my cheeks.

'I'm not sure what kind of point you're trying to make,' he says.

I grit my teeth, focus and take another step, my eyes slowly adjusting to the gloom. All I can make out is stuff. Piles of stuff everywhere. On the floor, on top of workbenches, stacked on shelves. No thick swathes of cobwebs like you see in the films, though. I breathe a sigh of relief and look around. There are old boxes, most of them water-stained and falling apart, pieces of machinery, rusty tools, broken furniture, bulging plastic bags and ... *aha*. The paint tins. Not too far from the door, thankfully. I quickly dart over and pick one up. Turning around with a triumphant smile, my face comes smack into contact with his chest.

'Ouch!'

He catches my arms to steady me. 'Sorry.'

I rub my nose with one hand. 'Why were you standing so close?'

'In case you needed protecting.'

'Protecting from what?' His proximity is unnerving, not to mention that this close I can smell his skin and feel the heat coming off his body. It's an intoxicating mix. I take a step backwards and his hands fall to his sides. I start to get a horrible sinking feeling in my chest when I notice that his eyes keep flicking upwards, to something on top of my head. *On my hair.* 'Protecting from what, Sam?' I repeat, my voice becoming high-pitched with terror.

He pulls a face. 'Just … promise me you won't freak out, OK?'

'Why … why would I freak out?'

He focuses his eyes on mine, attempting to keep me calm that way.

'Do you trust me, Ellie?'

I close my eyes and whimper. 'Please. Please God, no. Don't tell me …'

I hear a rustle as he moves. 'Just stand still. I'll get it.'

It. That's all I need to hear. That there's an *it* on my head. I don't even care what *it* is, although I have a strong suspicion, because he knows. Sam knows *exactly* what I'm most terrified of in this world. And it's not Chloe.

Sam

She's gone almost before I finish speaking.

'Ow!' It's my turn to exclaim in pain when she drops the almost full paint tin onto my foot. I watch, impressed, as she breaks into a sprint, like a racehorse released from the starting gate.

'Ellie,' I shout, hopping off on one foot after her, knowing I have zero chance of catching up. 'Wait.'

But she can't hear me over her own screams. She streaks across the lawn, towards the path that leads down to the beach. As she runs, she pulls off her T-shirt, ripping it up over her head and discarding it in her wake. I blink as she reaches for her black bra strap. She's not . . . is she?

She is. Her hands fumble behind her back, and just as she disappears over the crest of the sand dune, the strap comes undone and she flings the bra off to one side. Then she's gone, the screams trailing after her.

Hearing someone cough, I stop hopping. Chloe and Hamish are standing on the deck, staring at the spot where Ellie disappeared.

'What the hell?' Chloe says.

'There was a spider-related incident,' I tell her.

She nods. 'Ah. Yeah, she's not a huge fan of those.'

Hamish snorts. 'To put it mildly. There's still a hole in our garage wall from where she threw a tyre jack at one.'

'Great.' Chloe sighs. 'We've got to get to our last dance lesson for our first wedding dance, but I'd better go and check on her.'

Hamish checks the time on his phone. 'We're already late.'

'I know,' she says, 'But I can't leave without making sure she's OK.'

He rolls his eyes. 'It was a spider. I think she'll live.'

'Still,' Chloe says, doubtfully, 'we can't just leave her here. She came with us, remember?'

'I can run her home,' I offer. 'You guys get going if you need to.'

'Cheers, mate,' says Hamish, but Chloe lingers, unsure.

'I suppose we could just *not* do the choreographed dance,' Hamish offers. 'I have no problem with that.'

'Nice try,' she says drily. 'We're doing the dance.' She looks at me. 'Are you sure you don't mind dropping her home?'

'Not at all.'

'OK.' She nods. 'Thanks.'

After they leave, I test my foot out gingerly. It's tender, but takes my weight. Nothing broken. I pick up Ellie's T-shirt off the grass and pluck her bra from a tussock on the dune, feeling myself flush slightly as I try not to look too closely at it. There's a lot of see-through black lace, I do notice that much. Further down the track, I find her jean shorts and underwear, so I scoop them up too.

Down on the beach, it takes me a moment to spot her, and when I do, it steals my breath away. She's in the sea, only her head and shoulders above water. She's facing away from me, towards the horizon, where the sun is slowly setting. All around her the sky and the water glow with brilliant streaks of colour. I sit on the warm sand and wait for her.

Ellie

I let him wait for a while. Serves him right for making me go into the shed. He *knew* I was terrified of spiders. Of course I'm conveniently forgetting the fact that he offered to go in and get the paint for me but my own stubborn pride made me refuse.

Shuddering, even though I know there's no chance that the spider – if there really *was* a spider, that is; I wouldn't put it past Sam to have said that just to freak me out – could be still on me, I bob down underneath another wave just to make sure. The water is delicate and warm, the sunset spectacular. It's been a while since I've seen one quite as vivid as this, and I marvel at the colours, knowing all too well that they won't last long and soon the show will be over.

Eventually Sam gets up and wanders down to the water's edge, stopping ankle deep. The waves bubble back and forward around his legs. He's removed his work boots and socks and left them where he was sitting.

With my clothes.

Ah, yes. It comes back to me now, the fact that I am completely, one hundred per cent naked in the water. Thank God the sun is nearly down behind me. I know that from where Sam is standing, he won't be able to see my body in the water, only shadowy silhouettes.

'Are you going to stay in there all night?' he asks, his tone mild.

'Maybe.'

'Chloe and Hamish have gone. They had a dance lesson they needed to get to.'

'Oh crap, I forgot.'

'I said I'd run you home.'

'I can walk.'

'Or, here's a crazy idea, I could take you.'

'I don't mind walking.'

'Jesus, Ellie. I think we can be alone in a car together for five minutes without arguing, don't you?'

'Well, I know *I* can.'

He sighs, loudly. 'You grew up to be a bit of a pain in the ass, you know that?'

'Yeah, well … it takes one to know one.' As far as comebacks go, it's weak, but it's all I can think of on the spot.

He snorts with laughter. 'Come on. Time to get out.'

'You don't get to tell me what to do,' I reply with mild outrage.

'Of course not,' he sighs. 'I wouldn't dream of it.'

I swim in circles for a minute, more to make a point than

anything else. 'You could always come in,' I say. 'I'm surprised you haven't already. Once upon a time, any excuse and you'd have been in the water.'

He looks away. 'Yeah, well, things change. People change.'

'Since when does Sam Emerson say no to a swim?'

He doesn't answer.

I bob a little closer to shore, my curiosity piqued. 'Have you even *had* a swim since you've been back?'

He still doesn't answer.

'Sam?'

Finally, he looks at me, his face illuminated by the last rays of the sun. 'No. Not yet.'

I'm flabbergasted. 'Why not?'

I see his shoulders shrug. 'I haven't had a chance.'

'You live in a beach house, *on* the beach,' I remind him. 'It literally does not get any easier than that.'

'It's not a big deal,' he says brusquely.

'Are you kidding? It's a *huge* deal. Sam, you practically used to live in the water. We both did. When was the last time you even swam in an ocean?'

'Hong Kong isn't exactly known for its swimming beaches.'

'Maybe not. But you're here now. Come on, join me.'

'Ellie . . .'

'The water's amazing,' I coax. 'You won't regret it.'

He hesitates. I hear him swallow hard. Then a gentle sigh. 'Not tonight.'

I'm grateful that he can't see my disappointment. 'You've changed, Sam.'

'Can you just ... get out of the water, please. Before I have to ...'

'Before you have to what? Come in and get me? I'd like to see you try.'

'Ellie.'

There's something in his voice, something I can't quite put my finger on. Once upon a time, I knew everything this man was thinking, but not any more.

'Fine. I'll get out. But you owe me dinner for the spider prank.'

'It wasn't a prank.'

'There really was a spider?'

'There was. Not a very big one, though,' he adds quickly when he hears me whimper. 'And long gone by now.'

'How can you be sure?'

'Because you'd have drowned it ten times over,' he points out. 'I *knew* you were still terrified of them. Why did you try and pretend otherwise?'

I move my arms in lazy circles through the water. 'You kept going on about how none of us have changed. I guess I was trying to prove to you that I have.'

'You shouldn't care what I think,' he says softly.

'Of course I care.'

A loaded silence follows. This is dangerous territory, I realise.

'Well, I mean I *used* to care,' I clarify. 'Not any more. Of course I don't care any more.'

'Ellie?'

'Yes?'

'Please, *please* can you come out now,' he says. 'I'm hungry.'

'Hi, hungry,' I joke, grateful to him for lightening the mood. 'I'm naked. So maybe you could fetch my clothes, unless you want me to inflict that sight on you.'

'As traumatic as that would be, I think I'd live.'

It takes me a moment to realise he's echoing the words I said to him the other day, when he was standing at his front door in his underwear. There's amusement in his tone, and I take it as a challenge.

'You're right.' I stand up in the mid-thigh-deep water, and lean my head to one side, wringing the water from my hair. When I've finished that, I dip forward before throwing my head back. My hair arches above me, then lands on my back with a loud slap. I hear him give a sharp intake of breath.

'You OK, Sam?'

'Mm?' His voice comes out choked. He clears his throat. 'Yes. Fine.'

'Good.' Shoulders back, chest out, I stride out of the water, making no attempt to cover myself at all. Let him look.

Sam

Oh God. *Oh God.*

The last thing I expect her to do is stand and walk out of the water completely naked, smirking as she heads straight for me. I panic, rooted to the spot. At the last second she alters her path, brushing to one side of me instead, so close that I can feel the air whisper between us.

Even though I try not to notice, I can't help *but* notice. It's not like she's trying to hide herself from me; completely the opposite. She's lean and athletic, but also curvier than she was as a teen, her body matured into that of a woman. I wonder if she still likes to run and surf. We used to do those things together.

After she passes, I close my eyes, though the image of her is still seared across the inside of my eyelids.

She's beautiful.

Opening them again, I watch the colours in the sky fade for a few minutes, allowing her time to dress.

'You can look now,' she calls out. 'I'm decent again.'

Neither of us says a word as we make our way back up to the house, and I wonder if it's because she's reliving what just happened over and over in her head, as I am. Inside, she leans against the kitchen island and watches as I lock up and look around for my keys.

She points to a sideboard. 'They're over there. But I really don't mind walking.'

'So you've said.' I shove the car keys and my wallet into my pockets. 'Ready?'

'Oh no,' she suddenly exclaims, her hands flying to cover her mouth.

'What?'

'I didn't get around to fixing the paint I messed up.'

'Don't worry, I'll take care of it this week.'

'I can't ask you to do that.'

'You're not asking. I'm offering.'

'Maybe I should quickly do it now?'

I shake my head. 'I don't think Chloe would be too happy with one of your half-arsed repair jobs.'

'I have no idea what you mean by that.'

'Oh really.' I smile at her, amused.

'Yes,' she says. 'Really.'

'Remember that time we found a split in the seam of my wetsuit, right before the club champs?'

I see the moment the memory comes to her. Her eyes open wide and her mouth forms an O shape, before she closes it quickly. 'Vaguely,' she says, nonchalantly.

'You said you could fix it for me.'

'I did fix it for you.'

'Yes, you did,' I agree. 'With *staples*.'

'Hey, it worked, didn't it? The seam held together.'

'Yes, it held together. But the sharp bits scratched the hell out of my hip the entire time I was out on the water.'

'Pfft,' she snorts. 'It was hardly noticeable.'

'I was *bleeding*.'

She rolls her eyes. 'It was a couple of scratches, you big baby.'

'Oh, *I'm* a baby? Says the woman who just performed a strip show on my front lawn because of a tiny spider.'

'*That* is a genuine phobia,' she huffs. 'What kind of person makes fun of that?'

I shake my head at her. 'I'll fix the paint this week. It's not a problem.'

'*I'll* fix the paint,' she argues. 'Clearly I have a misguided reputation for poor workmanship, and I'd like to correct that.'

'I see you're still stubborn,' I say, flicking off the main light switch, leaving just the one over the kitchen island on. 'Painfully so.'

She ignores this. 'I'll come by one day this week after work, if that's OK with you.'

I hold the front door open for her. 'You mean I actually have a choice?'

She lifts her chin and swishes past me out into the night air. 'Of course not.'

I sigh as I lock the door behind us. 'Didn't think so.'

Ellie

We don't speak the whole car ride home, which is only a matter of a few minutes anyway. I wasn't kidding when I said I could have walked here. I walked between our houses so many times when we were teens, I could probably find my way blindfolded.

I risk a sideways glance at him to see if he's feeling as unsettled as I am, but his face gives nothing away. I don't know what *he's* thinking about, but I'm thinking about how weird it is that despite a decade apart, it's still so easy to be around him. No one has ever driven me crazy like he does – he's annoying and infuriating and . . . just a pain in the arse – but God, I've missed this. Missed *him*.

His headlights sweep over Nan's house as he pulls into the drive. A curtain twitches, and we see her face as she tries to peer past the glare of the lights to make out who it is.

'She's seen you,' I say. 'You'll have to come in.'

'She has no idea who this car belongs to,' he points out.

'True.' I open the door. 'But I'll tell her. So if you don't come in now, you know she's going to be hurt.'

He unbuckles his seat belt. 'You never did grasp the concept of fair play.'

Nan is *ridiculously* happy to see Sam again. Like, completely over the top. She even cries a little as she squeezes his face and kisses his cheeks, while I stand nearby and watch, amused.

'It's . . .'

Mwah.

'. . . nice . . .'

Mwah.

'. . . to see . . .'

Mwah, mwah!

'. . . you again too, Nan,' he says, begging me with his eyes to rescue him. I shake my head and he glares at me.

'How long has it been?' she exclaims, pushing him back to get a better look at him but not relinquishing her hold on his face.

''T's 'een a 'ile,' Sam replies. It comes out undecipherable because of the way she's squeezing his cheeks. His mouth is shaped like the mouth of a goldfish.

'Still so good-looking,' she says. 'Look, Ellie. Look how good-looking he is. Don't you think?'

I shrug. 'I guess. If you're into that sort of look.'

Sam's eyes narrow as Nan's head swivels in my direction. 'Almost every man you've ever dated has been a carbon copy of this one,' she says. 'You don't need Freud to tell you what *that* means.'

'Oh sweet Jesus, kill me now,' I mutter. 'Let him go. I'm sure he's got somewhere else he needs to be.'

'You shouldn't get so embarrassed, Ellie,' Nan says, finally releasing Sam's face. 'I've always known you two would—'

'Nan!' I warn. She shuts up, but with a knowing smile.

Sam pulls a few faces, trying to stretch his cheeks back into shape. Alfie sniffs his hand cautiously. His tail starts wagging and he gives Sam a lick.

I grab Alfie's collar and pull him away. 'Thanks for the lift home, but don't let us keep you. I'm sure you have places to go, people to see.'

Sam shrugs. 'Nope. My evening is wide open.'

'Wonderful.' Nan beams. 'You can stay for dinner.'

'Nan, I'm sure Sam doesn't want—'

'I'd love to.'

Sam

I feel like I've stepped into a time machine and gone back ten years as I sit on a bar stool by the bench and watch the way Ellie and her grandmother interact with each other. Shooing each other out of the way. Bickering loudly over what the correct temperature of the oven should be so that the meatballs don't dry out. Arguing over whether the water should be warm or cold *before* you put the eggs for the salad in.

'It's cold. You put them in *cold* water,' Ellie argues. 'Then you add salt and slowly bring it up to the boil before turning it down to simmer for ten minutes.'

'Ten minutes? Ten *minutes*? Sure, if you like eating rocks, maybe.' Nan pushes her away from the sink with her hip. 'Give me that pot. You put the eggs in *warm* water, add a splash of vinegar, then boil them vigorously for four and a half minutes. Not a second more.'

Ellie sighs. 'Like I keep telling you, that's why your eggshells sometimes split when you cook them. You lose half the egg in the water, it's a waste. But will you listen? No.'

Nan looks at me. 'Hark at her ladyship,' she says, rolling her eyes. 'She might be a fancy hoity-toity chef for rich people now, but I think she's forgotten who taught her how to cook.'

'Well it certainly wasn't you,' Ellie snorts. 'If anything, you taught me how *not* to do it.'

Nan goes deathly still. She reaches out one hand to turn the tap off and then places the pot down on the hob. Her movements are slow and exaggerated. I lean back on the stool. I ate a lot of meals here growing up, and although Ellie has a point, I'd never be so stupid as to say it to Nan's face.

'Is that so?' she says.

'Whoa, step too far, Ellie,' I say in a hushed voice. 'It was nice knowing you.'

She flicks me a panicked look and immediately tries to backpedal. 'What I *meant* was that, um . . .'

'You can leave my kitchen now, thank you.'

'Of course you can cook, Nan. I mean, your shepherd's pie . . .' She kisses her fingertips. 'Best in town. In fact, the world, probably. Definitely better than mine.'

'Go on.' Nan sniffs. 'Off you go. I'll call you when dinner is ready. It might not be up to the standard that you've become accustomed to, but it's good honest fare. Certainly didn't do you any harm when you were growing up.'

'Talk about dramatic,' Ellie sighs. 'I was only trying to help. Come on.' She jerks her head at me. 'I'll get you a beer.'

'I've been cooking since before you were even born,' Nan

188

grumbles as I follow Ellie. 'Before your mother and father even *thought* about . . .'

Thankfully we don't hear the rest once we step outside.

'As you can see, she's still a drama queen,' Ellie says, rolling her eyes.

I look at her thoughtfully. 'What was it you said earlier? It takes one to know one?'

She narrows her eyes. 'You're calling me a drama queen?'

'Hey, if the tiara fits . . .'

'You know what, I don't think you deserve that beer after all.'

I'm not listening to her any more, though, because something has caught my attention over her shoulder. 'Is that . . . ?'

Ellie turns and smiles proudly. 'My home. Yes.'

'You live in an old railway carriage?'

'I sure do.'

'Wow.' I walk across the lawn, taking in the sight. It's about twelve metres long, painted a kind of maroon colour. There's a small wooden deck built out in front of it, but I can see that the carriage itself is resting on its original undercarriage. Eight square windows line the front, four on each side of a door.

'Where did you find this?'

'I was actually looking for an old caravan that I could do up, then this came up in one of my online searches and I fell in love. The auction was touch and go, I nearly got outbid over my limit, but in the end I won.'

'You do realise that this is probably the coolest home I've ever seen?'

189

'Oh, I know. And you haven't even seen inside yet.'

'I'm afraid it won't live up to the outside.'

She reaches for the door handle. 'Don't worry, it does. Wait here while I turn on the lights. In fact close your eyes. I want to watch your face when you see it.'

'I'm not clos—'

'*Close them.*'

'Fine.' I do as instructed, and listen as she opens the door and a few switches flick on. I startle when I feel a slight pressure on my lower back.

'Sorry,' she says. 'Just me. Take three steps forward, but lift your feet so you don't trip over the door frame.'

'Can't I just open my eyes and look where I'm going so I don't trip over the door frame?'

'Indulge me.'

I take three steps, concentrating more on the fact that her hand is on my back than on worrying about tripping.

'OK,' she says, and the touch on my back disappears. 'Open your eyes.'

She's right. It does live up to the outside. In fact it's *better* than the outside. I stand in the middle of the carriage and try and look everywhere at once, but that system doesn't work. There's just so much to take in. So I focus my eyes on one end and start there, methodically running my eyes from floor to ceiling so I don't miss anything. The floor and walls are lined with timber, though not the same kind. The wood on the floor is darker, aged, with flaws and imperfections that have been neatly polished and incorporated into the overall look. The floorboards are laid widthways across the carriage, whereas the ones on the wall run down vertically. The ceiling is covered with some kind of cream-coloured ornate tin panelling, and it looks amazing.

To our right is a little living area, complete with a brown leather couch and an old grey armchair. I'm not much of an interior designer, but even I know that the cushions and throw blankets that seem to be just casually tossed have in fact been artfully chosen and placed. A bookshelf sits beside the armchair, and opposite it, I'm astounded to see, is a small black fireplace and chimney.

'Does that work?' I ask, pointing at the fireplace.

'Sure does.' She walks over to it and opens the little door. 'It's cleaned and empty now because . . . well, summer. But in winter it heats this place up beautifully.'

I turn my head. 'And you have a kitchen?'

'I sure do.'

She passes me and runs her hand over a white marble benchtop. 'Fully functional. You've got an oven and hob here.' She points. 'Sink, fridge freezer and even . . .' she bends down to open a door, 'ta-da!'

'You're kidding. A dishwasher.'

'Spoilt, right? Although I don't really use it.' She shrugs. 'I eat with Nan most of the time.'

Over her shoulder I notice floor-length curtains, drawn shut. 'Is that . . . ?'

'My bedroom.'

'You don't have to show me,' I say, afraid that she might think I'm hinting.

'No tour is complete without a peek at the master bedroom,' she says.

It's bigger than I was expecting – around a third of the carriage's length – and includes an en suite bathroom. I can see this, because she's left the door wide open.

'Sorry,' she says, darting inside to pick up a towel and some clothes off the floor. 'I'm normally a lot tidier.'

I can't help but smirk, and she looks up at the wrong time and notices.

'What?' she demands. 'What's that look for?'

'Well, this is me you're talking to,' I remind her.

She looks at me blankly. 'And?'

'I nearly got lost amongst all the crap on your bedroom floor once. In fact I came *this* close to calling for help.' I indicate with my fingers.

She rolls her eyes. 'Ha ha, you're so funny. I'm not *that* bad.'

'You have improved,' I agree. 'Astoundingly, your bed is even made.'

'Maybe I didn't sleep here last night,' she quips, and my stomach plummets right to the bottom of my feet. She notices the colour drain from my face.

'I'm kidding,' she adds quickly. 'I make it every morning before I go out. Start the day as you mean to go on, that sort of thing.' She lifts the lid of a woven laundry hamper and puts the towel and clothes inside. 'And I like climbing into a crisp, made-up bed at night rather than a messy pile of sheets and blankets. It just feels nicer.'

'It's none of my business where you sleep.'

'Here,' she says, pointing at the bed. 'I sleep here. Every night.'

'Like I said, it's none of my business.'

She narrows her eyes as if she wants to say something, but stops herself, walking back to the kitchen and opening the fridge instead. 'Beer?'

'Please.'

She takes one out, uses the bottom of her T-shirt to twist the top off easily and passes it to me, repeating the gesture with one for herself.

'Cheers.'

'Cheers.'

We tap our bottles together.

'God, that's good,' she says, smacking her lips together after a mouthful. 'I needed that after the trauma of today.'

'Trauma? Oh, you mean the poor, helpless spider that you drowned in the ocean?'

'It was either me or him,' she mutters darkly, shuddering.

'How do you know it was a him? I really hope it wasn't a mummy spider. There might be orphan baby spiders back in the shed right now, waiting for Mum to come home. Hungry, scared, all alone.'

'Joke's on you if you think that's going to make me feel bad. A baby spider is still a spider. They can starve to death for all I care.'

I laugh. 'You've become hard, Ellie.'

'Yeah, well, the world will do that to you. Anyway, what do you think?'

'Of . . . ?'

'This.' She makes a sweeping gesture that encompasses the carriage. 'I know it's small, but I don't mind. It's cosy.'

'It's great, it really is. Whoever renovated it has excellent taste.'

'You mean me. *I* have excellent taste.'

'You renovated this?'

'From scratch. Why do you sound so surprised?'

'Not *scratch* scratch, though, right?'

'Look at these, oh doubtful one.' She gestures with the bottle and I follow her to the living area, where she points at some framed pictures on the wall. 'This is what it looked like when I bought it.'

I peer at the photographs and let out a low whistle. 'What a dump.'

'Right? Completely run-down. Holes, dead creatures, manky smells . . . the works. I pretty much had to pull it apart and start again.'

'OK. Sure. But when you say *you* did it . . . '

'I did,' she protests. 'Ask Nan, or Chloe, or anyone. I mean, I had some help, of course. From various friends and tradespeople. But I did a fair chunk of the work myself.'

'Mm-hmm.'

'Why do you sound like you don't believe me?'

'Well, you're telling me that the woman who ran screaming into the ocean today when she had one teensy, tiny spider on her . . . *she* worked on a grotty old carriage like this?' I point at the picture. 'I mean, this is what, only six-by-four? And I can see the cobwebs from here.'

'I'm not saying it was easy,' she admits. 'I had to try and overcome my phobia, believe me, and there were some … incidents along the way that I'm not particularly proud of.'

I smirk. 'You didn't strip off in front of your neighbours too, did you?'

'No,' she says. 'Of course not.' Then she turns pensive. 'Well. Not *completely*.'

I laugh then. Properly laugh. Like I haven't laughed in a long, long time. I laugh so hard and for so long, tears actually well up in my eyes. She chuckles along with me at first, but then starts to look grumpy.

'I'm so happy you find my phobia amusing.'

I can't answer her. Every time I look at her face, I end up laughing harder.

'Seriously,' she says, glaring at me. 'It's fine. Don't worry about offending me or anything.'

'I'm sorry … it's just …' I can't finish the sentence, though. I'm too busy imagining her poor neighbours copping an eyeful.

She opens a drawer in the kitchen and rummages inside it. 'I'm sure I've got a balloon and a pin around here somewhere,' she mutters.

That stops my laughter almost immediately. 'You wouldn't,' I splutter, trying to catch my breath again.

'Not so funny *now*, is it?'

'Close the drawer.'

'Or what?'

After a brief stand-off when neither of us blinks, I call her bluff and lean against the counter, lifting my beer to my lips. 'It's OK. You haven't really got a balloon in there.'

'Oh yeah?' She pulls a silver one out and dangles it in the air between us. 'What's this then?'

I choke on the beer I've just swallowed. Some – unfortunately – gets sprayed out, some goes up my nose and some goes down the wrong pipe, probably into my lungs. I cough, unable to take my eyes off the balloon.

'I think it's one of the ones left over from Nan's eightieth birthday party,' she muses. 'That was a great night. We had one of those pigs on a spit, you know the ones I mean?'

I'm unable to answer because I'm coughing too much.

'The meat was really tender and juicy, and the crackling? Ohhh. It was crunchy and salty, just the way it should be. You know,' she muses, 'I'd never really been a big fan of pork until that night.'

I'm listening to her, but my eyes haven't left the balloon as she plays with it, stretching it out between her hands, pulling the neck and then letting it snap back into place. I carefully put my beer bottle down on the bench.

'Ellie, I'm very sorry that I laughed,' I say in a low, measured voice, keeping my tone steady like I'm negotiating with a bomb-wielding maniac. 'Now please can you put the balloon down?'

She grins at me.

Ellie

'I *could* put it down,' I reply, enjoying the power switch. Suddenly he's not so amused. 'But first I want an apology.'

'For what?'

'For laughing at me.'

'I wasn't laughing *at* you. I was laughing because you strip naked every time you see a spider.'

'Not *every* time.'

'OK. I'm sorry. But I've stopped laughing now, so you can put the balloon away and we'll just pretend this never happened. Sound good?'

'What's the name of it again?' I muse, stretching the tip of the balloon as far as I can.

He winces. 'What's the name of what?'

'Your phobia.'

'I'm not really—'

I lift the balloon to my pursed lips.

'Globophobia,' he says hurriedly. 'It's called globophobia.'

'Ah, that's right. I always thought it was such a weird name for a phobia about blowing up a balloon. I mean it would make more sense if it described a phobia of travel. Get it? Globe. As in, the world.'

He nods. 'I'll agree with anything you want, as long as you put the balloon back in the drawer.'

'Mm.' I look at it thoughtfully, waiting. He's never been able to resist correcting me, and this time he lasts less than five seconds.

'Although *technically*,' he says, 'it's not so much a fear of inflating balloons as it is of them popping.' He swallows hard. 'The noise it makes.'

'So I can do this?' I lick my lips, inhale deeply and put my mouth around the end of the balloon.

I don't even see him move, he's that fast. The balloon is whipped out of my hands, leaving me standing there with my mouth wide open, still exhaling. Only it's into his chest this time, because suddenly he's standing millimetres away from me. I blink, startled, then tilt my head back slowly.

His eyes are closed, and his chest is rising and falling like he's just finished a sprint. There's a twitch in his lower jaw, and I watch it, fascinated. This close, I can smell the freshly laundered smell of his shirt, along with another smell, muskier. The scent of him. He was actually really worried, I realise, and straight away I feel awful.

'I'm sorry.' I put my hands behind my back, between me and the counter, and lean on them. 'I took that too far, didn't I.'

He opens his eyes and looks down at me, and it's lucky I'm holding onto the counter, because my legs suddenly have no bones left in them. His eyes probe mine, searching for something, like he has a million questions and I hold all the answers. I feel like I'm drowning in them, but just as I'm about to slip under, he lowers his gaze to stare at my lips instead.

Is he thinking about kissing me?

The thought pops into my head with a jolt. If it was anyone else, I wouldn't question it. But this is Sam. *Sam.* And yet I swear he has that unmistakable look on his face, like he's parched and I'm what he's craving. His lips even seem to part in preparation.

'Dinner's ready!' Nan calls, her timing as impeccable as always. Sam's eyes widen a fraction and he jumps swiftly away from me, as if he's been in a trance and has just come to his senses. I swallow hard.

'I'm sorry,' he mumbles, running a hand through his hair.

'For what?'

'I don't know,' he says, and it's true. He looks as bewildered as I feel.

'I said DINNER'S READY,' Nan calls, louder.

'We're coming!' I yell back at her. 'God, she's so impatient.'

Sam clears his throat. 'Unlike you.'

I realise instantly that he's trying to lighten the mood again, get us back to even footing, so I play along, because it's easier than trying to dissect what just happened between us. 'I know, right?'

'I was being sarcastic.'

'I know. Come on.' I open the fridge and take out another

couple of beers to have while we eat. 'We'd better go before she gets mad and feeds everything to Alfie.'

'Would that be such a bad thing?'

It's actually nice having Sam join us for dinner, not that I'll ever admit that to him. Normally it's just Nan and me, and as much as I love her, I can only hear about the latest Dingle family drama on *Emmerdale* so many times. The three of us eat, talk and laugh, and it's just like old times. Nan asks Sam lots of questions about his life in Hong Kong, and for the most part he answers them. Sometimes he's a little guarded, especially when she asks about Mei, but that's understandable. Alfie sits beside him the entire time, resting his chin on Sam's thigh and gazing up at him adoringly.

'He's such a good judge of character,' Nan says.

'It's not that,' I retort. 'How many meatballs have you slipped him under the table, Sam? Four?'

Sam gapes at me, looking betrayed.

'You didn't like my meatballs?' Nan sniffs, clearly affronted. 'Even with my special ingredient?'

'Speaking of which, you know what the doctor said,' I remind her.

She waves a hand dismissively. 'He said a lot of things. I can't be expected to remember everything.'

'About food, Nan. You're not supposed to be adding *any-thing* "special" to your meals. The more basic, the better.'

'I don't recall him saying that,' she mumbles.

'That's because you're only choosing to remember the bits that suit you, not the bits that are going to help save your life.'

I point at the half a meatball left on Sam's plate. 'This is exactly what he told you not to do.'

'They're just meatballs.'

Sam looks back and forward between us. 'Am I missing something?'

'Her special ingredient,' I inform him, 'is cheese. Lots and lots of grated cheese.'

'Ah,' he says, poking the meatball with a fork. 'So *that's* what all the gloopy stuff around the bottom is.'

'It really adds to the flavour, doesn't it.' Nan beams.

'It's also high in saturated fat,' I point out. 'Which *you* are supposed to be cutting out.'

'What kind of life is a life without cheese?'

'Um, a *longer* one?'

'Maybe,' she concedes. 'But I'd rather die happy eating the foods I enjoy than miserable and eating stuff that tastes like nothing.'

I throw my hands up in the air and glare at her. 'Do you see what I have to deal with, Sam? She's so . . . *stubborn*.'

'I'm an old lady,' she retorts. 'Let me enjoy whatever time I have left.'

Sam blinks like a possum in headlights. 'I think that you both make excellent points.'

I stare at him. 'Coward.'

Nan grins like she's won, which I guess she has. She gets to her feet and picks up Sam's plate, putting it on top of her own. 'Dessert, anyone? It's a special occasion, so I thought apple crumble and vanilla ice cream.'

I frown. 'We don't have vanilla ice cream, *or* apple crumble . . . do we? I can tell by your face that I'm wrong.'

'I whipped one up while you were outside,' she says. 'It should be finished cooking by now. And there's some ice cream in the freezer. Underneath the peas.'

'Hidden, you mean?' I shake my head at her as she leaves the room.

Sam is looking at me with an odd expression.

'What?' I ask him.'

'It's just . . . I feel like I've gone back in time,' he says. 'Sitting at this table, in this room that hasn't changed in the slightest, listening to you two fight.' He looks around, shaking his head lightly.

'I wouldn't call it fighting. It's more like affectionate bickering. And it's only because I care about her.'

'I know. And it's great how much you love her. She's lucky to have you. I just . . . ' His face clouds. 'I wish I could have been there for Grandad at the end. I *should* have been here.'

'It was out of your control.'

He pulls a face. 'Maybe at first, with travel restrictions and then . . . Mei.'

He looks so forlorn that before I even realise what I'm doing, I've reached across the table and squeezed his hand. He looks down at my fingers, cupped over his protectively. For a second I think he's going to pull away, and I hold my breath. But then he gently flips his hand underneath mine so we're palm to palm.

'Thank you,' he says. 'For inviting me here tonight. It's been a long time since I felt like I belonged anywhere.'

The words are so simple and heartfelt that they fill me with a swell of emotion. I want to tell him that he's always belonged here. That he will *always* belong here. Then Nan reappears with dessert. Sam smiles at me and releases my hand. And just like that, the moment is over.

Sam

Dear S,

Once again, you're most welcome. I am glad my collection of words helped you. Maybe you're right, maybe I should become a therapist and write a bestselling book about waves. Who knows, I might make millions of dollars and become the first giraffe to travel the world on a book tour. To be honest, though, I'm not sure many others would understand the comparison as well as you have. Sometimes things that make perfect sense inside my head don't translate as well into words.

I hope you're doing OK.
DG

PS Of course I surf. Do you know anyone around here who doesn't?

Ellie

Dear Daisy,

   I'm doing ... better than I expected, actually. Thanks for asking. It's weird. When I came back here, I had a plan. Get the house fixed, get it sold and then get out. I planned on avoiding as many people as possible, though to be fair I had no idea half of my senior class were still here. I'm ashamed to admit that I judged them for that at first. What a wanker, eh? Comes back from overseas thinking he's all that and looks down on all the little people who never went anywhere.

   It wasn't really like that, though. Not really. I didn't consciously mean to judge anyone, because who am I to judge? What have I achieved? I'm back here with nothing and no one to show for the last five years of my life. I have a degree, sure. But no job, currently. No home. My grandparents' place still feels like exactly that ... my grandparents' place. I know it's legally mine now in name, but it's theirs in every other regard. Their design, their furnishings. All their things are still there, and I mean everything, including my grandmother's clothes. My grandfather never had the heart to throw anything out after she died. Her shampoo bottle and facewash are still on the little shelf in the upstairs shower, though the contents are probably solid by now. Her slippers sit on the floor by the bathroom, as if they're just waiting for her to pop them on, and her gardening shoes are on the deck by the back door, as if she just kicked them off on her way into the house. Her clothes, her shoes, her handbags and scarves, they're all still in their wardrobe. There's even a book on her nightstand that she must have been reading when she died. Her glasses are folded up on top of it. The house is filled with their things. The accumulation of a lifetime. When you look at it like that, it's kind of sad. That a pile of clothing, books and kitchen stuff is all that remains after someone has gone. There are some things I will keep, their photos and my grandfather's maps, but the rest I have no use for.

All I have left of Mei's belongings is a ring. Not her wedding ring, we buried her wearing that. I bought this ring for her on our first wedding anniversary. The stone is a round opal, the most brilliant blue. I don't think it came out of nature that colour, I'm pretty sure the sales assistant said something about it being manufactured. But it's stunning, and Mei fell in love with it the second she saw it in the window of the jeweller's. So I bought it for her. Not then, not when she was with me. I went back a day later and bought it, and I kept it hidden in my sock drawer for eight months until our anniversary. I remember she cried when I gave it to her, because she thought I'd searched the city for a jeweller's and a ring we'd seen in passing almost a year earlier. I didn't have the heart to tell her I'd been holding on to it for all that time. I just smugly banked the brownie points I'd been awarded for being a 'thoughtful and wonderful' husband and kept my mouth shut.

So that's it. That's all I have left of our life together. Her mother tried to get me to sort through her things a few weeks after she died, but I refused. I wasn't ready. I didn't think I'd ever be ready, if I'm honest. But when I made the decision to come back home, I had to do it. Turns out most of it was just stuff, at the end of the day. Furniture, kitchenware. I offered it all to friends and donated whatever was left to charity. Her clothes, shoes, make-up and so on was a little bit harder to let go. I took the ring and let her mother and sisters have the rest. Whether they kept it or not, I don't know. And I don't need to know. Because I realised that all that stuff was just that ... stuff. The emotional connection comes through the memory of the person wearing that jacket, or smelling of that perfume, so that's what I held on to. My memories. No one can take those away.

I remember looking around our empty apartment before I left it for the final time, and feeling guilty because it was like I'd just wiped all trace of her from the face of the earth.

Here I go again, babbling it all out to you. I'm starting to

207

feel like this correspondence is very heavily one-sided. Tell me something about yourself so I don't feel like I'm the only one spilling their guts here. Or maybe something about the person you lost. If you feel up to talking about it.

S

Dear S,

   The ring sounds beautiful, and I now know that you're a romantic at heart, because the story BEHIND the ring is beautiful too. I've decided that it's not fair that you know my name (or think you do), yet you still haven't told me yours. I mean, I'm assuming here, but I'm guessing your parents weren't just incredibly lazy and decided to name you a letter in the alphabet. Although that would be helpful when filling out forms, only having to sign an initial. A real timesaver.

   You asked me to tell you about the person I lost.

   He was ... incredible. Ambitious, kind, confident. The funniest person I've ever met. He made me laugh every single day. And he was really caring. He treated me like I was the most precious thing in his world, even when I was being a pain in the ass. (I know, it's hard to believe I can be like that, but it's true.) I adored him, everything about him, even his faults. He was stubborn, and could be extraordinarily bossy. He always thought he knew what was best for me, instead of letting me figure it out for myself. We argued a lot, silly stuff, but we could be honest with each other in a way that not many people can. He was my everything, for a while. The yin to my yang. The Batman to my Robin. I honestly thought fate had brought him into my life and that he'd be a part of it for ever, until he wasn't.

Daisy

Ellie

Dear Daisy,

First of all, fate? Sorry, but I'm not so sure I believe in 'fate'. Because if I did, that means I have to believe that Mei was always destined to die on the side of the road that day. That she was running late for a predestined reason. That from the moment she was born, it was already written in the stars somewhere that she would step off that footpath right at the wrong moment. That she'd die without us ever getting to say goodbye.

If that's fate, you can stick it.* I can't ... won't believe in that.

Secondly, what the hell? I've been going on and on like some self-absorbed jerk about MY grief, and MY loss, and how I'M feeling ... and then you go and completely dismantle my heart with your beautiful words. I mean, bloody hell, Daisy. I don't know what to say. I'm not as good with words of comfort as you are. I'm sorry. I wish I was. All I can say is that I'm here for you too, if there's anything I can do.

And thirdly, no. My parents weren't lazy. The S stands for ... drum roll, please ... Santa! That's why I chose a Christmas tree to put my letter in, see?

Santa

*Not you personally. I'm not telling YOU to stick it.

Sam

Dear S,

I'm sorry, but there's no way you're Santa. I met him once, in a bar in Ireland on St Patrick's Day. He was six foot two and built like a brick shit-house, with ginger hair and a ginger beard and eyes the colour of emeralds. He was also incredibly drunk, and I mean stupidly so. He serenaded the entire bar with a beautiful rendition of 'Molly Malone' and then fell sideways off his bar stool in slow motion while we all watched and wondered if it was part of the show. But he didn't get back up. Instead he curled up into a big ginger ball on the floor and went to sleep, and everyone just spent the rest of the night stepping over him.

So there you have it. I've met Santa. You're not him. Unless YOU'RE six foot two and built like a brick shit-house, with ginger hair and a ginger beard and eyes the colour of emeralds, and you just haven't thought to mention it yet. In which case, top of the morning to you, it's nice to see you again.

- Daisy

Ellie

Dear Daisy,

   Busted. Sadly, no, I'm not six foot two and built like a brick shit-house, with ginger hair and a ginger beard and eyes the colour of emeralds, but I wish I was. What a magnificent man I would be.

   I'm afraid I'm a fraction shorter than that, with ordinary blond hair and blue eyes. In case you're envisioning some kind of sexy Viking, let me stop you right there, because unfortunately, and not due to a lack of effort on my part, I've never been able to pull off a beard. The hair grows out kind of patchy and in weird directions.

   S

Sam

It makes me smile every time I read her last letter, and so far that's been at least ten times, probably more like fifteen. I have no idea who this Daisy is, or why she keeps writing back to me, but I'm happy she does. She's funny. She's also kind, and has a knack for taking my jumbled-up, confused thoughts and unravelling them in a way that makes perfect sense. Somehow it makes everything feel better. *She* makes everything feel better, brighter, and until now, there was only one other person in my life who could do that.

Ellie.

The letter also serves as a distraction from thinking about how close I came to kissing her the other night, because I'm trying really hard not to think about that. When I *do* think about it, I remember how I could see in her eyes that she *wanted* me to kiss her . . . and I end up not knowing what to think at all.

Ellie

'Ellie, hi,' he says when he opens his door on Friday evening and sees me standing there. His tone is surprised. 'What can I do for you?'

'Are you ready?'

'What?'

'I'm not late, am I?' I make a show of checking the time on my phone.

'Late for what?'

I sigh, sliding it back into my pocket. 'You forgot, didn't you.'

'No,' he says, quickly.

'I *knew* you'd forget.'

'I didn't forget,' he protests. 'I was just, ah . . .'

I clock his panicked expression and take pity. 'I'm just messing with you.'

His eyes narrow. 'You mean, we have no plans?'

'Nope. No plans,' I confirm, pointing past him to the inside of the house. 'Mind if I come in?'

'Actually, I do now.'

'It's not my fault you're still an easy wind-up.'

'It takes one . . .'

'. . . to know one.' I talk loudly over him. 'Jinx. You're getting predictable, Emerson.'

He leans against the door frame, crossing his arms over his chest. Even though it's more of a smirk, it feels good to see him smiling again. 'To what do I owe this pleasure, Campbell?'

I reach into my back pocket and pull out a paintbrush, brandishing it at him. 'I promised I'd come back and sort out that paint I messed up. Chloe's coming by tomorrow to plan out the placement of the seats, et cetera, so it needs to be done by then or I'm in serious trouble.'

'It's already done. I did it this afternoon.'

'Dammit, Sam, I said I'd take care of it.'

'You also said you'd be around "one day this week". It's Friday night, Ellie. I thought you'd forgotten.'

'Friday night is still technically this week,' I retort.

He sighs. 'You're welcome, by the way.'

We stare at each other for a few moments, and I realise he's waiting for me to say the actual words.

I shrug. 'I'm not thanking you until I inspect the work. For all I know you could have done a half-assed job, and I'll be the one who gets the blame for it.'

He moves to one side. 'Fine. Be my guest.'

'Ohhh, what's that divine smell?' I ask, breathing in

deeply when I get inside and a delicious scent hits me square in the face.

'Nothing too exciting,' he replies, closing the door behind me. 'A simple stir-fry.'

'It doesn't smell simple.' My stomach rumbles loudly as I sniff the air. 'Garlic? And . . . ginger?'

'You're good,' he says, clearly impressed. He walks over to where a wok sits on the hob, emitting a sizzling noise. He picks it up and expertly tosses the ingredients inside. It releases a fresh burst of exotically fragrant scent into the air. 'You haven't eaten?'

I follow him and lean against the bench by the stove so I can watch him. 'I had some crackers and cheese at Chloe's, but nothing substantial.'

'In that case, would you like to join me?'

My stomach rumbles again. 'Sure. I mean, if you don't think it'll be too awkward.'

He gives the wok one final toss then turns the ring off. 'Why would it be awkward? Because you're a professional chef and I'm merely an amateur? If you promise not to judge me too harshly, I think we'll be OK.'

'Of course I won't judge you. But that's not what I meant.'

'People eat together all the time, Ellie.'

'I know, but this is . . . us.'

He gives me a look. 'Stop overthinking things. We managed fine the other night, didn't we?'

'That's true.' My mind flashes back to that moment in my railway carriage, as it's been doing several times a day for the last few days. I get an excited swirl in my stomach every time I think about it, which is highly confusing, but not in an unpleasant way.

'Can you set the table, please?' he asks, pointing to a drawer with his tongs.

'Sure.' Inside the drawer, I find a pile of neatly folded tablecloths.

'Forks are in the top drawer by the sink,' he adds.

I choose a blue tablecloth and fetch a pair of forks, then head to the table, shaking the cloth out and smoothing any creases in the fabric, and lining up the forks opposite each other.

'How's Chloe?' he asks, as he uses the tongs to dish the stir-fry into the bowls.

'She's OK. Weirdly relaxed, actually. I'm worried it's the calm before the storm.'

He snorts. 'If the way she's acting now is the calm before the storm, I'd hate to be here for the *actual* storm.'

'She's not that bad.'

'No, I'm sure she's not. But don't you ever get tired of being bossed around by her?'

I sit down and continue smoothing out the tablecloth, mostly to give my hands something to do. I feel like I'm betraying Chloe's trust by telling Sam what I'm going to say next, but at the same time, I don't like him thinking badly of her.

'The thing you have to understand,' I tell him, 'is that to Chloe, this wedding kind of means everything.'

'I don't see why. It's just one day in your life,' he says, putting

219

the bowls down on the table. 'Basically a big, expensive party. And when it's over, everything is the same as it was the day before, except you now have an official piece of paper. The money is far better spent on buying a house.'

'They already own a house.'

'Something else then, something tangible, so you've got something to actually show for all the money you've spent. Or better yet, save it for the future. For when you start a family. Kids aren't cheap, from what I've heard.'

He heads back to the kitchen, and I watch him, wondering if it was his own wedding that has made him so jaded, or if he's always felt like this.

'Chloe can't have kids,' I blurt out.

'Oh. I'm sorry to hear that.'

'She got pregnant three years ago. It wasn't planned, but they were really happy when they found out. But when she was almost ten weeks, she got these awful pains and started bleeding. The pain actually got so bad that Hamish had to call an ambulance. They did scans at the hospital and realised it was an ectopic pregnancy.'

'What's that?'

'When the egg fertilises and implants outside of the uterus. In her case, it was still in one of her fallopian tubes, which had ruptured.'

'That sounds awful.'

'It gets worse. They had to operate, and when they opened her up, they realised the rupture had caused massive internal bleeding around her cervix. They removed the tube, but the next day she was still bleeding, so they rushed her back into surgery and had to do a full hysterectomy.'

His face has gone ashen, as some men's tend to do when you talk about things like fallopian tubes and cervixes. 'And a hysterectomy means . . . ?'

'It means that she can't have kids. Basically all the gear she needs is gone.'

He exhales audibly, shaking his head. 'How did she take it?'

'Not well. Understandably. She was devastated, as was Hamish, though he hid how he was feeling so that he could support her.'

'Ah yes, the great manly tradition of bottling up one's feelings.'

'Which is a stupid thing to do,' I snap, wondering if he's talking about himself too. 'You only have to look at the suicide rate of men in this country to realise that.'

He recoils. 'That's quite a leap.'

'Well, men hiding their feelings is not a good thing. It's not tough, or macho.'

He holds his palms out in a conciliatory gesture. 'I completely agree.'

'Good. Sorry. I get a bit worked up on the subject, but only because I saw how much it affected Hamish and how he didn't deal with it when it happened like he should have.'

'Is he OK now, though?'

'Yeah.' I nod. 'They both are. It took time, though, and counselling, and a lot of support from their friends. Logan started hosting regular boys' nights in his workshop. He has a bit of a den set up by the office. The guys hang out, drink, play cards or pool, and I guess they talk too. Chloe and I and a few girlfriends do the same, at least once a month, usually at her place. It seems to help, knowing how much love and support they have around them. And it gives people the chance to chat without fear of judgement if something's troubling them.'

Sam's listening, but I can tell by the faraway look in his eyes that his thoughts are also somewhere else. I remember his letters, how alone he felt in Hong Kong after his wife died. How their friends – and I use the term loosely – didn't even want to mention her name around him in case he got upset. From the sounds of it, he had no support at all.

'Anyway,' I say, changing the subject, 'what's a girl got to do to get a drink around here?'

'What would you like? I have beer, wine or . . . ' he opens the fridge and looks inside, 'juice.'

'What sort of wine is it?'

He lifts a bottle out of the fridge door and peers at the label. 'It's Gew . . . Gewürz . . . Nope, I've got no chance of pronouncing that.'

'Bring it here, you uncouth peasant.'

'It was a welcome-home gift from one of the neighbours,' he explains, bringing the bottle and two glasses to the table. 'Esmae and Bruce, in the Spanish-style house.'

'Oh, I love that place,' I say, watching him pour the wine. 'So eccentric.' When he's finished pouring, I pick up the bottle.

'Gewürztraminer,' I read off the label.

'Bless you,' Sam says, grinning.

I groan. 'Seriously?'

'What?' he protests. 'It's a quality joke.'

I pick up my fork and poke it down into the food, turning it around until I've captured enough of the noodles, then put it in my mouth. It's a taste explosion, and I close my eyes, appreciating and savouring all the individual flavours as I chew. It's a little bit spicy, just a tiny bit, but it's also sweet, sour and salty. Swallowing the mouthful, I open my eyes again to see that Sam is watching me.

'Well? Do you like it?' he asks.

'I'm impressed.'

'Really?' He beams proudly.

'Seriously. When did you learn how to cook? I mean, this is restaurant quality, and if my memory serves me right, you used to burn two-minute noodles nine times out of ten.'

'You can't burn two-minute noodles.'

'And yet somehow you managed. That's how much of a non-cook you were. But this, this is really good.'

He looks down at his own bowl. 'It's just something simple I learned to throw together. Prawns, ramen noodles, bok choy, mushrooms, carrots, snow peas, ginger, garlic, soy, sesame oil, rice wine, brown sugar and some chilli oil, because I prefer it with a bit of a kick.'

'You could be my sous chef any day,' I say, before realising how it sounds. 'On the ships, I mean,' I add hastily. 'That's not a metaphor for life ... or anything.'

He suppresses a smile. 'It's not that complicated to prepare,' he says. 'Fifteen minutes, start to finish. Mei and I ...' He pauses when he mentions her name, then carries on. 'We used to cook it all the time on a Friday night.'

'Well, it's really good.' I ignore the stab of jealousy I feel at the mention of her name. How can I be jealous of his dead wife? 'She taught you well.'

'Thanks. Obviously it's nothing like what you probably create.'

I pull a face. 'Used to create. Not much call for French cuisine at the café.'

'Do you miss it? That life?'

I'm quiet while I give his question proper consideration. 'I do,' I say eventually. 'But I try not to think about it much. That life almost feels unreal sometimes, like I dreamt it all.'

'I bet Nan wasn't too happy that you gave it all up for her.'

I snort. 'That's an understatement.'

'Do you regret coming back?'

'No,' I say firmly. 'I would have regretted it more if I hadn't. I'll always be grateful for this time with her.'

He puts his fork down and instantly I realise my mistake.

'I'm sorry,' I say quickly, laying a hand on his arm. 'I didn't think.'

'It's OK. You're right. I *do* regret not being here when Grandad ...'

'It's not like you had a choice, with everything that was going on. The world was a crazy place to be.'

'Still, there's always a way,' he says softly. 'I should have tried harder to find it.'

I squeeze his arm lightly, wishing there was more I could do to make him feel better. Bring back that smile again.

'I'm proud of you, Ellie. Of everything you've achieved.'

I feel my cheeks warm under his praise. 'Thanks.'

'I'm really sorry that I was so judgemental the first time we ran into each other. Saying all that stuff about you still being here, working in the café, living at your nan's. I was—'

'Being a dick?'

He snorts back laughter. 'That's the second time you've called me that, but yes, that pretty much sums it up.'

'I forgive you.'

'Thanks. Of course, you could have mentioned that you own the café, and that you live in a railway carriage. Then I wouldn't have made horrible assumptions.'

'You didn't give me a chance to mention anything.'

'That's true. It's just . . . I came here with a clear plan. Avoid everyone, get the house ready for sale as quickly as possible, then sell it and move on. I honestly thought you'd be long gone, so I hadn't prepared myself for how I'd feel running into you again.'

I put my own fork down. 'And how *do* you feel?'

His eyes hold steady with mine. 'Honestly? Confused.'

Sam

'Confused . . . in what way?' she asks, picking up her wine and taking a large mouthful, like she needs a bit of Dutch courage to hear my answer.

'Ellie, I've tried not to think about you that much, over the years.'

'Ouch,' she says with a wince.

'On purpose,' I add gently. 'Because losing you was one of the hardest things I've ever gone through.'

'It wasn't exactly a picnic for me either,' she retorts, her eyes flashing. '*You* walked away from me, Sam. You left me. I never in a million years thought you could do that.'

'I was angry.'

'Misguidedly at me.'

I shrug. 'Sort of. Maybe.'

'What do you mean, maybe? I didn't do anything wrong.'

'It's hard to explain.'

She pushes back her chair; it scrapes on the floor. 'You know what, thank you, Sam, for dinner. But I really can't be doing this right now. So I will check that paint job and then get out of your hair.'

I blink. It's all happened so suddenly. One moment we're having a conversation and the next she's on her feet and ready to leave.

'Ellie, wait . . . ' I reach for her hand, but she pushes it away like my touch hurts.

'Where's the switch for the outside light?' she asks, looking around. I can hear a tremor in her voice and I hate myself for causing it.

I stand up and follow her towards the outside doors.

'Ellie . . . '

'Switch,' she mumbles. 'Where's the damn switch?'

'It's over there, on the right, but I'm not sure you're going to be able to see the paint very well through those tears.'

'Dammit, Sam,' she says. 'You're supposed to pretend you haven't noticed.' She wipes her face quickly. 'That's what normal people do.'

'Since when was I normal?'

She snorts through her tears. 'Good point.'

'I didn't mean to upset you. What can I do?'

'You can look the other way while I go to the bathroom and attempt to salvage any dignity I might have left. Can you do that?'

I nod. 'I can.'

She heads off down the hallway. I walk slowly back to the

table and sink down onto my chair, picking up my glass and taking a large mouthful of wine myself.

'I'm sorry,' I call out to her. There's no answer, so I sit and chastise myself. Everything had just started to go so well between us again.

When five minutes turns into ten and she's still not back, I go looking for her. The bathroom door is open, the light off. For a moment, I think she's left, either slipped past me to the door without me noticing, or – and I wouldn't put it past her at all – climbed out of the bathroom window and absconded into the night.

'Ellie?'

'In here.'

She's in my grandfather's study. I hover in the doorway for a few seconds, observing her. She's standing in front of his large floor-to-ceiling bookcase, her head tilted as she reads the spines, her fingers trailing gently down the lettering.

'I forgot how much stuff he had,' she says, turning. Her tears are gone, but her eyes are a little red, like she let herself have a good cry in the bathroom. 'I'm sorry, I probably shouldn't have come in here without asking.'

'It's OK.'

'Are you sure? Your face kind of says otherwise.'

'Yes, I'm sure. It's fine. I just . . .' I look around the room. 'I always feel a bit emotional in here. It's the one place in the house I can still feel his presence. I know that probably sounds silly.'

'No, it doesn't,' she says softly. 'I know what you mean.

This room is so ... *him*. I wish I'd ...' She sighs. 'I wish I'd made more of an effort to visit him, because he was always so nice to me when we were friends. But I was scared of what he might tell me about you. Especially after ...' She stops and looks downs at her feet.

'After what?' I prod her gently.

'It doesn't matter.'

'Ellie, please. After what?'

She takes a deep breath and lets it out slowly. 'After you got married.'

'Oh.'

'I know I shouldn't have cared. I mean, things had ended so ... horribly between us.' She lifts her chin and looks me straight in the eye. 'But the truth is, I was devastated. More than I'd ever thought I could be.'

My chest feels like it might burst from the shallow breaths that are suddenly all I can take. 'Why?'

'I don't know. I think it just finally sank in that I'd really lost you. That you were gone and were never coming back.' She sniffs and wipes one cheek with the back of her hand 'After that, I avoided your grandfather in the street if I ever saw him. And if he came into the café, I'd hide out the back.'

'I'm sorry.'

'For what?' She laughs bitterly. 'Getting married? No you're not. And I don't expect you to be.'

'No, I'm not sorry for getting married. I loved Mei. I'll never regret that. But I'm sorry you got hurt.'

She buries her face in her hands. 'How, Sam? How was it

so easy for you to walk away from me? You were supposed to be my best friend.'

I swallow hard, suddenly scared to say what I need to say, but knowing that if I don't, I'll never get the opportunity again. It's now or never. 'What if I had wanted to be more than that.'

She blinks owlishly at me. 'What?'

I take a deep breath. 'Why do you think I was so angry. I hated Logan, yes. I hated seeing you with him, watching him kiss you. I thought at first that I couldn't stand it because of how much I hated him, but then I realised. It was because of how much I loved *you*.'

'I loved you too.'

'No, Ellie. I mean ... I *loved* you. More than just as your best friend.'

She doesn't answer, just stares at me with her big, beautiful eyes.

'I wasn't honest enough to admit that to myself until later. I missed you like I'd left an actual part of myself here in Seclusion Bay. But I couldn't come back. Couldn't face seeing you with him, especially knowing that your loyalties lay with him now, not me.'

'I ...'

'It's OK. I understand, or at least I think I do. When I met Mei and fell in love with her, I realised how impossible it must have been for you. It didn't matter what you did, you couldn't make both of us happy. One of us was always going to be upset, and Logan was the guy you loved.'

'No.' She shakes her head violently. 'I *never* loved him. I mean, I thought I did, like every seventeen-year-old girl thinks they're in love. But it wasn't love. I broke up with him not long after you left and I wasn't even sad about it. Because no loss could *ever* compare to how it felt losing you.'

I swallow hard. Her words are doing strange things to my insides, like all my organs have liquefied and are running through my veins like quicksilver. Slowly she lowers her hands from her face, and the pain in her eyes hits me in the chest like a bullet. I feel in that moment that I'm standing at a crossroads. I can either go to her, or I can turn and walk away. My head is torn, it has no idea what to do, but my heart does, and I let it take the lead, striding across the room until I'm standing right in front of her. She takes a step backwards, until her back is pressed against the bookshelf. Her eyes have welled up with tears again; I see them more clearly when I'm this close to her. I see everything. The way her gaze overflows with uncertainty and heartache. The way her bottom lip is quivering, actually fucking *quivering*. The sight of it almost breaks me. The effort required to keep my hands by my sides and not put them on her is enormous.

'I'm sorry,' I say, and this time it's *my* voice that breaks.

She lets out a choked sob, and that small sound tips me over the edge. My hands fly to her, and I bury them in her hair as I lower my head and press my forehead against hers. Her hands touch my arms, briefly, before coming up inside my embrace to settle on my cheeks, her fingers warm against my jaw and so achingly familiar.

'So am I,' she whispers. 'I wish—'

I cut her words off with my mouth. I intend to kiss her gently, but my lips have a mind of their own. This is a kiss of frustration, for everything that has happened between us. She whimpers under my onslaught, her mouth opening to meet mine, and our teeth and tongues clash briefly in the best possible way. Our first kiss feels like coming home.

'Oh Sam ...' she moans breathlessly when I drag myself away from her mouth for a moment to kiss her cheek, her jaw, then nuzzle into the side of her neck. Her lips are right beside my ear when she says it, and the words have a frenzying effect on me. *I want her.*

I run my hands down her waist and behind to cup her ass for a moment, giving it a rough squeeze that causes her to moan again, then down to her thighs. I tug at them and she allows me to lift her, her legs wrapping around my waist as I burrow myself against her, feeling her whole body welcome me. The bookshelf isn't attached to the wall, I realise, as it wobbles under our weight and a book topples off an upper shelf, narrowly missing my head.

'Ever had concussion from sex before?' she murmurs.

'No, but there's a first time for everything,' I manage to reply, although it's a miracle I can even muster words at this point, so incredible does it feel to be touching her, finally, after all this time. Feeling her touch me back. Her hands cup my jaw as we kiss and my hips grind against her, wishing all this goddam fabric between us would somehow magically disappear. I can't get enough of her, the taste of her, my tongue teasing and tantalising hers as we stimulate each other, driving each other to the brink of madness. Another book falls. This one connects with her shoulder and she flinches.

'Are you OK?' I ask, my voice husky with desire and concern.

Her pupils are dilated and massive, and it takes her a second to focus on my face after I pull away. I want to dive into them, into *her*. She nods, tries to pull me close again. 'Don't stop, please . . .'

'Oh, I'm not stopping,' I reassure her. 'Just moving you out of the firing line before this whole shelf comes down on us. Hold on tight.'

Her arms go around my neck and her legs tighten around my waist, nudging me in a way that brings both pain and pleasure. It's my turn to moan. She tightens her legs even further, until my erection is nestled in that place between her legs it so desperately wants to enter. 'Don't,' I say weakly into her hair, 'unless you want this to be over before we even really get started. It's been a while. It won't take much.'

She chuckles, enjoying her power.

'I mean it,' I warn, lumbering backwards until I feel the couch against the back of my legs. Turning, I detach her grip and drop her down onto it.

'Hey,' she protests, blinking up at me. 'I was enjoying that.'

I arch my eyebrows. 'Then you're *really* going to like what happens next.'

Ellie

He practically throws himself over the back of the couch, landing on top of me awkwardly.

'Oof,' I say, feeling the air forced out of my lungs. 'You rescued me from the bookshelf only to break one of my ribs in the process?'

'Sorry,' he says guiltily. 'I didn't mean to land on you so heavily. Are you OK?'

'I'm fine.' I reach for him, but he lifts himself further away, resisting my attempts to pull him down. His forehead furrows as he looks at me.

'Are you sure you're OK?' he asks.

'I'm a *little* hurt,' I say. 'Maybe you should kiss it better.'

'Oh, I should definitely do that ...' His eyes run over the top half of my body. 'Where does it hurt?'

'Everywhere'

He lowers himself back down, his face disappearing into the curve of my neck. I feel his lips lightly touch my skin.

'Here?' he murmurs.

I giggle involuntarily and he looks up at me, outraged.

'Did you just *giggle*?'

'No,' I say. 'Of course not.'

He lowers his head and kisses me again, the tip of his tongue tracing its way from my collarbone up to my ear lobe. I can't help it, I giggle again.

'That was *definitely* a giggle,' he says, his breath hot on my face, his eyes boring into mine.

'I can't help it,' I squeal. 'Remember on *Friends*, when Ross and Rachel start dating, and they're kissing for, like, the second time, and she keeps laughing?'

He frowns at this change in direction. 'Maybe. What's that got to do with—'

'It's just that it's the same thing.' I cup his cheeks, stroking one thumb over his cheekbone. 'This is *you*. Sam. My best friend. Kissing me.'

He pouts mockingly. 'Well, *trying* to.'

'I'm sorry.' I adopt a sober expression. 'I won't giggle any more.'

'Ellie, serious question, do you want me to stop?'

I shake my head emphatically. 'Don't you dare. I just need to get past that thought, that it's you ... us.'

He lowers his head and kisses me, urgently and passionately. When he draws away for breath again, I whimper.

'Did that help?'

I nod.

'Good. Now I can back to what I was doing. Is this where I

hurt you?' He places a finger on my throat, in the little hollow dip at the bottom.

'No, not there,' I reply, closing my eyes.

The air shifts and his lips trace kisses along my collarbone. 'How about here?'

'Not there either.'

My shirt is tugged upwards, over my ribs, then he moves down the couch and I feel his lips on my stomach, causing me to suck in air sharply, arching my body up to meet his mouth. Light butterfly kisses leave a path along my waist. 'Here?'

I can't speak any more, so I just shake my head, knowing what's coming next and wanting it so badly that I almost yank his head up and guide him there myself, because he's torturing me and he knows it. But I muster every ounce of willpower instead and play his game, because surely another few minutes won't kill me. Then again . . .

He scrunches my T-shirt up even further, until it's above my chest. I feel his fingers hook into the material of my right bra cup, then there's a slight pause where we both hold our breath, before he pulls the material down roughly. I hear him moan as my breast is exposed. Hearing how much he wants me is intoxicating.

'Oh Ellie,' he whispers softly. 'You're beautiful.'

I move underneath him, wriggling until I capture him between my legs again. Only his thigh, though. Frustratingly, he keeps his hips out of my reach. I want to feel that bulge of his again. I want to touch it while he—

His tongue teases my nipple, just one quick little lick, and it's like he just poked me with an electric cattle prod. My whole body jumps and shudders.

He looks back up at me. 'Is this where it hurts?' he asks, his voice thick with arousal.

I don't answer. Instead I grab the back of his head and push his face back down. He licks my nipple again, runs his tongue around it, over it, then gently tugs at it with his teeth. I whimper as he takes the whole thing into his mouth and sucks. It feels fucking amazing. I reach my hands down, in between our bodies, searching for the button on his jeans, wanting to get my hands inside to find his erection, to feel how much he wants me.

'No,' he growls. 'Not yet.'

He forces my hands above my head, one of his holding both my wrists together easily.

'Not fair,' I protest.

'Totally fair,' he argues mildly, his tongue already back on my breast. 'Wow, this is . . .' *lick*, 'very . . .' *suck*, 'sensitive,' he remarks, as I arch and buck every time his mouth touches me. 'Is the other one the same?'

With his free hand he pushes my bra up to join my T-shirt. Now both of my breasts are exposed, and he smiles down at them like it's Christmas morning and he's just found his present underneath the tree. He cups one, using his thumb to tease the nipple into a peak, like he's discovering just how his new toy works. 'Look how hard I can make it,' he says. 'And *that's* just with my thumb. Imagine what my tongue can do.'

'This is torture,' I complain, writhing as I try half-heartedly to free my hands. 'How come you're allowed to touch me and I can't touch you?'

'Because, Ellie,' he explains patiently, 'it's been quite some time for me. I am about as sensitive as it's possible to be right now. One touch from you and it's all over, I'm afraid.'

'It's been a long time for me too,' I retort.

'Really?' His eyes lift to probe mine.

'Really.'

They darken as he digests this. It seems to turn him on, because he finally lowers his body between my legs and I wrap them around his waist again. With my hands trapped, it's the only control I have right now, and I intend to fully utilise it. I arch my back, and as his erection rubs up against me, I cry out with the intense pleasure of it.

'Oh, I'm sorry, does it hurt there too?' Sam mumbles as he lowers his hand to touch me through my shorts. Lying there with one of his hands holding mine above my head, his mouth on my breast and his other hand massaging me, it is mind-blowing how fucking pleasurable this is, and I can't help but wonder if it's because it is Sam who is doing it.

Sam

She comes with my name on her lips, and I almost join her in release as she shudders and convulses against me, even though we are both still technically fully clothed. Watching her, knowing that I did that to her, makes me want to do it again and again and again. I abandon her magnificent breasts just as I feel her start to go, and kiss her hard and hungrily as the vibrations roll through her body, before she goes weak underneath me.

'Oh my God, Sam,' she mutters between kisses, with her eyes closed. '*Oh my God.*'

'So?' I nibble on her bottom lip. 'Did I make it all better?'

A smile tugs at the corner of her mouth. 'Maybe a little bit.'

I push myself up so that I can see her better. 'Only a *little*?'

Her eyes fly open and I see she's teasing. 'Enough for now, but I'm sure I'll require further attention again later.'

'So greedy,' I chastise her.

'It's your turn.' She wriggles her hands, freeing them from my now loose grip. 'Roll,' she instructs, and I do as I'm told, shifting sideways until I am on my back and she is on top of me. She straddles my lower stomach, which I'm grateful for, because my dick is incredibly sensitive right now and I wasn't kidding when I told her one touch from her will probably send me crashing over the edge. She pulls her T-shirt and bra off over her head, fully revealing her breasts, and I reach for them again. To my dismay, she pushes my hands away as she tugs at *my* T-shirt.

'Shirt off first,' she demands.

'Fine,' I grumble, then half sit up to make it easier for her. She yanks it off and tosses it over her shoulder before pushing me back down flat again.

'Hey, I get it,' I say. 'You're in charge now.'

'Damn right I am,' she says, her eyes fixed on my chest. Her fingers trail towards my nipples, and I rest my hands behind my head and watch her explore.

'They're not as sensitive as yours,' I remark mildly, then yelp when she gives one a pinch.

'Are you sure about that?' She grins.

'I was, but I'm not any more.' I moan as she tweaks the other one as well. She leans forward, her long hair trailing across my face as she kisses my chest. I breathe in deeply, recognising the salty smell of the sea.

'Have you been swimming?' I ask, wrapping a tendril around my finger.

'Mm?' She lifts her head briefly to look up at me.

'Your hair, it smells like the sea.'

'I went for a surf after work,' she says, returning to concentrate on what she's doing. Her tongue trails down the centre of my stomach, towards the waistband of my jeans. 'Now shush,' she murmurs, her lips against my skin.

'It's great that you still surf.'

'Of course I still surf.' She undoes the button on my jeans and starts sliding the zip down. I close my eyes and grip her hair tightly as I feel her breath on me.

'Well *hello* there,' she murmurs, and then she runs her wet tongue over the tip of my penis and I almost explode right then and there. I try to think of anything except what she's doing. I don't normally have a problem lasting the distance, but when it's been as long as it has, and with the memory of her coming as I touched her fresh in my mind, I feel as close to the edge as it's possible to be.

'We should go for a surf together tomorrow,' she says, starting to pull my jeans down to expose all of me. 'Just like in the old days. Of course, that's if we can tear ourselves away from doing *this*. We could lock the doors and spend the whole day in bed.'

I freeze, letting her hair fall from my fingers. An image, a memory of doing that with Mei, just came into my mind. Not long after we'd started seeing each other. Spending an entire day in bed.

Mei.

Ellie feels my body stiffen and looks up, confusion darting across her features.

'What's wrong?' she asks.

'Stop.' I sit up carefully, holding her upper arms, pushing her gently up too. 'I'm sorry. We shouldn't be doing this.'

'Why not? You seemed to be enjoying it two seconds ago.'

'I was. I am. But this is . . . It's too fast. I'm sorry. I shouldn't have let it happen.'

She covers her chest with her arms. It's heartbreaking to watch her switch from the confident seductress of a few moments ago to this unsure, vulnerable woman. I curse myself for letting it get this far. The thought of stopping is impossible. But so is continuing. Either way, she gets hurt.

'I thought we both wanted this,' she says softly.

'I do. I did. I'm sorry, Ellie. I don't think it's a good idea, not with me leaving again soon.'

'Oh my God,' she says, but it's a very different *oh my God* to the one she uttered a minute ago when I kissed her. 'I'm so stupid,' she says, clambering off me and fumbling on the floor for her bra and T-shirt.

'Don't say that,' I scold. 'Don't *ever* say that. This is nothing to do with you, and everything to do with me.'

'Oh please.' She laughs bitterly. 'Spare me the "it's not you, it's me" speech.'

'It's true, though.'

She pulls on the T-shirt, stuffing the bra into a back pocket.

'Can we talk about this?' I plead, though I'm unsure what I could say to make it any better.

'Sure,' she says, her expression a mixture of anguish and heartache. 'Go ahead. Talk.'

I open and close my mouth a few times. 'I don't know what to say,' I manage eventually.

'Just tell me this,' she says. 'Do you still *want* to leave the bay? Even after what just happened? Or will you stay this time? Stay here with me and work whatever this is out. Together.' She swallows hard.

I stare at her, a million confused thoughts in my head. I never wanted to come back here, let alone live here again. As hard as it was, I'd moved on. Not just from the town, but eventually from Ellie, too. Could I really settle back here again? With the same people? I can't promise her anything, that's the only thing I'm sure of. And she deserves more than that.

'Answer me, Sam. You owe me that at least. Do you still want to sell the house and leave?'

'Yes.'

She shakes her head, her eyes confused. 'I don't understand. You told me that you were in love with me all those years ago, and we just almost . . .' She gestures to the couch. 'How do you feel about me now?'

I take a deep breath, wanting to be truthful with her, but knowing I can't give her the answer she wants to hear. 'I honestly don't know.'

She flinches. 'Wow.'

'I care about you, Ellie. Of course I do.'

'But not enough to stick around.'

I shrug, unable to deny it. I see it on her face, the actual moment her heart breaks. I recognise it because I've seen it before, that day on the beach.

'Then the answer is no, Sam.' She angrily wipes tears from her eyes. 'We can't talk.'

She heads for the door and I watch her leave, fighting the part of me that wants to run after her, knowing that it will only make it worse for her if I do. In the doorway she hesitates.

'Can you promise me one thing?' she says, her tone flat.

'What is it?'

'Don't let what happened between us tonight stop Chloe from having her wedding here. Please. I'd never forgive myself.'

'Of course not. I'd never do that.'

'Thank you.'

Then she's gone.

I stay where I am until I hear the front door close behind her, then I walk to the window and push aside the curtain. There's no sign of her; she's already gone. Dropping the curtain again, I feel close to tears myself. I messed up, but I was telling her the truth. I can't stay here. There are too many memories, and this town has never felt like home.

And yet being with Ellie feels exactly like coming back to where I'm supposed to be.

Ellie

It's just as well I've walked the path between our houses a thousand times, because I can't see a hell of a lot through my tears.

I can't believe what just happened.

I've been fooling myself for years into thinking I hated him when it turns out the opposite is true. But it's been easy to do, because I never thought he'd come back.

Cars pass by, going in both directions, but I keep my head down, my hair hiding my face. It's a small town and I'm a business owner, so the likelihood of seeing someone I know is fairly high. I'm only a few minutes from home when headlights coming towards me slow as they pass, and I hear the unmistakable sound of a car pulling over before turning and coming up behind me. The vehicle pulls to a stop, but I ignore it and keep walking. Whoever it is, I don't want to see them. I don't want to see *anyone*.

I hear a door open.

'Ellie,' a man says. 'What's wrong?'

Fuck.

'Nothing,' I call over my shoulder.

'Bullshit.' Logan jogs to fall into step beside me. 'I could see in the street light that you're crying.'

'Well done, Sherlock,' I say. 'Your medal is in the mail.'

'Why do you always have to do that?' he asks.

'What? Why do I always do what?'

'Talk to me like I'm an idiot.'

I stop walking and face him, resigning myself to the fact that he's not going to leave. 'I don't.'

'Yeah, you do.'

'I promise you, I'm just as sarcastic with *anyone* who won't leave me alone when I ask them to.'

'At least let me drive you home.'

I snort. 'Like hell.'

'What did I ever do to make you hate me so much?'

'I don't *hate* you.'

'Then why can't you accept a ride?'

'Because I don't want to do anything that might give you the wrong idea.'

'When was the last time I texted you, Ellie?'

'I don't know.'

'Think.'

'It's late, Logan.'

'Please.'

I rack my brains, but I honestly can't remember. 'I have no idea.'

'Exactly. It's been years. Have I showed up at your house out of the blue recently? Or your work?'

I shake my head.

'No, I haven't.' He sighs. 'Look, Ellie. I know I behaved like a dick after we broke up. And believe me, I look back at how I acted and I'm ashamed. But you have to understand, I was so in love with you—'

'That doesn't excuse stalking,' I interrupt.

'Stalking?' He reels away from me, his face genuinely astonished in the murky yellow of the street light that cuts through the darkness. 'Is that how you see me? A stalker?'

'Maybe not any more,' I admit. 'But back then you wouldn't take no for an answer. You kept calling, messaging, showing up anywhere I was, like you somehow knew I'd be there.'

He rubs the back of his head with his hand. 'Jesus, Ellie. We live in the same fucking small town. We have the same friends. I didn't mean to always be in your face. It just worked out that we both got invited to the same things.'

'I guess you have a point.'

He looks at the ground for a few seconds, then back at me, his face serious. 'Have you ever loved someone so much that when you lose them you wonder how you're supposed to carry on and pretend like nothing's wrong?'

I swallow hard, aware of a sinking feeling in my stomach. *Of course I have.*

'It's like you're just supposed to forget about how much you love them, and all the plans you had for the future.'

I hold up a finger. 'Whoa. Hold up. We *never* made any plans for the future.'

'*You* might not have. But everything I've ever done, Ellie,

I did for us. That's always been the goal.' He starts counting things off on his fingers. 'Finish school, learn the trade, open my own business, save for a house. Get married like Hamish and Chloe, and one day ... a family of our own.'

'Are you serious?'

He nods. 'Very.'

'I can't help how you feel, Logan, but I've never wanted any of that with you. I'm sorry, but it's true.'

'I know,' he says sadly. 'I think I've always known it. But hey, a guy can dream, right? I always knew I was your second choice.'

'What are you talking about?'

He pulls a face. 'Sam, of course. I knew you had feelings for him, even when we were together. But I always hoped that'd change, especially after he left. Then you fell to pieces, and I knew it was always going to be him.'

'We were just friends.'

'Nah. Ask anyone. You two were always more than that. You just didn't know it.'

I stare at him, unable to answer, my mind working furiously. Is it true? Sam pretty much admitted tonight that he'd loved me but hadn't realised until it was too late. Is that why I was so devastated when he left? Because I'd been in love with him too?

'Ellie,' Logan says. 'We were friends once. Before all the drama happened. I'd really like us to be friends again. You're Chloe's maid of honour and I'm Hamish's best man. We kind of have to get along, at least so we can give them the wedding day they deserve.'

'Yeah, you're right. We do.'

He swallows hard. 'If Sam is who you want, I'll be happy for you.'

'I honestly don't know what I want. And even if I did, it doesn't matter. He's still leaving as soon as the house is sold.'

'I can't say I'm sorry.'

'Why do you hate him so much? Because he was a better surfer than you?'

He snorts. 'I couldn't give a fuck about that.'

'Then why were you always so horrible to him when we were growing up?'

'You know, for a bright girl, you can be a bit thick sometimes.'

'And you're a misogynistic prick,' I shoot back.

He shrugs. 'I hated him because *you* loved him.'

Which apparently everyone knew but me.

I rub my forehead wearily. 'OK, Logan. I won't avoid you any more. But you can't say the kind of stuff you said to me the other week at Chloe's. You have no say in anything to do with my life. OK?'

He nods. 'OK. That was out of line, I accept that. I'd heard Sam was back in town and it brought back some of those old feelings.'

'That can't happen again.'

'I promise. Friends?'

'Friends. On probation, though,' I warn. 'Any drama and we're done.'

He smiles. 'Got it.'

Sam

I barely slept after Ellie left, tossing and turning all night, going over and over everything in my head, trying to pin down exactly how I was feeling, and failing. Everything was too confused, too muddled by time, guilt and grief. How could I know whether what I was feeling for Ellie wasn't just the comfort of familiarity? I'd felt all alone in the world the past two years, but being back here with her had made the loneliness go away. She'd given me that sense of belonging again, something I hadn't had since Mei's death. She'd reminded me what it was like to laugh. To not wake every morning focusing on what I'd lost, but to look forward instead to what the day might bring.

When I hear knocking on the door, I almost run to it, but it's not her.

'Morning,' Chloe says, holding out a takeaway cup. 'I brought you a coffee. According to Kelly, this is how you like it.'

I take the offered cup and feel the warmth soak into my hand. Steam rises from the little sippy hole, along with the smell of freshly brewed coffee beans. I breathe it in gratefully as Chloe steps inside.

'I had no idea that you were such a regular customer that Kelly knows your usual,' she says.

'Did you see her this morning?' I ask.

'Who, Kelly?'

I stare at her.

'Ah, you mean Ellie,' she muses. 'No. I didn't. She wasn't there. Probably gone to the beach for a run or a surf. Unless she's at work or helping me with something, she can usually be found there.'

She turns to put her diary and phone down on the table and freezes when she sees the detritus from last night's dinner. 'I'm sorry, do you have company?'

'No,' I mutter, picking up the bowls and wine glasses and taking them to the kitchen sink. 'I wasn't sure what time you were coming.'

'Oh, no apology needed. And no need to organise your life around me. You're the one doing me the favour after all. Did you have a nice evening?'

'Yes.' Which is true, up to a point. But I'm not telling her what happened.

'Someone I know?' she asks.

'It's a small town, so probably.'

Sensing she's not going to get any more information out of me, she sits down and opens her diary. 'I just wanted to run through a few things with you, if that's OK. Just timeline stuff, like what's happening when.'

'It's fine.' I sit opposite her and pick up the coffee again.

'OK.' She runs her finger down a checklist. 'First thing Saturday morning the chairs and tables will be delivered. The DJ will come mid-morning to set up his gear. He's playing the music while I walk down the aisle, as well as covering the reception. I've given both him and the party planners a map so they know where everything needs to go.'

'A map?'

She pulls a piece of paper out of her book and unfolds it, revealing a large plan she's drawn of my back yard. It's surprisingly accurate, and to scale. 'This is a copy for your reference, but I don't expect you to oversee them or anything. For the amount I'm paying, they know exactly what they need to do.'

'I thought *you* were the party planner.'

'No, I'm the bride. I delegate. The events company people will set up the chairs and the wooden archway where Hamish and I will say our vows. We're not going to have a traditional sit-down dinner,' she adds. 'We *were*, at the other place, but there's not really room for that here.'

'Oh, I'm sorry.'

'Don't be, it's worked out much better. Everyone around here hires the fancy wedding venue, with the sit-down salmon-or-chicken meal thing. *My* wedding is going to be the complete opposite. It will blow all those other weddings away.'

I baulk at her competitive tone, then remember what Ellie

told me, and why this wedding means so much to Chloe. 'I'm sure it will.'

'We've hired food-truck vendors and a drinks van. If it's OK with you, they'll park up around the wedding area after the ceremony, and then while Hamish and I are having our photos taken, they'll put out canapés and nibbles for the guests to snack on while the party planners rearrange the chairs and add tables and get the place ready for the reception.'

She uses a long white fingernail to point out on the map where they'll park.

'The cake maker will set up the cake on a table *here* by the speakers.'

'It's all fine with me, honestly. Do whatever you want.'

'Hamish and I come back, we do speeches, cut the cake, and people can wander around the food trucks getting whatever they feel like to eat – they'll have a more extensive menu going then. Basically, everyone drinks, eats, socialises and dances. Oh, and of course, most importantly, everyone enjoys themselves.'

'Of course.'

'It's going to be perfect.' She smiles. 'Informal, fun and just a beautiful day and night with all of our friends and family. That's what I want.'

I watch her talk as she runs through the rest of the schedule: what time the florist, hairdresser, make-up artist, etc. will arrive. She's full on, definitely. I wonder, as I listen to her tell me about the guys who will set up the lighting, whether she knows how lucky she is to have the friends she has. The way they rallied to get this house ready for the wedding, and the way they banded around her and Hamish after their loss, shows *exactly* how much these people care about her. Not everyone has that kind of community. I know that from bitter experience.

'OK,' she says. 'I think that's everything. Any questions?'

'No, none.'

'And it's all OK with you?' She runs a finger down her list. 'I mean it's all just temporary stuff. Your grass might get a little hammered from the stilettos, but nothing will be permanently affected.'

'Chloe, think of this place as your own for the day and do what you like.'

She snaps her diary shut. 'You're a good guy, Sam.'

'"Tell that to Ellie,' I say, without thinking.

'Ellie?' Her tone is sharp, her expression shrewd. 'That's who the other wine glass was for?'

I briefly consider lying, but what's the point? Ellie will probably tell her anyway. 'Yes.'

'What happened?'

'Nothing. She came over last night to fix up that bit of paint she mucked up.'

'And?'

'And I happened to be cooking dinner, so she joined me. That's it.'

'Judging by the way you opened the door and looked extremely disappointed to see that it was me standing there, that's definitely *not* it.'

'I don't know what else you want me to say.'

She sighs heavily. 'I want you to reassure me that nothing happened last night that might set my best friend back in her recovery by about ten years.'

'Recovery?'

'Yes, recovery. From *you*.'

'That seems a bit dramatic.'

Her expression hardens. 'Is it, Sam? Is it really? Because I don't remember you being around to pick up the pieces. *I* was.'

'We were just kids, Chloe.'

'We were eighteen. Adults, technically. And yes, I know friendships at that age don't always last and people get over it. But *she* didn't. Not for a long, long time. To Ellie, you were . . .' She looks to the ceiling as she fumbles for the right words. 'You were like oxygen to her. She needed you. And yes, *that's* being dramatic. But that's how much you meant to her.'

'It wasn't easy for me, either.'

'Maybe not. But you *did* get over her. You married someone else. And we all know how well she took *that* news.'

'What do you mean?'

She flushes. 'Nothing.'

'Chloe . . .'

'All right.' She shrugs. 'But you won't like hearing it.'

I frown, unsure what to expect.

'The night she found out you were getting married, we were all round at our place. Having a few drinks in the garage, playing darts. Just hanging out. She got really, really drunk, and . . . her and Logan kind of ended up together again. Just the one time.'

She was right. I don't like hearing it. In fact, I fucking *hate* hearing it.

'Don't,' Chloe says warningly, holding up one finger. 'Don't you dare judge her.'

'I'm not.'

'I know you hate him, but he's not as bad as you think, and he adores her. Always has.'

'He's a jerk,' I snap. 'But if that's who she decides she wants . . .'

'Well, now that's the problem. She's not interested in Logan. Never really was. By her own admission it was just a stupid mistake.'

The thought brings me little comfort. I'm still stuck on a mental loop of the two of them together. 'It has nothing to do with me.'

Her eyes narrow. 'Are you sure? Because you seem bothered.'

'I just . . . Why *him*, of all people?'

'He was better than some of the others.'

'Others?'

'Did you think she's been single this whole time?'

'No, of course not. I—'

'Because I hate to be the bearer of bad news, but there have been a few men in the last decade or so.' She starts counting them off on her fingers. 'After you, there was Hudson – he was really nice. Not her usual type, but nice. The thing with Logan. The odd summer fling with guys who were only in town for a few nights or weeks. You know what it's like here. Then she went overseas for all those years. I can't even imagine the fun she must have had on the yachts, I mean, you've seen the shows, right?'

I shake my head.

'Probably best you don't. Lots of alcohol, spa pools and bunk-hopping. Anyway, then she came home and met Josh. He was so in love with her. Younger, a surfer like you. More of a free spirit, though. Less intense. He wanted her to sell the café and move to Bali with him.'

She carries on as if she has no idea how much I hate what she is saying, how much I don't want to hear her words. Yet I can't seem to walk away either.

'Why are you telling me all this?' I ask, my voice strangled.

'Honestly? To see your reaction.'

'This is some kind of sick joke?'

She shakes her head. 'More like a test. And judging by the way you looked when you heard about those guys, I'm right. You have feelings for her.'

'I think you should go.'

'OK.' She picks up her phone and diary and holds them against her chest. 'But before I go, I want you to know that even though some of those men were legitimately really nice guys, she never gave any of them a chance. Not properly. Because there was one thing wrong with all of them. You know what that was?'

I shake my head.

'None of them were you.'

Ellie

Dear Daisy,
   That man you lost, how did you know when you were ready to
move on again?
   S

Sam

Dear S,

   To be honest, I don't think I ever really did move on. I thought I had, but lately I've started to question everything.

   All I know is that everyone is different, and there's no right or wrong amount of time to grieve. You'll know when you're ready to love again. It could be months, it could be years, because love is not something you decide, it's something you feel. Feelings are our conscious experience of an emotional state. Emotions manifest in our unconscious mind. In other words, we can control how we react to an emotion, but we can't control having the emotion itself.

   Basically, we like who we like.

   But here's the thing. Emotions can co-exist with each other. It is possible to feel both grief and joy at the same time. Our hearts have a remarkable capacity for unlimited amounts of love, and I mean love in all its wondrous guises.

   I don't think you ever completely get over losing someone you loved, but somehow you learn to adapt, and hopefully in a way that doesn't prevent you from being open to any future joy that life might bring. Because you deserve joy, you deserve love. And falling in love with someone new doesn't mean you have to stop loving your wife, or that you're over her. Moving forward doesn't mean forgetting what's already been. It's about being open to new possibilities, no matter how scared you might be.

If there is one lesson we should take from grief, it's that life shouldn't be taken for granted, and neither should love.

Daisy

Ellie

'Wake up wake up wake up wake up wake up wake up!'

The door of my room – or rather the spare room at Chloe and Hamish's house – is thrown open, and three seconds later the curtains are pulled back, letting the sunlight flood in, half blinding me in the process.

'Look,' Chloe says. 'Ellie, look outside.'

'Can't. You've fried my retinas.'

She ignores me. 'There's not a single cloud in the sky, it's the perfect day for a wedding. MY wedding!'

I open my eyes and smile at her as she bounces up and down by the window. She's already wearing her white satin dressing gown with the word BRIDE embroidered in pink flowery lettering across the back. My MAID OF HONOUR one is hanging on the bedroom door.

'I'm so happy for you,' I tell her. 'But why are you waking me up so early? The ceremony doesn't start until three p.m.'

'Can't sleep. Too excited. Feeling slightly stressed.' She waggles her head. 'Bordering on the edge of panic, possibly. Definitely mild hysteria.'

I sit up and arrange the pillows behind my back. 'OK, let's take it down a notch. Everything's going to be fine, I promise. You have organised this day with military precision.'

'I have, haven't I.'

'You really have. Everyone knows what they need to do and when they need to do it, so all you have to do is relax and enjoy your day.'

She nods. 'Yes, enjoy my day. Shift over, will you.' She sits down on the bed and I scoot my legs to make room for her.

'Before we make this day all about me, are you sure that *you're* OK?' she asks.

I haven't told her what happened with Sam, but I know she suspects something, because I've been subdued this past week, even though I'm trying really hard not to let my mood affect her big day.

'Yeah.' I plaster on a smile. 'Of course I'm OK. I'm just still waking up properly. On YOUR WEDDING DAY.'

She squeals. 'Can you believe it?'

'What's the game plan?'

'First off, champagne breakfast, cooked by you. So get up.'

'You're in the way.'

She stands and picks up the blankets, peeling them off me. 'Up.'

'Yes, ma'am.'

She crosses the room and lifts my gown off the door. 'Here

262

you go, my very special maid of honour and very best friend in the world.'

'Don't,' I warn, taking it from her and slipping my arms inside. 'You'll make me start blubbing, and you don't want me looking all red and blotchy in your photos.'

'I mean it,' she says, seriously. 'I don't know how I would have gotten through the last few years without you.'

'Hey, it's what friends are for, just like how you've always been there for me,' I remind her.

She takes my hands in hers. 'You know you're going to find a Hamish of your own some day, right.'

'I hope not. He's not really my type.'

'You know what I mean. Unless ...' She trails off questioningly.

'Unless what?'

'Unless you've already found someone.'

'You know, don't you?'

'If you mean that you're in love with Sam, yeah, I know.'

'Is it that obvious?'

'Only to anyone with eyes.'

'So ... everyone, then.'

'Yes. Everyone.'

'How long have you known?'

'Longer than you, I suspect. You know how they say men and women can never really be "just friends". We all knew you and Sam had something special back in the day, even if you two were blind to it.'

'What am I going to do? He's leaving again.'

'Tell him how you feel. Maybe he'll change his mind and stick around.'

'I doubt that. He can't wait to see the back of this town, and us.'

She smiles at me sadly. 'I wish I knew what to say.'

'How about "hurry up and cook my damn breakfast, woman"?'

She snorts. 'You actually *want* me to order you around?'

'Today, yes. It's all about you. I refuse to even think about him.'

She gives me a strange look. 'You know he's going to be at the wedding, right?'

'No.' I frown at her. 'No, I did not know that. That's the kind of information you probably should have mentioned before now.'

'I had to invite him, it's his house.'

I cringe at the thought of seeing Sam again after what we did the other night and how it ended. 'Is it too late for me to resign as maid of honour?'

She peels me off the wall and starts pushing me towards the kitchen. 'Yes,' she replies firmly. 'It's too late, and you have too many things to do. Starting with cooking my breakfast, please.'

Sam

I keep out of the way as much as possible while around me the house is transformed into something out of a fairy tale. The chairs and tables arrive just after 8 a.m., as per the schedule, the florist and lighting people not long after that. As they bustle around and take over the place, I hide myself away in my grandfather's study, sitting at his desk and attempting to read one of his books while studiously trying not to look at the couch and remember what happened there barely a week ago.

But of course, the more I try not to think about it, the more I do. I take out the letter from DG to read again. It's textbook advice really, only delivered in her signature way that somehow gets through to me, even when I've already had – and dismissed – the same thoughts myself. Deep down, I've always known that if – when – I move on, it won't be a betrayal to Mei. I won't be cheating on her, or her memory, or the memory that was us. She will always be a part of me, and

I will never forget her, or how much she meant to me. DG's letter has reminded me that you can both grieve and live at the same time.

Love is not something you decide, it's something you feel.

She's right. And just as you can't decide who you fall in love with, you can't simply decide to fall *out* of love either. I never stopped loving Ellie, and if Mei had been anything like her, then maybe I'd have a reason to feel guilty, as if I'd married her as some kind of substitute. But they're nothing alike. Either physically or in character.

Ellie is a child of the sun, golden-limbed, salt in her sun-bleached hair. Strong-willed and vibrant, she is laughter, fun and passion, and does what she wants, when she wants.

Mei was gentleness and serenity. A safe haven in a stormy world. Petite, raven-haired and delicate-featured. Self-sufficient and content with her own company. She was the opposite of drama, and I was drawn to her compassionate nature, though I never got the sense she really needed me. She loved me, I know that, and if the shoe had been on the other foot and it had been *me* who had died that day on the street, she'd have handled her grief a hell of a lot better than I have, I know that too.

But she did die. And as much as that hurts, I'm still here, still alive.

If there is one lesson we should take from grief, it's that life shouldn't be taken for granted, and neither should love.

I trace my fingers over my grandfather's map, his destinations marked in pencil, small comments here and there to remind him of particular places and stories. I remember him telling me a story about how one day, on a complete whim, he turned up at the airport with a rucksack and his surfboard and bought a ticket for the next available flight out, not caring where it was headed. He was so open to life and everything it had to offer.

None of us knows when our time is up. I could go to sleep tonight and not wake up in the morning, and the thought of that happening without Ellie knowing how I really feel scares me. But more importantly, it scares me *more* than the idea of letting my guard down and letting her in.

Ellie

The morning passes in a bit of a blur really. The other brides-maids, Tash and Fiona, are both cousins of Chloe's who I've known almost as long as I've known her. Together we spend the time reminding Chloe to breathe and reassuring her that everything is organised, because she's convinced she's forgotten something. Around 11 a.m., as we pile into my car to head to Sam's house, where we'll be getting ready, something clicks inside her and she decides to just let it all go. Resign herself to the fact that what will be will be. She even plays 'Que Sera' through my stereo Bluetooth on the short drive over. Not the old version, the Justice Crew one. And every time it gets to the bit about friends, she sings louder, right in my ear.

'I'm driving,' I remind her the fourth time she does it.

'I'm GETTING MARRIED,' she sings back.

'How many drinks have you had?' I ask as we pull into Sam's driveway and park. There are service trucks and people everywhere, but an area of the front lawn has been cordoned off for us, and also for the groom's cars when they arrive. Some guests will park on the road, but Chloe has also organised shuttle vans to bring people to and from town.

She unclicks her seat belt. 'Two. I've had two small glasses since breakfast. I'm not drunk, Ellie. I'm happy.'

We get out of the car and start removing garment bags and shoeboxes from the back. After one final check to make sure we've got everything, I close the door. Chloe is staring up at the house.

'Ready?' I ask her, trying not to drop anything.

She nods. 'Today I get to marry the love of my life. The man who rubs my feet when I've had a bad day and brings me a coffee every morning in bed.'

'That is so cute,' Tash coos. 'You should mention that in your vows.'

'I can't wait to be Mrs Searle,' Chloe continues. 'Married to my fuzzy-wuzzy Hammy-Wammy.'

'That's . . . *less* cute,' comments Fiona, her nose crinkled.

'What?' Chloe pouts. 'It's my nickname for him. Seriously, his back is so furry, he's like a teddy bear.'

'Come on, guys,' I say. 'Let's go. The hairdresser is probably already waiting.'

'Eww, Chloe,' Tash grumbles as they follow me inside. 'I haven't had enough drinks to cope with *that* mental picture.'

'Yeah, definitely don't mention the furry back thing in your vows,' Fiona concurs. 'No one else needs to hear that today.'

I've stopped listening to them, because as soon as we traipse inside, Sam is there. Standing in the hallway as if he's been waiting for us.

'Hi,' he says, staring at me, not appearing to notice the others at all.

'Hi.'

'Oh my God, look at it,' Chloe gasps, dropping her wedding dress bag onto the couch and practically floating to the open doors that lead out to the back deck and lawn. 'Guys, look at everything set up. It's even more beautiful than I imagined! Look at the lanterns in the trees, and the arch. Ohhh, the arch is perfect.'

Tash and Fiona follow her, but I don't want to dump my precarious load and then have to try to pick it all up again. 'I'll take this stuff upstairs,' I call to Chloe, but she's already outside and doesn't hear me.

'Are you OK?' Sam asks.

'I'm fine.'

'Do you want any help?'

'No.'

But it's too late, he's already taking one of the boxes off me. At least it helps me get a better grip on the rest of the stuff.

'Thanks.'

'No problem.' He points to the bag Chloe left on the couch. 'I take it this needs to go upstairs too?'

I nod. Seeing him again is even harder than I thought it would be.

He picks up the bag. 'I was hoping we could talk.'

'No point.'

'Ellie.'

I head for the stairs.

'It's OK, honestly,' I say, forcing my voice to sound light-hearted. 'You were pretty clear the other night. I don't think we need to rehash it. Especially not today.'

'The other night—'

'Was just a bit of fun.'

We've reached the top of the stairs and I head for the master bedroom at the end, the one that used to belong to Sam's grandparents. On the way, we pass the open door of *his* bedroom, and I almost – *almost* – instinctively turn into it. I spent a lot of time in that room once. I wonder if he still has the surfing posters on his wall, and the small basketball hoop on his wardrobe door. Whether his numerous trophies still line the shelf above his desk, and whether my initials are still carved into the inside of his wardrobe door, next to his.

'It was more than that and you know it,' he says, following me into the master bedroom and hanging Chloe's garment bag on the wardrobe door.

'Are you sure it's OK for us to use this room?'

He nods. 'It's fine. Stop changing the subject.'

'I'm not changing the subject, I'm asking a question.' I put the shoeboxes against the wall underneath the windowsill, out of the way. 'This feels weird, being in your grandparents' bedroom.'

'You *are* changing the subject, and I'm telling you it's fine. My grandmother would have loved all this. I think she always hoped that one day I'd . . .' He trails off.

'Get married here?' The words feel like knives in my heart.

'Ellie, the other night, I—'

271

Chloe bursts into the room. 'Ellie, you need to see the drinks caravan. It's the cutest ... Oh, hi, Sam.'

He smiles at her, but it's a tight smile. 'Chloe. All set for the big day?'

She shrugs lightly. 'As much as I can be. You haven't seen my hairdresser or make-up girl anywhere, have you?'

'Don't panic, I'm right here.' On cue, Tessa Headley sweeps into the room, her assistant/husband Glen behind her, carrying all her bags. We've known Tessa since school days, although she did leave the bay after we graduated, spending a few years travelling round Europe before studying hairdressing in the UK. She came back about two years ago with her English hubby Glen in tow, and opened a salon just down the road from my café. 'And Stacey's here too, she just had to use the toilet first. She has a shockingly small bladder, that one. We had one glass of bubbles before we left my place and she already needs to pee.'

'IT'S MY WEDDING DAY!' Chloe screams.

'I KNOW!' Tessa screams back.

Sam winces, sticking a finger in one of his ears and wiggling it.

Tessa starts unpacking curlers, straighteners, hot brushes etc. onto the bed and instructs Glen to hunt out all the power points as she and Chloe run over the plan for her hair again. Sam takes advantage of the distraction to gently take hold of my arm, pulling me towards the window. My treacherous heart immediately starts beating faster at his touch.

'Please can we talk?' he asks. 'I know I'm not very good at expressing how I feel the majority of the time ...'

'Understatement.'

272

'. . . but I'd like to try.'

'Where's my dress?' Chloe starts spinning in panicked circles. 'WHERE'S MY FUCKING DRESS?'

'It's right there,' I snap at her, pointing to where Sam hung it on the back of the walk-in wardrobe door. 'Now calm the fuck down.'

Tash and Fiona gasp and look at Chloe, waiting to see if she's going to roast me for swearing at her on her wedding day. She stares at me. I stare back at her defiantly.

'Tough love,' she says finally, nodding. 'Good. That's probably what I need. And wine, actually. I need another glass of bubbles while Tessa does my hair.'

'I'll hunt out a couple of bottles,' Fiona says eagerly, already halfway out of the room.

I turn back to Sam. 'As you can see, it's pretty much organised chaos in here.'

'Five minutes?'

'I can't. Chloe needs all hands on deck. This is her big day, I have to be here for her. Whatever you want to say, it'll have to wait. Sorry.'

He lets go of my arm and nods. 'I understand. You're a good friend, Ellie. She's lucky to have you. I'll catch up with you later, OK?'

I nod, but in my head I'm already planning on avoiding him as much as possible. The last thing I need is to hear a breakdown of reasons for why he has to leave town, and why he can't be with me. A rejection is still a rejection, no matter how many nice words you use to try and cushion it.

Sam

I know that all eyes are supposed to be on the bride when she makes her big entrance, but I honestly don't even see her at first, standing at the top of the stairs, her bridesmaids in front of her.

All I see is Ellie.

She's always beautiful to me, even when she's been painting all day and her hair is messy and I can smell the sweat on her skin. But I've never seen her look more stunning than she does right now. Her beautiful blonde hair is a mass of curls, draping gracefully down her back, a few strands hanging loosely around her face. I can see pretty little flowers woven through the curls and around her head, like she's wearing a floral crown. Her dress is pale pink, delicate and whimsical, with a plunging V-shaped neckline. Her shoulders are bare and tanned, as is the leg I glimpse through a long split in the floor-length dress.

I can't take my eyes off her as the music starts and one by one they come down the staircase. Guests gather on each side of the aisle to watch as Chloe follows her bridesmaids to where Hamish is waiting underneath an arch made of driftwood and decorated with flowers. When she gets there, we take our seats. I sit near the back, but in an aisle chair so that I can clearly see Ellie throughout the whole ceremony.

As if she senses my eyes on her, she flicks a quick glance my way while Hamish tearfully chokes his way through his vows. When our eyes make contact, her smile falters briefly, and my heart skips a beat at the sadness I see on her face.

Ellie

I can feel the weight of his eyes on me the whole time, and consequently I can't focus on anything that Chloe, Hamish or the celebrant say. When it's all over and the new husband and wife are kissing, I send up a silent prayer that she doesn't ask me what I thought of their vows, because I didn't hear a word of them.

He looks . . . incredible. When we first came down the stairs, I didn't even have to search the room; my eyes were drawn to him immediately. A man in a beautiful blue shirt amongst a sea of black, white and other pale colours. I've always loved him in blue, and he knows it. It brings out the colour of his eyes, and contrasts perfectly with his hair and his skin. Standing there looking up at me, he was more like the Sam of old than the ghostly version who first returned here.

I feel incredibly vulnerable, standing in front of everyone, knowing that I've always been terrible at hiding my emotions.

At least I can draw comfort from the fact that people will assume I'm tearful because I'm watching my best friend get married, not because I've finally realised that I am one hundred per cent, madly, deeply, head over heels in love with a man who doesn't love me back.

After the ceremony, Sam lingers on the edge of the immediate congratulatory crowd. I know he's trying to catch my attention, but I can't do this. I can't listen to his reasons for leaving me again when I've only just got him back in my life. It hurt badly enough back then, but now that I've realised I actually love him? No. I can't do it. Not now. Not here. Thankfully, the whole bridal party is required down on the beach for photos, so I slap on a bright smile and laugh and joke around with my friends. We lift our dresses out of the water, the men roll their pants up to their knees, and we jump up and down in the shallows until the photographer is sure he has the perfect shot. Being in the water is calming, as always, and I wish for a brief moment that I had a surfboard handy. The thought of paddling away from the inevitable confrontation with Sam is tempting.

When we eventually get back up to the house, the lawn has been completely transformed. There are tables for people who want to sit down to eat, and taller ones for those who prefer to stand. Cool stripy beanbags and deckchairs have been placed at the top of the bank overlooking the ocean. People are sitting there drinking and watching the sun as it sinks lower in the sky.

A cute little mint-green caravan is all lit up with fairy lights and bunting. A wooden board in front of it has Chloe and Hamish's names and the date, and a cocktail menu listed underneath. I vaguely recognise the woman inside as someone I've seen at town events before. Charlotte, I think her name is. There are also a couple of food trucks. I take a glass of wine off a passing tray and wander over to look at the menu boards in front of them. One is serving finger foods – little cups of fish-n-chips, burger sliders, mini hot dogs, prawn skewers and crumbed scallops, that sort of stuff. The other is a coffee and dessert truck, serving ice cream tacos, gelato, churros dipped in chocolate, crêpes, doughnuts and waffles. Unbelievably divine smells are coming out of both vans, and normally I'd be lining up to sample everything they have to offer, but my stomach is in knots. I might not know where Sam is, but I do know he's here somewhere.

As if he can hear my thoughts, he appears beside my right elbow. 'Drink?'

I lift my glass. 'Already got one.'

He pulls a face. 'Wine? Bor-ing.' His playful tone is completely at odds with the way we left things last week, or even the way he's been behaving since he came back, for that matter.

'Excuse me?'

He takes the glass from me and puts it down on a nearby table.

'I was drinking that,' I protest as he takes my hand in his and pulls me towards the drinks caravan.

'Hi, Charlie,' he says to the woman inside, and I feel a tiny stab of jealousy. He's on a nickname basis with this woman already?

'Hey, Sam.' She smiles, taking his empty glass from him. 'What did you think of that one?'

He pulls a face. 'To be honest, I didn't like it as much as the first. Remind me what that was called again?'

'Mai Tai the Knot.'

'Ah yes. That's right. Can I get another two of those, please?'

'Sure.' She reaches for fresh glasses.

Sam grins at me. 'Do you get it? Mai Tai the Knot. *Tie the knot.*'

'I get it.'

'They're all like that. Wedding themed. I've had that one and a . . . ' he peers at the board, 'You & Me G & T.'

So that explains his mood, I realise. He's drunk.

'I know what you're thinking,' he says. 'But I'm not drunk.' The way he's smiling, I'm not sure I believe him.

'Have you had anything to eat?'

He shakes his head. 'No. Been waiting for you. I was hoping we might do that together.'

Taking his elbow, I gently try to pull him towards one of the food trucks. 'OK, well why don't we grab something now.'

He puts a hand over mine, firmly resisting all attempts to shift him. I'm strong, but he's stronger. 'Plenty of time for that. I think we should try the Wedding Bell-ini next. Or maybe the Bloody Marry Me. That's pretty clever. Did you come up with these names yourself, Charlie?'

'Is there a drink called Who Are You and What Have You Done With the Real Sam?' I mutter underneath my breath.

Charlie puts our drinks on the counter in front of us. 'I'd love to take the credit, but someone else thought of these.'

'Well whoever it was, I'm sure they don't make them as well as you do.' Sam lets go of my hand and picks up both drinks. 'Now, there's got to be a quiet spot around here somewhere.'

Nerves kick in at the thought of being alone with him. Especially with the mood he's in. *He* might be tanked up on cocktails and feeling jovial, but I'm still stone-cold sober.

'Actually, Sam,' I say, 'I probably should check on Chloe. Maid of honour duties include holding her dress up while she pees, and after the pre-ceremony wines, she's probably due for one right about now.'

'Are you for real?'

'What?'

'You have to hold her dress up while she pees?'

'Haven't you ever watched a rom com when there's a wedding involved?'

He squints at me. 'Rom ... com?'

'It's short for romantic comedy,' I say slowly.

'I knew that.'

'No you didn't.'

'No, I didn't. Look, there's a free table. Quick, let's grab it before someone else does.'

He nudges me in the small of my back towards the table and I take a few steps. But just then the music stops, and I'm saved by the whiny feedback of the microphone as the DJ turns it on.

'Damn.' I pull a face. 'It looks like it's time for speeches and toasts.' I take my drink from him and gulp half of it down in one hit. He's right. It's delicious.

'Stop trying to avoid me, Ellie. Please.'

'I'm not. I just take my job as Chloe's maid of honour seriously, as any good friend should.'

He studies my face for a moment. 'Fine. Go. But afterwards, we *need* to talk.'

'Absolutely,' I call over my shoulder as I hurry away from him. 'You'll be my first priority.'

Sam

I nurse my drink as the speeches take place, listening to stories of Hamish and Chloe's life together, and I realise that in my haste to tell Ellie how I feel, I've haven't really given much thought to what that means. For us, for the future. Am I going to keep the house and stay here in the bay, or sell and ask her to go with me, leaving behind her business, her friends and her grandmother? Or is there another option, one that I can't think of right now but that would somehow make us both happy?

The happy couple cut the cake, and then the DJ announces the first dance. Hamish looks like he's sweating bullets, but he pulls it off. They both do. I watch them move around the dance floor to a country song about love, and I feel the last layers of hesitation crack and peel off my heart. I want this too. Straightening up, I scan the crowd, searching for Ellie. I need to tell her how I feel *now*. I can't wait a second longer.

Unfortunately, just as I find her, Chloe gestures to the bridal party to join her and Hamish. I'm forced to watch as Logan holds his hand out to Ellie, who accepts it graciously. He leads her onto the dance floor and wraps one arm around her waist. Jealousy bubbles up my throat like stomach acid, and I swallow it down. I don't want to feel jealous, I really don't. I'm not usually that kind of guy. It's just the fact that it's *him*. The one man on this whole planet who I can't stand.

As I watch, he pulls her in closer until his chest is ever-so-slightly touching hers. I'm not a violent person, apart from that one incident in Hong Kong, which was out of character, but seeing him touch Ellie makes me want to do violent things to him. He bends his head to whisper something in her ear, and she laughs. I chug back the rest of my drink and bang the empty glass down on the table. *Enough.*

Ellie

'Mind if I cut in?'

'I do, actually,' Logan snaps at Sam, tightening his arm round my waist. I wriggle to try and loosen his grip, but he simply holds on even tighter. Two seconds ago, we were joking about Hamish's two left feet; now the air is thick with tension and I'm completely taken aback by how quickly the mood has changed.

'Let go of me, Logan,' I say.

'No. We haven't finished our dance.'

I reach behind and peel his fingers off me, pulling them backwards until he yelps. 'Yes, we have.'

Logan nurses his fingers and glares at Sam. 'What's your fucking problem? She's the maid of honour, I'm the best man. We're just dancing like we were told to.'

Sam tears his eyes away from Logan to look at me. 'I wanted to ask you for a dance, but I think this piece of trash had plans to hang onto you all night.'

'Who the fuck are you calling a piece of trash?' Logan clenches his fist.

'Was it not obvious?'

'Guys,' I say. 'Come on, this is Chloe's wedding. I'm not going to let you ruin it. If you're going to fight, you'll have to fight me first.'

I slap one curled fist loudly into my other palm a couple of times. They both look at me like I'm crazy.

'Yeah, that's what I thought. Logan, go find your girlfriend and dance with her.' I glare at Sam. 'You, follow me.'

I don't even check to make sure he's behind me as I weave my way through the crowd, away from the dance floor, towards the top of the sand dunes where the beanbags are. Strings of fairy lights and lanterns hang from poles and trees all around, giving the place a beautiful soft, romantic vibe. The night is filled with the sound of music, conversation and laughter, but my mood is dark.

'What was that?' I ask when we're far enough away from other people.

'I wanted to dance with you.'

'And you couldn't wait until I'd finished dancing with Logan?'

His face darkens, confirming my suspicions.

'You're jealous.'

He snorts. 'Of Logan? Hell, no.'

'So if I were to go back right now and, I don't know, kiss him, you wouldn't have a problem with that?'

He scowls at his feet.

'That's what I thought.'

He exhales heavily. 'I'm sorry for acting the way I have. I'll apologise to Chloe.'

'Luckily for you, I don't think she saw anything.'

'I just can't stand that guy. And seeing you with him again was . . . ' He trails off.

'Was what?' I prod.

'Horrible. I hate it.' His eyes flash in the dark, his jaw tight.

'Why?'

'Because of you, Ellie,' he blurts out. 'Because of how I feel about you.'

'I thought you didn't know how you feel.'

His jaw clenches as his eyes bore into mine. 'I didn't. Or at least, I was confused. But now . . . '

'Now what?' I prompt when he trails off.

Sam

It's here, the moment I've been trying to find all day, but now that it is, I can't seem to do it. I can't say the words. Not because my feelings have changed, but because they're even more intense than I thought they were. Seeing her with Logan and feeling my reaction has shown me just how much I love her. How much I *need* her. And that kind of vulnerability terrifies the hell out of me.

What if I lose her too?

'Now ... *what*, Sam?' she asks again, her lip trembling. 'How do you feel about me?'

'I ...' This is harder than I ever thought it would be.

'You know what, just forget it,' she says, as her eyes fill with tears. She turns away from me and starts walking.

It's now or never. I find my words.

'Ellie, wait.'

She keeps walking.

I take a step after her. 'I love you.'

She freezes. Her shoulders stiffen. She doesn't turn, but that's probably just as well, because one look at her face and I might lose the ability to speak again.

I take another step. 'I love everything about you, Ellie. I love your smiles, all of them. The cute little one you have when you're thinking about something and you don't realise anyone's watching you. And the loving one you give when you see someone you care about. That big, beautiful smile you have when you're out on the water, in your element, riding a wave. But most of all, I love that special one you have just for me. Soft and reassuring, tender and irresistible, it promises me that you'll always accept me for who I am. Even tonight, when I'm not exactly being the best version of myself.'

I hear her breathing choke a little, as if she's crying. I take another step.

'I love your eyes,' I say. 'Even when you're rolling them at me, which is alarmingly often, by the way. I love the freckles on your nose, and the dimple in your cheek. The way your hair smells, the way your skin feels and the way your kisses taste. I love you even when you're driving me crazy with your stubbornness and the fact that you have to argue about almost *everything*. I love how you pretended not to be scared of spiders any more to impress me, even though you clearly still are, and the way you've built this amazing home and life for yourself. I love your kindness, your loyalty, the way you never pretend to be anyone but who you are.'

I'm standing right behind her now. I pick up her curls and

push them gently to one side, exposing her neck. I see a ripple pass over her throat as she swallows.

'I love the way you look at me,' I whisper into her skin. 'The way you make me laugh even when I feel like crying. I love you, Ellie. All of you, with everything I have.'

I kiss her neck, and she shudders, turning slowly until we're face to face. The intensity in her eyes threatens to rip my heart out. It's love; raw, exposed, vulnerable love. She's scared too, I realise. I sweep her into my arms, squeezing her as tightly as I can against me.

'Say something,' I breathe into her hair. The flowers in her crown tickle my nose. She pulls back, just enough to look up at me. Her eyes are glassy with tears.

'You had me at "wait",' she says.

Ellie

Of course he's been stuck under a rock somewhere, and the reference goes straight over his beautiful head.

His face crinkles, puzzled. 'Wait?'

'*Jerry Maguire*,' I explain, wiping my tears away. 'The movie? Tom Cruise, Renée Zellweger? He gives her this big, soppy speech and at the end she tells him that he had her at hello.'

He kisses the tip of my nose. 'Ah, I see. This is one of those rom coms you were talking about.'

I stand on tiptoe and kiss him on his chin, my hands splayed across his broad chest. 'You really should try getting out some time.'

He slides his hands down to my waist and pulls me in tightly against him. 'Why would I want to go out when I have *you* to be staying indoors with?'

'You're assuming an awful lot there,' I say breathily.

He leans back to study my face. 'I *do* have you, don't I?'

'Always,' I reply simply, and his pupils flare in the soft light, before he crushes my mouth with his.

Neither of us hears her at first. I hear *something*, but honestly, a meteorite could have hit the ground next to us and we'd probably still have kept kissing. Eventually, though, her voice gets through.

'Ellie?'

We reluctantly draw apart, although he doesn't let go of me. I feel a bit dazed and confused when I look at her. Who is she again? Ah, that's right.

'Hi, Chloe.'

'Hi, Ellie.'

She tries to communicate with me without speaking, and I do try my best to understand, but it's all just head-waggling in Sam's direction, her eyes wide as she pulls various faces.

'I have no idea what any of that means, Chloe.'

She rolls her eyes. 'You OK, Ellie?'

I swivel my head to Sam, who's watching us, amused, then back to Chloe.

'Bit busy, actually. Was there something you wanted?'

'Nothing major, just due a bathroom break and need a bit of help with the dress. But I can find Fiona or Tash, it's not a problem.'

I look up at Sam, torn.

'Go,' he says, kissing me lightly on the mouth. 'I'll get us another drink.' He kisses me again, then heads for the drinks caravan.

I watch him walk away, resisting the urge to run after him.

What if he changes his mind when I'm out of sight? I mean, did that really just happen? Or am I having hallucinations brought on by hunger? I touch my lips. They're tender. It definitely happened.

Getting to the bathroom takes longer than it should because everyone wants to chat to the bride. She has to keep stopping along the way to smile and make small talk. Everyone wants to tell her how much they put into the wishing well to go towards her and Hamish's honeymoon, even though it's supposed to be anonymous. I hover behind her while she laughs and talks, resentfully thinking about how I could still be kissing Sam right now. My thoughts are whirling. This is Sam. *Sam.* And we've just told each other we love each other. It should feel . . . weird. Maybe even awkward. But it doesn't. It feels like the most perfectly natural thing in the world.

As soon as we get inside the bathroom, Chloe's demure bride act *completely* disappears. She whirls on me as I'm locking the door.

'Ellie!' she shrieks, so loudly I jump.

'What?'

'Don't *what* me. You know *exactly* what.'

I nudge past her meringue skirt and lean close to the mirror, wiping smudges of lipstick from the corner of my mouth. 'Oh, you mean Sam?' I ask innocently, as if my world hadn't just completely changed.

'*Oh, you mean Sam?*' she mimics in a silly voice. 'Yes, I bloody mean Sam! When did . . . ? How did . . . ? Who made the first move? Is this a *thing* thing? Or a we're-at-a-wedding-so-let's-fuck-and-then-tomorrow-pretend-it-never-happened thing.'

'It's a thing thing.'

She makes a cooing noise in her throat and looks at me like I'm the last puppy in the shelter left for adoption. 'Are you sure? I mean, has he said that in actual, exact words?'

'He told me he loves me.' The words sound like music in my ears. *He loves me!*

She claps her hands to her cheeks. 'Tell me everything.'

'It was so romantic,' I bite my bottom lip and smile as I remember the words he spoke, the way he kissed my neck. 'He had a whole speech, about how he loves my smiles, and the way I smell, and my skin . . .'

She screws up her nose. 'That sounds—'

'OK, yes, I know it sounds creepy, I'm not doing it justice. It was beautiful, trust me.'

'Are you sure he's not drunk?'

'He's not drunk.'

'Lonely and horny?'

'No,' I protest. 'Well, maybe. But he really loves me. He said so. Over and over and over. I feel like I'm in a dream right now. Quick, pinch me . . . *Ow.* That hurt.'

'Sorry.'

I rub my arm. 'OK, so it's definitely not a dream.'

'Oh God.'

'I know.'

'*Oh God oh God oh God.*'

'Believe me, I feel the same way.'

'No, it's not that. I mean, it is that, but also, I *really* have to pee.' She jiggles on the spot. 'I've been holding it in for hours.'

'Oh, right. Sorry.' I lift the toilet lid and help her gather all the layers of fabric and tulle, holding them above her head while she feels her way to the seat and sits. She wasn't joking. She pees for ages.

'Ohhh, I needed that,' she sighs, relieved. 'Nearly left it too late.'

'*That* would have made it a wedding to remember for all the wrong reasons.'

'Definitely. Anyway, back to you and Sam. What does all this mean? Are you guys together now? Is he going to stay here? Does this mean he's not selling the house any more?'

'I don't know,' I reply, trying not to sound like I haven't been wondering the exact same things. 'You came along and interrupted us five minutes after he said he loved me. We haven't had time to talk yet.'

'Just time to shove your tongues down each other's throats.'

I flush at the memory.

'Hamish hasn't kissed me like that in years,' she sighs wistfully.

'You guys show your passion in other ways,' I reassure her.

'Yeah,' she snorts. 'Choosing curtain samples and arguing over whose turn it is to have control of the TV remote.'

'Exactly.'

'That kiss looked pretty good. How did it feel?'

'Honestly?' I smile at her. 'It felt incredible. I never wanted it to end.'

'You know what,' she says after we've rearranged her dress back into place. She studies her reflection in the mirror while she washes her hands. 'I'm going to go out there and get me some of that.'

'Sam?'

She rolls her eyes at me. 'No, Hamish, obviously. My husband.'

'Oh. Yeah, that makes more sense.'

She dries her hands on the towel and reaches into the corset of her dress, cupping each breast and lifting it up before letting the dress go again, giving them both a bit of a boost. Her cleavage wobbles alarmingly. 'We are going to find ourselves a dark, quiet corner of this house and we are going to consummate our marriage right here, right now.'

'Won't people notice you're missing from your own wedding?'

'I doubt it. Not as long as there's still free food and booze on offer. If anyone asks, cover for me.'

'Of course.' I salute her. 'Your maid of honour is here to serve. I'll tell them that you guys are ... um. That Hamish is showing you ... uh ...'

She gives me a hug, laughing. 'You're a terrible liar, Ellie. But you're the best maid of honour any bride ever had.'

Sam

'Alone, finally,' I say, closing the door after the last of the guests and locking it. The clock above the fireplace tells me it's just gone one in the morning. 'Now come here.'

'That was a very successful wedding, don't you think?' Ellie picks a cushion up off the couch and plumps it like a pillow, puts it back down, decides she's not satisfied and tweaks its position a few times. 'Chloe looked so happy when they left, and at the end of the day, that's all that matters. Her happiness. Well, *obviously* Hamish's happiness matters too, but not as much as hers. Guys don't really care about the details, do they. Not like girls do. But I thought it was all perfect, don't you think everything was perfect?'

She's babbling. I don't blame her. I've been wanting to get her to myself all night, and now that I have, I'm a bundle of nerves too.

'Everything that happened tonight was perfect,' I agree.

'We should probably make a start on the clean-up,' she says, looking around the room.

'Leave it. The caterers took all their own stuff with them, and Chloe said the chairs and tables will be picked up on Monday. Whatever's left can wait until tomorrow.'

She bustles to the kitchen bench and starts opening drawers. 'It won't take long, though. And it'll mean less to do in the morning. Do you have any rubbish bags?'

'Ellie.' I watch her, amused. 'Forget about that. We need to talk.'

She puts her fingers in her ears. 'No we don't.'

'What are you doing?'

'I don't want to hear what you have to say in case I don't like it.'

'But we should—'

'La-la-la-la-la.'

I walk to stand in front of her and pull her fingers out of her ears. 'What makes you think I'm going to say something you won't like?'

She stares me, her eyes pools of vulnerability. 'You did the last time I was here. I mean, I left thinking that was it, you and I were done for good. But then tonight there you were, saying the sweetest things. And I don't *think* you're drunk, at least I hope that's not all it is. You can't blame me for being a little confused.'

'I'm not drunk, and I meant everything I said. The other night, I was confused myself. But things have changed since then.'

'Why?'

'Someone recently reminded me that love shouldn't be taken for granted.'

A flicker crosses her face and she looks down at the floor, clearly feeling overwhelmed.

I cup her chin and gently lift her head until I can look into her eyes. 'Especially the kind of love I feel for you.'

She swallows hard. 'So you really did say that? I didn't just imagine it?'

'Say what, that I love you?'

She nods.

'Oh, I said it.' I take her face in my hands, using my thumb to gently wipe away a tear. I kiss her forehead, and she presses hard against me as if she's trying to sear my kiss into her skin. 'And I meant it. I meant every word. Don't get me wrong, I'm scared. When you've lost someone . . . ' He takes a deep breath. 'When Mei died, I realised that bad things can happen to good people, and everything really can change in an instant. These last couple of years, I've been living in fear. No, not living. Existing. Does that make sense?'

She nods, sniffing. 'It's understandable. You've been through something traumatic.'

'Still, I don't think I handled my grief as well as I could have. As well as some others do.'

'I don't think there's a wrong way or a right way, and it's *definitely* not a competition.'

'I did the best I could, I guess. I can't change anything now, so all I can do is try to really live again, like Mei would have wanted me to. I don't want to be scared any more. I want to grab life in both hands and live the hell out of it. With you by my side.'

'I want that too,' she says. 'I love you.'

I burrow my hands into her hair and pull our faces together, kissing her. She has no idea how much those words mean to me. The way my heart skips a beat when she says them. I want to hear them from her lips again and again, every day for the rest of my life. For the first time in two years, I feel excited about what's to come. And it's all because of her.

'I love you too,' I say, in between kisses. 'And whatever we do from here, we'll work it out together.'

She nods in my hands. 'I have no idea how this is going to work, but I don't want to worry about any of that tonight.'

I lift her up and sit her down on top of the bench. 'I can think of at least three things I could do that might help distract you.' I lower my head to kiss her in the soft part of her neck beneath her ear, and she moans.

'Only three?' she says breathily, arching her neck to give me more access.

I chuckle, feeling her heartbeat through the skin under my lips. 'I'm always up for a challenge.'

She wraps her legs around my waist. The split in her dress falls open, the material draping to the floor, leaving her leg exposed. I run a hand along her smooth thigh, feeling the muscle clench beneath my fingers. When I reach her knee, I move my hand to the inside of her thigh and head back up again. Her muscles clench even tighter as my fingers brush against the front of her knickers. I use my thumb to stroke her through the fabric, and she arches upwards.

'*Oh God.*'

'I've been wanting to do this ever since you walked down those stairs,' I tell her.

She reaches for my shirt buttons and starts undoing them. 'What else?'

I pull the sheer fabric to one side. Straight away I can feel how wet she is already, and I feel more turned on than I've ever been in my life.

'Do you want me to tell you, or just shut up and show you?'

'Both,' she says, ripping the last two buttons off my shirt in her impatience. She shoves the material over my shoulders, and I shrug my arms, helping her to get it off. She starts exploring my chest, shoulders and back urgently with her fingers.

'Lift,' I instruct her, tugging the elastic on her knicker waistband. She uses her arms to lift her body off the bench, and I pull her underwear completely off, dropping it to the floor. I catch a glimpse of her, soft and inviting. She's still wearing her strappy shoes, pale pink to match the dress, the heel on them tall and skinny. Dangerous. I hook a finger in the strap on the back of each heel and peel them off, letting them fall to the floor.

'God, you're so sexy,' I marvel, touching her again.

'Compliments are all well and good,' she says, squeezing her thigh muscles around my hand. 'But I'd much rather be touching you too.'

'I just . . .' I feel almost drunk as I take in the half-naked sight of her. 'I want to savour every single moment of this.'

'I like the sound of that,' she murmurs, trying to recapture my mouth.

'Uh-uh,' I scold her, leaning just out of her reach. 'Just because I'm happy to oblige doesn't mean you can do whatever you want. There's a process to these things.'

She groans. 'Sometimes you have to let me be in control too, you know.'

'Sometimes, yes. But this is not one of those times.' I reach for the dress strap on her left shoulder, and she watches as I glide it across her skin. As I move it over her shoulder and down her bicep, she quickly glances at my face, just in time to see my expression the moment I realise something.

'Hey,' I exclaim. 'You're not wearing a bra?'

She shakes her head.

I slide the dress even further, and her whole breast pops out of the fabric. My breathing quickens. 'You've haven't been wearing a bra at all today?'

'Nope,' she confirms.

'So *all day* you've been naked underneath this dress?'

She smiles, amused. 'People are generally naked underneath their clothes, Sam.'

'Yes, but ...' I splutter. 'Not *naked* naked. Good God, woman, what if your strap had come undone on the dance floor?'

'It didn't.'

'But it might have.' I cup her breast in my hand, watching as the nipple hardens in front of my eyes. I lower my head and flick it a few times with my tongue, feeling smug when I hear her moan.

'If I had known you were naked all this time, I would have made everyone leave straight after the ceremony.' I tug roughly at the strap on the other side, and she lifts her arm to help. In seconds, she is sitting with her dress bunched around her waist, both breasts completely exposed.

'Hey, you two,' I say, like I'm greeting old friends. 'I've been dreaming about you every night for the past week.' I cup them, enjoying the weight of them in my hands. Ellie's breath quickens as I explore her perfect curves, and I can't help but smile at the way she squirms with pleasure. She loops her feet together behind my back, pulling me towards her.

'Not yet,' I croak hoarsely as my penis bumps against her. Even through my clothes I can feel the intense heat of her, and God, do I want to be in there.

'Yeah, yeah, I know.' She breathes in sharply. 'It's been a long time, it won't take much, et cetera, et cetera.'

'It really won't,' I mumble against her skin.

She grabs my jaw roughly and pulls my head up. 'Well tough,' she growls. 'Because I want to feel you inside me *now*.'

I groan, her words lighting an uncontrollable fire in my groin. I reach for the button on the front of my pants and her hands join mine in a desperate fumble.

'Wait,' she says, pulling a face. 'Not here. The kitchen bench feels wrong ...'

I stare at her questioningly.

'It's where food is prepared,' she elaborates.

'Ah, of course, Chef Campbell.'

I slide my hands underneath her and lift her off the bench.

Her arms wrap around my neck and she hangs on as I head for the sofa.

'No, wait,' she says again.

'What now?' I moan, trying not to concentrate on how her breasts feel squashed against my chest.

'The bed. Not the sofa. More room to do ... things.'

'I like the way you think.'

I change direction, heading for the stairs, feeling the strongest I've ever felt in my life as I charge up them. We bang into the wall a few times because I can't stop kissing her long enough to see where I'm going, relying on instinct and memory only. Kicking open my bedroom door, I lurch across the room and throw her onto the bed. She bounces, but only briefly, because I quickly cover her beautiful half-naked body, searching again for her mouth with mine.

Ellie

I can't wait any longer, it's just not physically possible. I reach for the waistband of his trousers and underwear and shove, wriggle and manipulate them while he jerks his body, helping me. All I can think about is freeing his penis, and a sudden heavy weight against my thigh tells me I've done that. Immediately I reach for it, circling it with my fingers. It's so much bigger than I anticipated, but then he is all man now. Hard, large, wonderful man. I stroke the length of it up and down a few times, and he moans into my mouth, pulling away from our kiss.

'Where do you want me to come?' he asks. 'Because that moment is not too far away, believe me.'

I feel a slickness on the tip of his shaft that confirms this.

'Inside.' I guide the tip between my legs to where it belongs. 'I want you to come inside me.'

His pupils flare at my words and he nudges into me, so close to going inside, teasing, tantalising. But then he pulls back. 'I can't. I don't have a condom,' he says, frustrated.

'I'm on the pill,' I reassure him. 'And I haven't slept with anyone since my last check-up, which was clean.'

'I haven't been with anyone except Mei in the last decade, and there were no problems with either of us.' He shifts, using his fingers to part my skin. 'Are you sure?'

I don't answer with words; instead I lace my feet behind his body and pull him in, *all the way in*. It's all the confirmation he needs.

We both gasp as that first thrust fills me completely. He lifts himself up so we can stare into each other's eyes, both of us in complete and utter wonder at how *fucking* incredible this feels. Then he pulls back and thrusts again, and I almost scream from the pure pleasure of it. I dig my fingers into his biceps and move with him again and again and again.

'Jesus Christ, Ellie, I don't know how much longer I can hold on.'

I shift my hips, widening my legs so that he can go even deeper. I can feel every inch of him inside me. *Fuck.* He adjusts his weight onto one arm, licking his thumb and reaching down between us to rub me, never pausing in his thrusts, his eyes wide, every muscle in his shoulders and arms stretched and defined.

'Ellie,' he moans. '*Ellie.* I'm sorry, I can't wait, I'm going to come.'

'I'm right . . . there . . . with you.'

He drives into me harder and faster, his thumb rubbing

me the whole time. I clench myself around him internally, squeezing him as tight as I can. He pulls back and gives one massive final thrust that drives me up the bed, and we come together in a giant ball of flaming chaotic energy that explodes around us like a supernova. I swear I see stars. He shudders inside me as wave after wave of intense, mind-blowing pleasure rolls over me.

Afterwards, he collapses beside me and pulls me into his arms, still with him snug inside my body. We lie there forehead to forehead, panting, dripping with sweat.

'Holy hell,' he says.

'I completely agree.'

'That was ...' He kisses the tip of my nose. 'I'm sorry I couldn't last any longer.'

'Neither could I.'

'Feeling you come when I was inside you ...' He blows air out of his mouth, imitating a bomb going off. 'Do you have any idea how tight you just squeezed me?'

'Can you blame me?'

He groans, giving a little thrust with his hips. 'I want to do it again.'

'I'm not stopping you.'

'I might need a few minutes to recover. I want the second time to last a hell of a lot longer.'

'Round one *was* always bound to be a short one.'

He runs his hand up my stomach and cups my breast, absent-mindedly stroking my nipple with his thumb. I feel the waves start to build again.

'You're right,' he agrees. 'It was. Now that we've got that first time out of the way, we can take our time. I have so many things I want to do to you.'

'*To* me, or with me?'

'Both.'

I kiss him. 'We've got all night.'

He shakes his head. 'No. We've got the rest of our lives.'

Sam

Every morning since Mei died, I've had these moments when I wake up and briefly forget everything that's happened. When everything is as it was, before reality comes crashing back in and I remember. Mei is dead. I am alone.

But not this morning. Not any more.

I wake to the sight of Ellie sleeping next to me, her hair tousled on the pillow from our night of fervent lovemaking. It almost doesn't seem real, but the only thing that feels weird about it is that it doesn't feel weird at all. There was no awkwardness between us; in fact I couldn't get enough of her. I doubt I ever will. I lift the hair that covers her face and she smiles without opening her eyes.

'No regrets?' she murmurs.

I roll onto my side and gently wrap my leg over her hip. 'Not a single one,' I say emphatically.

'Whoa,' she says, her eyes flying open. '*Someone* woke up ready to go again.'

'Can you blame me?' I kiss her cheek. 'Look at you.'

She pulls a face. 'Considering I didn't take my wedding make-up off last night, and the amount of kissing we did, I'm guessing I probably look a bit of a mess.'

'Wrong.' I kiss her again. 'You're absolutely beautiful.'

'There's a possibility, just a slim one, that you might be a little biased.'

'Maybe.' I tuck a persistent curl behind her ear. 'Does this feel at all strange to you?'

She scrunches up her nose while she thinks, then shakes her head. 'Surprisingly, no. You?'

'No. I mean, I've known you since you were an annoying, stroppy little . . . Actually, I guess not much has changed.' I burst into laughter at her look of outrage.

'*I* was annoying?' she says, her fingers diving to tickle and poke my waist until I convulse in protest.

'All right, all right,' I concede. 'We both had our moments. My point is, I wanted it, believe me, I wanted it so bad. But I never in a million years thought you and I would . . . we'd end up in . . . that this might . . . '

She lays a finger on my lips to shush me. 'It's OK, I understand what you mean. All I know is that having you back in my life brings home just how much I've missed you.'

'I've missed you too,' I admit.

'And now I don't want to wake up next to anyone else ever again,' she says softly, her eyes gazing into mine.

I kiss her, slowly at first, then more urgently as my need increases. She pushes my leg off her, hooking her own over mine. Then she fumbles between us, guiding me inside her with her fingers, gasping into my mouth as I enter her. Immediately I stop kissing and stop moving, concerned.

'Are you OK?'

'Just a little sore,' she admits. 'It's been so long and we were pretty . . . energetic last night.'

'Do you want me to stop?'

'No.' She frowns. 'Don't you dare.'

'I don't want to hurt you.'

She pushes me onto my back and straddles me, moving her hips as she lifts herself up and down, controlling our rhythm, almost completely lifting off me, pausing as we both stare at my exposed penis, only the tip still inside her. Then she plunges herself back down and I marvel at how she fits all of me inside of her so perfectly. It's tormenting, incredibly so, and I take it for as long as I can before I reach for her and swiftly roll us over, putting myself back on top and in control.

'You're a tease, Ellie,' I say, grinding myself into her again and again.

'You love it.' She smiles contentedly, her nails digging into my shoulders, her hips opening wider to let me all the way inside.

'*I love you.*'

Ellie

I seriously didn't think I'd be able to walk. My legs feel like jelly. All wobbly and weak. And if it wasn't for a text that came through from Kelly just after 9 a.m. reminding me that the deadline for finalising next month's food order was two days ago, I would have happily stayed in bed with Sam all day. All *week*, probably.

'Can't we just stay here,' he grumbles, as if he's read my mind. I fumble with the straps of my very crinkled bridesmaid dress, letting my feet adjust to supporting my weight again.

'I wish.'

'We can lock the doors,' he continues. 'Pull the curtains. Order food in. Live like hermits. Make love all day and all night.'

'As wonderful as that sounds, I have a business to run. Zip me up, will you?'

He kisses my back, then gently slides the zip. 'This is wrong,' he complains. 'I want to be taking this thing *off* you, not putting it on.'

I turn and kneel on the bed, kissing him. 'I'll be back as soon as I can. But if I don't go and send this order off, I won't have any food to sell. And food is kind of a critical thing in my line of business.'

'Can't it wait until tomorrow?'

Pulling myself from his grasp reluctantly, I search the floor for my shoes. 'Considering it was due Friday and I completely forgot because I was preoccupied with last-minute wedding stuff, not to mention thoughts of you, no. It can't wait. They're already doing me a favour by letting me put it in late.'

'Fine,' he sighs. 'I guess I can live without you for a few hours. It'll be a struggle, though.'

'I'll miss you too. Have you seen my shoes?'

'Downstairs, I think.'

I have a flashback of him pulling them off my feet in the kitchen, then where he touched me next, and I feel my cheeks flush.

'I'm pretty sure you just remembered the same thing I did,' he muses. He's lying back on the pillows, his hands laced behind his head. The sheet covers half of him, but only just. I can see the bottom of his stomach, right at the top of his . . .

'I have to go,' I blurt, knowing that if I stare any longer, I'll lose all willpower to leave.

On my way out, I pause by the mirror that hangs on the wall by his door, and reel back in horror. It's worse than I thought.

'Oh my God, I *told* you. My make-up is everywhere! And

I look like I've had about an hour of sleep, if that. Look at all these flowers!' I start picking the remains of my floral crown out of my hair and give up. 'I need a shower. Stat.'

'Sorry.'

'No you're not.'

'No. I'm not. You're still beautiful.'

'And you're still biased.'

Downstairs, I find a pile of napkins left from the wedding and wet a few under the tap, rubbing most of the make-up off my face, cursing whoever invented waterproof mascara.

'You look like a really cute panda now,' he says, zipping up the fly on a pair of denim shorts he's thrown on to follow me.

'Great, that's exactly the look I was going for when I do the walk of shame home.' I pull on my shoes, hanging onto the bench for balance.

He grins. 'Good point. If people see you still in that dress, with your hair all messy, and your make-up like … that, they're going to know *exactly* what you've been up to. Your reputation will be ruined.'

I shrug, walking to wrap my arms around his waist. 'Ah well, never really had much of one to begin with.'

He laughs and kisses me on the top of my head. 'So it was worth it?'

'Definitely.' I pull away reluctantly. 'Keys?'

He plucks them off the top of the fridge and holds them behind his back. 'Payment first. I'll accept kisses and … anything else you'd like to offer, really.'

'Sam.'

He sighs, holding them out. 'Fine.'

'I'll be back as soon as I can.'

'Half an hour?' he asks hopefully.

'Longer than that, sorry. I need to head home first for a shower. Can't exactly go into town looking like this.'

'And smelling like me,' he murmurs.

'Exactly. Shower, the café to send in the order, and then I'll probably check in on Chloe before I come back here.'

'She's a newly-wed,' he points out. 'If she has any sense, she'll be in bed with Hamish doing what *we* should be doing.'

'Maybe. But remember they've been together for almost eleven years. I don't think they go at it like rabbits any more.'

'Just a heads-up. I don't care how long we're together, I'm *never* going to stop wanting you.'

'Good.'

'I'm going to want you *all* the time.'

'The feeling is entirely mutual,' I reassure him. 'I'll see you in a few hours, OK?'

'OK.'

He leans against the door frame and watches me walk out to my car. 'What are you going to tell Nan when she asks you where you've been all night?'

'I'll tell her the truth,' I reply, opening the door and putting the windows down to let fresh air in. 'She loves you. This is going to make her day.'

His face suddenly turns serious, and he bolts down the steps and across the lawn to where I'm standing. He takes my face in his hands, and I feel my heart skip a beat at the pained look in his eyes.

'What is it? What's wrong?' I ask, and when he takes a long time to answer, seemingly because he can't find the right words, I start to panic. 'Sam, what's the matter?'

'I . . .' He takes a deep breath in, then exhales slowly. 'I just wanted to screenshot the moment. Freeze time. I never want to forget how I feel right now.'

'I thought you were maybe having second thoughts.'

He shakes his head furiously. 'No. Never.'

I cup his cheek with my hand, feeling his jaw twitch beneath my fingers. 'Don't look so worried. Everything is going to be OK. Better than OK. Everything's going to be perfect.'

'Do you think so?'

I nod.

'I'm sorry,' he says.

'For what?'

'Being afraid. If something happened to you . . . I couldn't survive losing you as well.'

I reach up and press my lips hard against his. 'You won't lose me. I promise.'

He closes his eyes. 'You can't promise me that. Mei didn't wake up that morning knowing she was going to die.'

'None of us can predict the future. But Sam, look at me.'

He opens his eyes and I flinch at the fear I see in them.

'I can promise you that I will love you for however long we have together,' I tell him. 'Whatever happens, I'll always love you.'

He presses me firmly against his chest. 'I love you too.'

It's not until I'm halfway home that I remember getting ready for the wedding at Sam's house the day before, which means I could have changed into my other clothes and spared myself the embarrassment of arriving home in a crumpled bridesmaid dress. A curtain twitches as I get out of the car, but Nan will have to wait until later for all the gossip.

Sam

I'm pathetic after she leaves. Like a lovesick teenager. Keeping one eye on the clock, checking to see how long she's been gone. I have a shower, then change the sheets on the bed, breathing in the smell of her from the old pillowcase before I put it in the machine.

I never expected to feel like this again. It's not necessarily a pleasant feeling, the kind of love where you miss someone so much with such an ache inside of you. I'd completely forgotten what it was like, this first flush, and I can't shake the feeling that it's all just too good to be true.

After a couple of hours of moping around the house, I decide I need coffee, proper coffee. Of course if Ellie still happened to be at the café, that would be a bonus, but when I get there, it's Kelly who's behind the counter.

'Hey, S ... A ... M,' she says cheerfully, then gives a low whistle. 'You look rough.'

'Thanks.'

She reaches for the metal coffee scoop thing. 'Usual?'

'Please. A large one.' I hand her my cup.

'Big night, I take it.'

'Yeah, it was. Chloe's wedding.'

'I heard you let her use your place after the venue stuff-up. Nice move, S . . . A . . . M. Really decent of you.'

'Anyone would have done the same.'

'What's the goss?'

'Goss?'

'From the wedding. Any fights?'

'Uh.' I cast my mind back to Logan and me squaring off on the dance floor. 'None that I saw.'

'OK, well who hooked up? People always hook up at weddings. It's all the sentimentality in the air.'

'Um . . .' A mental image of a half-naked Ellie sitting on my kitchen counter springs into my head. 'I wasn't really paying attention, sorry.'

She sighs, clicks the lid shut on my coffee cup and hands it to me. 'I'm disappointed. Not even any dancing on tables? Surely you got up there and had a crack?'

'I'm not really a dancing-on-tables kind of guy.' I crane my neck, trying to see if Ellie's in the kitchen.

'Don't worry, she's not here.'

'Actually,' I feel my cheeks flush, 'I was kind of hoping to catch her.'

Kelly's eyes narrow. 'Why?'

'Um . . . she, uh, she left something behind. After the wedding.'

She crosses her arms. 'Oh really. What?'

'Sorry?'

'What did she leave behind?'

'It's a . . . um . . . ' I cast my eyes around for inspiration, but find none. Then I have a genius idea. 'A bag. Like a make-up bag or something.' *Nice one.* I take a mouthful of coffee.

'Are you sure it wasn't her knickers?'

I almost spit the coffee back out. Half of it goes up my nose.

'Bingo,' she says. 'I *thought* she looked unusually happy this morning.'

'Did she?' I smile, feeling ridiculously pleased and smug that I did that.

'Look at you, all smiley and stuff. You've got it bad, haven't you?' She smirks, then rings through the purchase and holds out the card reader. 'Old people in love,' she says. 'It's kinda cute.'

'We're not even thirty,' I protest, tapping my card on the screen.

'Middle-aged, then.'

'I think you'll find that middle-aged is . . . Oh, whatever. Youth doesn't last for ever,' I remind her. 'So enjoy it while you can.'

'I intend to.'

I raise my cup in the air. 'Thanks for the coffee, and the insults.'

'You're welcome. Thanks for shagging my boss and making her happy.'

'You're . . . ' I stop. I don't know why, but my eyes are drawn

319

to a notepad beside the till. The top page is covered with writing, a list of some sort. 'What's that?'

Kelly follows the direction of my eyes. 'Food order. Ellie just phoned it through to the supplier. Why?'

'Can I see it?'

'Why?'

'*Please.*'

She shrugs. 'I guess so. It's not like it's state secrets or anything.' She hands the pad over and starts cleaning the coffee machine.

I scan the page, feeling confused. It's not the contents of the list I'm interested in, it's the handwriting. I've seen this writing before. Recently. The way the d's have a little curl at the top, and the o's don't quite join up.

'Who wrote this,' I ask, already knowing the answer but needing to hear it confirmed.

'Ellie. Why?'

I stare at the list. Ellie wrote this.

Ellie is DG.

Ellie

Even though it's a beautiful sunny day, Chloe is inside nursing a hangover when I arrive at her house.

'I didn't even think I'd drunk that much,' she complains, a cold flannel over her eyes as she lies on the couch.

'I guess you *did* start at breakfast,' I point out, dropping my keys on the bench. She winces at the noise.

'Shush.'

'Sorry. Where's Hamish?'

'Out. He and his parents are showing some of his relatives the sights around town before they head home tomorrow. I think they were going to go to the beach for a swim too.'

'You didn't want to go?'

'I wasn't in any state to go, put it that way.' She peels the flannel off her eyes and sits up. 'I do feel a bit better now, though, after a nap.' She peers at me. 'You look ridiculously chirpy.'

'I didn't drink as much as you.'

'That's not it.'

I shrug. 'It's a nice day.'

'It's summer, we have lots of nice days. What aren't you telling me?'

'Nothing,' I say, in a way that indicates there clearly is something.

She gasps. 'You didn't.'

'That depends on what you think I did or didn't do.'

'You slept with Sam?'

I pull a face. 'Well, I'm not sure how much *sleeping* actually happened, but yes.'

She squeals and picks up a cushion, throwing it at me. 'Why didn't you text and tell me?'

'Because we're not sixteen any more. I'm telling you now.'

'How was it? How was he?'

'It was amazing.' I smile contentedly. 'Absolutely perfect. You know those movies where when they make love it always seems so intense and passionate and they do it fifty ways in fifty different places and positions and it's so sexy but the whole time you're thinking about how real life isn't like that?'

She nods, eyes wide.

'Well, it was like that. Like we were in a movie. He knew just what to do and when to do it, and I have never felt so desired and wanted in my entire life. The way he undressed me, bit by bit, and carried me up the stairs, and the way he touched me … I swear to God, we couldn't get enough of each other.'

She sighs. 'Oh Ellie. You lucky, lucky girl.'

'Hey, you're a newly-wed, that's pretty awesome too.'

'Yeah, I know.' She sounds wistful. 'And Hamish and I *did* have sex against the counter in Sam's grandparents' bathroom. Don't tell him, though.'

'As if I would.'

'So what does this mean? Are you guys a couple now?'

'I think so. We haven't really discussed the logistics yet.'

'You're not worried that this is moving too fast?'

'No.' I shake my head vehemently. 'We already have a shared history. It's not like we don't know each other.'

'You haven't seen him in a long time, though. People change.'

'I don't think they change that much. We have some catching-up to do for sure, but there's something comfortable about the idea of being with him.'

'Uh-oh. Using the word "comfortable" already to describe a relationship?'

I smile. 'Oh, believe me, last night was anything *but* comfortable.'

'I'm really happy for you.'

'Thanks. It still doesn't feel real,' I admit. 'I mean, Sam and me? *Sam?*'

She gets up gingerly. 'I hate to bring you back to reality, but I need a favour. Can you drive me to Logan's? I think I'd still be over the limit if I got stopped by the cops.'

I pull a face, remembering the run-in between him and Sam last night. 'Do I have to?'

'Yes, maid of honour, you do.'

'You do realise that's not a lifelong position, right?' I pick up my keys. 'The wedding is over, so I'm not going to be at your beck and call any more.'

'I know, but technically this is wedding business. Hamish put Logan in charge of rounding up all the cameras at the end of the night, those Polaroid instant ones, and the book for people to stick the photos into. I may have to wait weeks for the professional photographer to work her magic, but at least I can see these straight away.'

'Fine. Hurry up, though, I told Sam I'd only be gone a few hours.'

In the car, she directs me to Logan's new house. I didn't even know he'd moved, but she tells me he and Sarah officially shacked up together a few weeks back.

'Maybe this will make him grow up and start treating her properly,' I say, without any real hope. 'I'll wait in the car.'

She gets out and bends to look at me. 'No you won't.'

There's no answer at the front door, but that doesn't deter her.

'He's probably in his shed,' she says. I follow her reluctantly around the side of the house. The shed door is open. Music blasts out, some kind of screaming rock stuff that makes my skull ache. Logan is underneath the bonnet of a beat-up-looking classic car. An open bottle of beer sits on the concrete near his feet, and seeing it, my heart sinks. He's on the booze already. That can't be a good thing.

'It's his current project,' Chloe mutters to me. 'Hamish says he's already sunk around six grand into it. Looks like it's going to need a hell of a lot more.'

Logan turns, frowning. 'I heard that.'

'I don't know how,' she retorts. 'That music is fucking loud. Your new neighbours must hate you.'

He shrugs and walks over to the stereo, turning the dial to lower the volume. 'I hate them too,' he says. 'They've called noise control on me a bunch of times already. But that just makes me turn it up even louder,' he shouts in the direction of the fence.

'You're such a dick sometimes,' Chloe tells him.

He grins. 'I suppose you're here for the cameras.'

'It's sure as hell not for your cheerful company.'

'They're inside. I'll get them.' He doesn't move, though. Instead he shuffles his feet, then looks up at me. 'Hey, Ellie, I'm sorry about last night. That guy just pisses me off.'

'Forget about it,' I say shortly. 'I have.'

But he's not finished. 'You know, you used to give me shit, saying I was being jealous and possessive and all that. Well, what about him? How come it's OK when he does the same thing I get crucified for?'

'Sam is *nothing* like you.'

His eyes run up and down my body. 'Oh, he wants the same thing, believe me.'

'I'm not going to get into this with you.' I turn to go. 'Sorry, Chloe, but I'll wait for you at the car.'

'OK.'

'I'm just saying,' he continues as I start to walk away. 'He still wants you, just like he did back then. He hated me because I had you.'

I stop and face him again. 'You're wrong,' I tell him, my cheeks flushed with anger. 'He hated you because he could see what most of us couldn't, that you are a horrible, toxic excuse of a person. And for the record, I was never yours, but I'll always be his.'

He frowns. 'What are you saying, you guys are together now?'

'Yes,' I tell him, lifting my chin high. 'Not that it's any of your business.'

He looks me up and down again, but this time it's with open disgust. 'Which means you let him fuck you already. Classy.'

'What the hell?' Chloe stares at him, aghast. 'Shut up, Logan.'

He shrugs. 'At least that's killed any last feelings I might have had towards you. I don't do sloppy seconds.'

'I wouldn't go near you if you were the last man on earth,' I tell him. 'I don't know how Sarah can stand to let you touch her.'

He glares at me. 'You're an idiot if you think he cares about you.'

'No, I was an idiot for ever going anywhere near *you*.'

He takes a step towards me, and Chloe moves quickly, putting herself between us. 'Enough, Logan. Just get the cameras so we can get out of here and *you* can cool down.'

He doesn't take his eyes off my face, his jaw tight. I stare back at him defiantly.

'I mean it,' she snaps. 'Cameras. *Now*.'

'You always were a desperate slut,' he tosses out to me as he turns to head inside.

'What the hell has gotten into you?' Chloe shouts after him, incredulous. 'When did you turn into such an asshole? You wait until I tell Hamish about this!'

He disappears inside without answering, and she turns to me, putting her hands on my upper arms, peering into my face with a concerned expression. 'Are you OK?'

'I'm fine.'

'I can't believe he just spoke to you like that.'

I snort bitterly. 'Oh, it's not the first time.'

She shakes her head. 'All these years, when you said he was being a jealous prick, I had no idea you meant like *this*. I'm so sorry.'

Despite my bravado, I feel a bit tearful. 'Why do you think I avoid him?'

'I'm so sorry, Ellie. Believe me, when I tell Hamish what just happened, he's going to be pissed off.'

I shrug. 'I honestly don't care any more. I gave him one last chance and he's well and truly blown it. I want nothing more to do with him.'

'I'm sorry I made you get out of the car. Go back and wait. I'll be there as soon as I've got the cameras.'

I nod, but as I turn to leave, something colourful catches my attention in a dark corner of Logan's shed. With a quick glance at the house to make sure there's no sign of him, I hurry across to it, stopping when I'm barely a stride away. A retro-looking surfboard, leaning up against the wall. I see surfboards nearly every day, but not like this one. My heart rate quickens. It can't be, can it?

'Ellie?'

It is. I'm sure of it. I reach out a hand and run my fingers down the smooth, shiny surface. A green, orange and yellow striped design runs the length of it. I've seen this board before, many, many times. I take hold of it carefully and pull it away from the wall. There it is. I trace it with my fingers to be sure, the small crack in the red fin underneath. It's been repaired, but the crack is still visible through the resin. Closing my eyes, I remember a long-ago night on the beach in front of Sam's house. We sat around a campfire and listened to his grandfather tell us stories of surfing around the world, including the one about how he'd come in on a rocky beach on St Maarten and cracked his fin. *This fin*.

I hear Logan's voice behind me. 'Oh shit.'

'It *was* you,' I say.

'I can explain.'

I turn. 'It was *you*, Logan.'

He shakes his head, defensive. 'Not just me.'

Chloe looks from me to him. 'What are you guys talking about?'

I lift the board, standing it beside me. 'This is Sam's grandfather's board, Chloe.'

She frowns at Logan, understandably confused. 'Why have you got it?'

'Hamish was there too,' he tells her. 'We all were.'

She throws her hands up. 'I don't understand, were *where*?'

'This is the board Sam used on the day of the championships,' I explain, trying to keep my voice level but feeling fury

328

rising inside. 'It was in his car. The car that was stolen that night and set on fire.'

I see her mouth form the word *no*, and she shakes her head as realisation finally dawns. 'There's got to be another explanation, surely.'

'Why did you keep it?' I ask Logan, thrusting the board forward. 'Some kind of sick trophy? A memento of your crime?'

'I don't know. I wasn't really thinking. I just grabbed it before the fire spread and then panicked. I hid it in the shed at my old place, and honestly, I'd forgotten about it until we moved. I've been trying to figure out what I should do with it.'

'Oh my God, Sam was right.' I squeeze my eyes tightly closed, feeling the emotion bubbling to the surface as I realise that everything, *everything* could have been different. 'He was right all along. You guys stole the car and torched it.'

'No, that was an accident,' Logan replies quickly. 'We never meant for any of that to happen. It was just supposed to be a prank, but it went wrong.'

'A *prank*?'

'Yeah.' He rubs his hands through his hair. 'I was pissed off, OK. He won the comp and he was so fucking smug about it. I couldn't stand to see him win every single time. So we took his car.'

'Oh Hamish,' Chloe moans. 'Why didn't he tell me?'

'You weren't even with him then,' Logan barks at her. 'And we all swore each other to secrecy.'

'I can't believe this,' she says.

'We were just going to drive it up the coast a bit and ditch it, Ellie. I swear.'

'What happened?'

'I'd had a few drinks, and I honestly thought I was OK to drive. But I took a corner too fast and lost control.'

'Wait ... Malcolm's arm,' Chloe says. 'You guys told us the next day that he broke it in a midnight game of rugby on the beach.'

'Yeah, that wasn't exactly true. He broke it in the accident.'

'Accident?' I spit the word out. '*Accident?* That implies an unintentional act. What you guys did was *not* an accident.'

Chloe is looking at Logan as if realising she doesn't know him at all. 'You lied. You *all* lied.'

I shake my head at him in disbelief. 'I stood up for you.'

'We *both* did,' she shouts. 'For fuck's sake, Logan. We asked you straight to your faces whether you knew anything about it, and you all swore blind it wasn't you.'

'We couldn't tell you, could we,' he shouts back at her. 'You'd have dobbed us in for sure.'

'I stood up for you!' I say again, hot tears pouring down my face. 'I lost my best friend because of you!'

'Hey, it was his decision to leave, I didn't make him. You were better off without him anyway. If you think about it,' he says earnestly, 'I actually did you a favour.'

'Do me another favour,' I say, tucking the board under my arm. 'Stay the fuck away from me.'

I storm past him, heading for the car. Chloe jogs beside me, struggling to keep up. Logan follows us.

330

'Wait, what are you going to do?' he asks. 'Are you going to tell him?'

'Of course I'm going to tell him,' I snap.

'Just . . . think about it first. What's it going to achieve? All you'll do is rake up a whole lot of old drama. Everyone has moved on, why not just leave it be?'

'Get out of my way,' I warn him.

'I'd do as she says, Logan,' Chloe advises him.

He gets to the car first and stands in front of it, blocking my way. 'No. Not until you promise you're not going to say anything.'

'I'll tell you what I'm going to do,' I say levelly. 'I'm going to go and find Sam, and I'm going to spend the rest of my life apologising to him for being a stupid, *stupid* idiot and believing you instead of him.'

'You're not an idiot,' Chloe says. 'Not unless I'm one too. I believed them as well.'

He looks over the roof of the car at her. 'Look, for what it's worth, Hamish tried to stop us from doing it. He was against the whole thing, but he went along with it because—'

'Because you're a bully,' I cut in. I look him up and down the way he did me earlier. 'Sam saw you for *exactly* what you are. And *that's* why you couldn't stand him. Now get the fuck out of my way.'

He hesitates a moment too long, so my kick finds him right where I aim it. He folds like a house of cards, hands clutching his balls, his face contorted with pain.

'You deserve everything that's coming to you,' I tell him,

pushing him aside with one foot. I put the surfboard between the seats as I climb in. Chloe gets in the other side.

'What are you going to do?' she asks as I pull away from the kerb.

'Give Sam his board back, of course. Tell him he was right all along.'

'OK. OK, you *could* do that. Or . . .'

I flick a sideways glance at her. 'Or what?'

'Let's think about it for a second.'

'What's there to think about? If Logan and the others had just confessed instead of being cowards, Sam and I would never have had that stupid fight and he wouldn't have taken off.'

'Maybe,' she says tactfully. 'Or maybe he'd have left town anyway. We'll never know.'

'Oh my God.' I stare at her for so long she gets nervous and puts a hand on the wheel.

'Watch the road, Ellie.'

'You want me to lie to him to protect Hamish.' I can barely believe I'm saying the words.

'No,' she protests loudly. Then, quieter, 'Maybe.'

'I don't believe this.'

'I don't see the point in people getting into trouble for something that happened a long time ago. We were teenagers, Ellie. Teenagers do dumb shit all the time.'

'And they should face the consequences for that dumb shit.'

'At the time, sure. But now? Hamish, Logan, Malcolm, these guys all have real lives. Marriages, businesses, kids. You bring this up and it could really hurt their reputations.'

'I don't give a fuck about their reputations,' I say bitterly. 'And I highly doubt anything would happen to any of them. It's been too long, there's probably some sort of . . . statute of limitations in place or something. They'll get off scot-free, like they always do.'

'I can't speak for the others, but Hamish will be sleeping on the couch for a while, don't worry about that.'

'I don't care about Hamish, or Logan, or any of them. All I care about is Sam, and that he was right. I should have listened to him.'

'I understand that you're angry, and I'm not trying to excuse what they did, but these guys are your friends too, Ellie.'

'Not any more,' I say emphatically, pulling up outside her house. 'Now can you get out before you say something that wrecks our friendship too.'

'Ellie—'

'I mean it.'

'Fine.' She gets out and closes the door, leaning to look at me through the open window. 'I'm sorry, OK? Whatever you decide to do, I'll understand. I love you, Ellie, and I don't want to fall out with you over this.'

'Then don't ask me to lie to protect your husband.'

I drive away. She stands there watching me until I turn the corner.

Sam

I don't go home after I get the coffee, because I don't want to see her. I can't, not until I straighten things out in my head.

Ellie and DG are one and the same.

I head to the beach instead. It's a Sunday in the tail end of summer. Most of the tourists have gone, so I only need to walk south for a hundred metres to find a quiet spot at the bottom of some sand dunes. A private spot where no one will be able to see me unless they're almost on top of me.

The sea is playful today. I watch as a handful of kids bodyboard in the shallows.

Ellie is DG.

A bigger set of waves comes along. The third one curls, and in its stomach I see a black shadow darting along. Small, a snapper probably. It disappears as the wave breaks, and something inside of me clicks.

DG.

Dolphin Girl.

That's what I sometimes used to call her when we were young. She always looked so at home in the water. Could read the waves and currents better than most other surfers I knew. I told her she was like a dolphin.

Putting aside my questions about how she even found my letter, why wouldn't she simply tell me it was her? Why pretend to be a stranger? I can hazard a guess. I behaved horribly the first time I saw her. So dismissive and condescending. I can't exactly blame her for not wanting to talk to me after that.

I pick up a shell, and as I rub my thumb over the surface, feeling the tiny bumps of each ring that was added over time as the mollusc inside grew, I work out something that's been bothering me. In the letters, she mentioned losing someone herself. Did she say that purely to appear sympathetic to what I was going through? But then she never actually said that the one she'd loved had *died*. I assumed that. She said only that she'd lost someone she loved.

Did she mean . . . me?

She'd lost me.

It isn't comparable to a bereavement, but I understand where she was coming from. After all, I'd lost her too. My best friend, the girl who'd been a fixture of my youth. Overnight, we'd gone from seeing each other every day to nothing. No talking, no messages . . . nothing. I'd been so angry at her for so long, I never really stopped to think about how it might have affected her. As far as I was concerned, she'd made her choice when she believed Logan over me. I knew the loss of our friendship wouldn't be easy for her, but I *wanted* to hurt her, the way she'd hurt me.

She was right: I *have* been a dick.

When I get back to the house, having worked up a sweat in my eagerness to see her, she's not there. I feel a flood of disappointment. I want to tell her that I know she's the one behind the letters, but that it doesn't matter. Because I know now why she did it. All she has ever done is care about me, in some form or other. These letters have just been an extension of that. She saw I was lost and alone and she reached out a hand, just as she did all those years ago when I moved here and knew no one.

There's a note stuck between the front door and the frame.

Dear Sam,
  I waited as long as I could, but the neighbour called to say Nan isn't feeling well, so I've had to go home. I'll try and get back later, but it depends how she is. Maybe you could come to mine? I really need to talk to you.
  Love,
  Ellie

Ellie

'I'm fine.'

'You don't look fine,' I fret. 'People who are fine usually don't look as grey as you do.'

Nan rolls her eyes, her hand rubbing Alfie's ears. Even he looks worried as he sits with his head in her lap, staring up at her. 'I'm old. Old people are grey.'

'I'm not talking about your hair.'

'Stop fussing.'

I place the back of my hand against her forehead. 'It's part of the job description, I'm afraid.'

Nan looks reproachfully at our neighbour. 'Sue shouldn't have called you.'

'Well I'm not sorry,' Sue says. 'When you keeled over in the potatoes, I thought it best to let Ellie know.'

I survey the clammy sheen on Nan's forehead. 'I think we should call an ambulance.'

337

'Don't you dare,' Nan protests. 'I'm not wasting those poor people's time.' She shuffles awkwardly to the front of the couch and tries to stand up. I pull Alfie out of her way.

'Where do you think you're going?'

'I think I left the hose going, and until we see some rain, the council has us on water restrictions.' She manages to get to her feet, and smiles triumphantly before nearly toppling over. She grabs my arm to steady herself.

'Please sit down, Nan.'

She ignores me and heads for the door.

'Stubborn old bat,' Sue says. 'I'll get her a glass of water, shall I?'

'Thanks. And thanks for calling me, you know she wouldn't have.'

I follow Nan outside and stop short when I see Sam standing in the yard, supporting her with one arm around her shoulders and the other holding her forearm. My heart doesn't know whether to soar or drop to my feet at the sight of him, so it kind of does both.

'Hey,' he says.

'Hey.' I smile nervously back. It's only been a few hours, but so much has changed since then, including everything I thought I knew and believed about the past. When I tell him – because I know I *have* to tell him – am I going to lose him again?

'I caught this one trying to escape,' he says, leading Nan to the outdoor bench seat and lowering her down. Alfie jumps up beside her and nudges his head against her arm until she lifts it and drapes it over him.

'I was just going to turn the hose off,' she grumbles, but I notice her knuckles are white against Alfie's fur.

'I'll get the hose.' Sue emerges from inside and holds the glass of water out to Nan, who looks at it like it's poison.

'What's that?'

'What does it look like?' Sue says exasperatedly.

'Can I have a sherry instead?'

I take the glass from Sue. 'Drink the water, Nan.'

'Fine,' she grumbles.

'You don't look so good,' Sam says, studying her.

'I forgot to put my blusher on this morning. I wasn't expecting company.'

He shrugs. 'At least her sense of humour is still intact.'

'Yes,' I answer drily. 'Thank heavens for that.'

Sue rejoins us. 'The hose is off.'

Nan frowns at her. 'Are you sure you did it properly?'

'I know how to turn a hose off, Audrey.'

'Not this hose you don't. It's tricky. There's a knack to it.'

'How can it be tricky? You turn it one way to get water, and the other way to stop it. It's hardly rocket science.'

'Well *excuse* me, Madam Scientist. Apparently you know everything . . .'

'Can I have a quick word?' Sam whispers in my ear, pulling my attention away from the bickering between the two old ladies.

I glance at Nan. She seems OK now. Happy in her natural, argumentative element. 'Sure.'

He takes my hand and leads me around the corner of the house.

'I know,' he says.

'Sorry?'

'I *know*.'

My blood turns to ice, explanations darting to my tongue. How does he know? Logan wouldn't have said anything, neither would Chloe, I'm sure. And yet he's looking at me like . . . Wait. Why is he smiling?

'Know what, exactly?' I ask cautiously.

He pulls a piece of paper from his pocket and unfolds it, then passes it to me. I scan it, frowning when I realise what it is. 'My food order? What are you doing with this?'

'I went into the café to get a coffee and I saw it on the counter. That's when I realised.'

'Realised what?' I stare at him, uncomprehending. 'I don't understand. Why are you interested in my shopping list?'

'I'm not. It's the handwriting. *Your* handwriting.'

My handwriting? I look down at the list again, swallowing hard. *My handwriting.*

'I can explain,' I say, the words spilling out in a rush. 'I was going to tell you eventually, but the right time just never seemed to come up, and then we got close again, and I was scared that if I did tell you, you'd be angry and not want to speak to me any more. I know that's no excuse, though, and that you're probably furious with me.'

'Ellie—'

'I only did it to try and help you, I promise. You seemed so . . . lost in your first letter. It broke my heart and I wanted to comfort you, but you were very clear about not wanting anything to do with me.'

'Ellie, it's—'

'So when I saw you tie the letter to the tree, I thought, hey, here's a way I can help you. I know it was so wrong of me to read it, and I wasn't following you, I swear. I was out for a run when I saw you on the beach, so I hid and I waited for you to leave because I knew I was the last person you wanted to see, but then you went into the trees and I was curious, you know me. So I had a look after you left, and I'm so sorry—'

'Ellie.' He says it really loudly this time, and immediately I stop babbling.

He takes my hands in his. 'Don't be sorry. If you'd shut up for a second and let me get a word in, I'm trying to tell you that it's OK. I'm not mad. I *was* a bit upset at first, but I know your heart was in the right place. We can talk about your lack of morals when it comes to privacy later.' He grins. 'But I'm not upset with you.'

I nod, blinking away the tears that are threatening. I thought I was going to lose him again. I came so close. But he's not upset with me; in fact, he's smiling.

And then he's not. The smile turns into a frown so quickly I miss the moment it transitions.

'Is that . . . ?'

I turn to see what he's staring at over my shoulder, although to be honest, I already know. My car. His surfboard.

Sam

Part of me knows without a shadow of a doubt that it is what I think it is. My grandfather's surfboard. The one he passed down to me. The one I haven't seen since the night my car was stolen. The night that led to the end of my friendship with Ellie. But my mind is struggling to reconcile what I'm seeing with what I know. For years, I've believed this board was destroyed when my car was. I've mourned for it, and now here it is, in Ellie's car?

'OK, *that* I can explain too,' she says, repeating her earlier words, though with more panic now.

Pushing past her, I open the car door and carefully pull the board out, feeling a tide of emotion rising inside my chest as I touch it again. For my grandfather, this board was the beginning and the end of every adventure he'd ever had. Every nick, scratch and fibre held a memory, of a place, a time, a wave, a person. It had travelled the world with him, his most prized possession. He loved it almost as much as he loved my grandmother, and that was saying something. It wasn't the only board he owned, but it always remained his favourite.

I coveted it from the moment he taught me to surf, and when he gave it to me on my sixteenth birthday, I vowed to hold on to it always, at least until I had my own son one day and could pass it down to him. When my car was stolen, I told the police I didn't care if they never recovered it. All I wanted back was the board that had been inside, and I was prepared to do whatever it took to recover it. Media interviews, offer a reward, anything. Of course they looked at me like I was crazy. To them, it was just a surfboard. Easily replaced. But not to me.

After the confrontation on the beach, I made my grandfather drive me to where they'd found the wreck. All that was left was a charred metal shell and a pile of ashes. The board was gone. Destroyed. I was devastated, but not as much as my grandfather was, and that ate me up inside. Knowing he'd entrusted me with something that meant so much to him, and it was gone because of me. I knew it was my fault. I knew *exactly* who had taken the car, and why.

Logan. He'd always hated me, and that day, after I won the surf comp, he didn't even bother to try and hide it. All night at the awards party he glared at me like he wanted to kill me. I was young, smug and stupid, I made sure to flash my win in his face. In return, he made sure I knew Ellie was there with him. Kissing her in front of me, keeping an arm or a hand on her at all times. His message couldn't have been more obvious, and I felt it like a knife in the ribs. My best friend was now *his* girlfriend, and even though she'd reassured me it changed nothing, it did. It changed everything. I could feel her slipping away from me.

So when they called me up to receive the award, I dragged her up with me, hugging her right there on the stage in front of everyone. In front of him. When my car disappeared a few hours later, I knew who had taken it; there was never any doubt in my mind. But of course he denied everything, and his friends backed him up. And the one person in the world – besides my grandfather – whose opinion mattered to me, the person I most expected to be on my side, believed him too.

'This is . . . ' I run my hands along the familiar length of the board. It's in desperate need of a clean and a wax, but the bones of it are still solid.

'Your board. Yes.' I feel her hand settle on my shoulder, and shrug it off.

'Ellie.' I turn to face her. 'You of all people knew how much this board meant to me. You've had it all this time, and you let me believe it was destroyed?'

She shakes her head fervently. 'No, Sam. I thought it was gone too.'

'I don't understand.'

'I found it today and I was bringing it to you, but you weren't at your place, then Sue called so I had to come home. I didn't want to just leave it there for you to find without any context.'

'What context? Where did you find it?'

'That's ... complicated,' she says, wringing her hands in frustration.

'How is it complicated?'

She looks torn.

'Ellie, if *you* didn't have the board, then you know who did.'

'I do, but ... Knowing is not going to change anything. And the most important thing is that you have it back now.'

'I can't believe this.' I step away from her. 'You're covering for them?'

'No, I don't *want* to,' she says quickly, then lets out a frustrated wail. 'God, why does this always come down to me? I was caught in the middle back then, and now here we are and it's happening again.'

'Who's putting you in the middle?'

'You, Chloe ...'

'Logan.'

She sighs. 'Yes.'

'You're protecting him?'

'No.' She shakes her head emphatically. 'It's not how you think.'

'Ellie, did Logan have my board? Did he steal my car?'

'Yes.'

I feel anger flush through my veins. 'I knew it. I *told you* that he did it.'

'I know, but he told me that he didn't.' She stares at me helplessly. 'What was I supposed to do?'

'You were supposed to believe *me*.'

'I know. I'm sorry.' She steps forward and puts her hands on my chest. It rises and falls underneath her palms with every frustrated breath I take. Nothing is making any sense. This is exactly why I didn't want to come back here. This town and these people, all the bad memories. The feelings of betrayal. I take a step away from her, and her beautiful face crumples.

'No,' she says, shaking her head. 'Please, Sam. Don't go.'

'I don't know what's going on here, Ellie, but the fact is, you're *still* covering for him ... and I can't do this again.'

'I'm not covering for *him*. But Hamish and the other guys, they're not bad people. Chloe asked me not to say anything, she was worried it would upset things. But I was going to tell you.'

'I hope your friends appreciate how loyal you are. I just wish that loyalty would sometimes be directed at me.'

'That swings both ways,' she says bitterly.

'What's that supposed to mean?'

'Where was your loyalty to *me*, Sam? To our friendship? I didn't think anything could ever come between us, then you left town and never looked back, like I meant nothing to you.'

'You think that was easy for me?'

'You certainly made it look that way.'

'You're kidding, right?' I feel my heart beat wildly in my chest. 'Until I lost Mei, leaving you was the hardest thing I've ever had to do.'

'And losing you was the worst thing I've ever gone through,' she retorts.

We stare at each other, both of us frustrated.

'But Sam,' she says finally, 'none of what happened then, or today . . . ' she gestures at the surfboard, 'matters now. All that matters is that we're back in each other's lives. Together we can figure everything else out.'

I exhale heavily, wishing I could believe it was really as easy as that. 'I don't think love is supposed to be this hard.'

'What are you saying?'

I can't think when I'm around her, when she looks at me like that. I turn and start walking away from her. 'I need some time alone to think. I'm sorry.'

'Sam, stay. We need to—'

'Help!'

Sue comes hurtling around the corner, her face a picture of panic. 'Call an ambulance,' she cries, one hand on her chest. 'She's collapsed again, and this time she's not breathing.'

Ellie

It takes a few seconds for Sue's words to register. When they do, I run, hearing Sam hot on my heels behind me. I'm not prepared for the sight of my grandmother flat out on the ground. It stops me in my tracks. No. She can't be . . .

Sam's warm, firm grip on my shoulder snaps me out of it.

'Call an ambulance,' he says firmly.

I nod, pulling out my phone, my fingers shaking as I swipe the screen. Sam drops to the ground beside Nan as I dial the emergency number. Alfie keeps trying to push his way in, licking at Nan's face.

'Keep him out of the way,' Sam snaps at Sue.

'Ambulance, please hurry,' I say, as soon as someone answers. 'It's my nan.'

There's a click as the call is transferred.

'What's the address of your emergency?'

I tell her as I push the icon on the screen to put her on speakerphone.

'Is the patient breathing?'

'I don't know,' I stammer. I feel like I'm walking through quicksand to get to Sam's side. *Oh my God.* She's so pale, her eyes closed but her mouth wide open. Her face is contorted, as if she's in pain.

'Tell me exactly what's happened.'

'It's my grandmother, she had a heart attack two years ago and they put a stent in. She's just collapsed again.'

'OK. We've got help on the way. In the meantime, I need you to tell me every time she takes a breath in. OK? Starting from now.'

I watch Nan for signs of movement, but see nothing. 'I don't know,' I say, panicking. 'I can't tell if she's breathing or not.'

'She's not,' Sam says gravely. 'No pulse either.'

'OK, I'm going to need you to perform CPR,' the lady on the other end of the phone says. 'I'll talk you through it. We're going to start now and continue until the emergency services get there.'

'This can't be happening.' I sink to my knees on the grass beside Nan.

'I'll do it,' Sam says.

'Make sure she's flat on her back,' the operator says. 'Remove any pillows or cushions. Can you see any food or vomit in her mouth?'

Sam checks. 'No, nothing.'

'I need you to place one hand under her chin and tilt her

head back. Pinch her nose shut with your fingers, cover her mouth with yours and give two rescue breaths. Do that now.'

I watch Sam do as she instructs.

'OK, he's done that,' I tell her. 'Now what?'

'Now place the heel of your hand on her breastbone, between the nipples. Put your other hand on top of that hand and press down firmly, with only the heel of your lower hand touching her chest.'

Sam immediately starts pumping Nan's chest, as I watch her face for any signs that she's still here. There's nothing.

'You need to be doing two chest pumps per second,' the woman on the phone says. 'Keep it rapid. One, two, three, four . . . One, two, three, four . . . OK? Keep doing that, rapid and firm compressions.'

I've never felt as helpless as I do in that moment, watching Sam as he furiously pumps her chest. Everything goes kind of muffled as I reach down and stroke her forehead, remembering how she used to do the same to me when I was unwell. This woman has been the one constant in my life. Always. I can't picture my world without her in it.

'How're we going? Has she started breathing at all?' the operator asks.

'No, not yet.'

'Keep doing the compressions. Take turns if you get tired, but keep up that pace.'

I quickly wipe away my tears. The shock is wearing off and I feel a determination bubble up inside me. This is not happening, she is *not* dying. Not on my watch.

'Let me take over, Sam.'

'Not . . . yet . . .'

I hear the exertion in his voice, his breathing heavy.

What feels like an eternity later but is probably only a minute or two, he says, 'OK, get ready.'

I kneel over her, on the opposite side of him, and get my hands into the right position. As soon as he pulls his away, I replace them, thrusting down on her chest with everything I have in me. Over and over and over and over and over. I don't stop even when I hear sirens. I keep going as voices fill the night air around us and questions are fired at Sue and Sam, who do their best to answer. Red and blue lights flicker across Nan's face. A hive of activity is happening around me, but all I can see is my hands. My fingers laced together, my knuckles white with effort as I press down on her heart and silently will it to start beating again. I feel like I'm floating above, watching myself.

One, two, three, four . . .

'We'll take over now,' someone says, breaking through the vacuum of noise. My peripheral vision expands, and I see people touching Nan, cutting the sleeves of her shirt with scissors, attaching things to her.

One, two, three, four . . .

'She's got a pulse,' a male paramedic says. 'And oxygen stats are slowly rising. She's breathing, but not well.'

'Ellie,' Sam says gently. 'You need to move aside and them let them take over.'

I shake my head. *One, two, three, four . . .*

351

'Come on.' He tugs at my shoulder. 'They know what they're doing. Let them help her.'

I finally give in to him, letting myself fall backwards, exhaustion claiming my body. Various heads and shoulders immediately fill the space I have just vacated as paramedics start to work on her.

'You did good,' Sam tells me, pulling me into his chest, his chin on top of my head. 'You did good, Ellie.'

His shirt soaks up the tears that have started flowing again. 'Is she . . . ?'

He squeezes me tighter. 'I don't know. We just have to let them do their job.'

'I don't know what I'll do without her. She can't die, Sam.'

I feel him swallow next to my ear. He can't reassure me, as much as he wants to. He knows as well as I do that it's out of our hands now. We've done our best; all we can do is wait and see.

Sam

My grandfather's death happened from afar. One night I received a phone call to say he was unwell and had been taken into hospital. The next morning, another to inform me that he had died. They made it sound peaceful, as if he'd simply slipped away. He was so heavily medicated that I couldn't even call and speak to him. They said he would have been unaware he was dying, and I couldn't decide whether that was a good thing or not. Living a full life only to die without ever knowing it had come to an end.

Mei bled to death internally on a street corner. The people who stopped to help her had no idea she was dying in front of their eyes. Plenty of times I tried to imagine how it was for her, stepping off that footpath and being hit by that car. Did she see it coming? Or was she looking somewhere else, down at her phone maybe, composing a text message or flicking through Facebook? I imagined the impact, how I thought it might have sounded. Whether she went flying into the windscreen, the way you see in movies. At the hospital, they cleaned her up and laid her out on a bed before they let me see her. With her dark hair stark against a clean white sheet, she looked as beautiful as a sleeping princess. Only a graze above her left eyebrow gave any indication of the trauma and violence that had been inflicted on her. Other than that, she looked at peace.

Any death of a loved one hurts, but being told that someone has died, or only seeing the aftermath when death has been prepared for viewing, is *nothing* compared to the reality of watching it happen right in front of you. Ellie's grandmother's death is confrontational and violent. Her jaw contorted with pain, her clothes wet and reeking from where she has soiled herself, and I'm fairly certain I break one of her ribs when I give her CPR. I keep hearing the loud crack replaying in my mind, over and over and over.

She doesn't die right then on the grass in front of us. We bring her back, long enough for them to tentatively stabilise her and load her into the ambulance. Sue stays behind to lock up the house, and offers to take Alfie home with her. I drive Ellie in her car to the hospital, following the ambulance the whole way. Halfway there, the lights and sirens come on and we know she's taken a turn for the worse. Ellie doesn't speak the whole way, and I don't know what to say. There is nothing I can think of that will help her in this moment.

Ellie

At the hospital, they 'officially regret to inform' me that the last time Nan was here, she requested a DNR be recorded on her file.

Do not resuscitate.

They tell me matter-of-factly that they have to respect her wishes and let her go. The Nan I know is already gone. They tell me that even with the machines, it is highly unlikely she will last the night, but that she is in no pain. They can't guarantee that she can hear me, but they tell me that now is the time to say anything I need to say. To say goodbye, so that they can turn off the machine and let her die peacefully and with the dignity she deserves. On her own terms, that's what she'd have wanted.

I sit beside her bed and hold her hand while machines breathe for her. I tell her how much I love her. How grateful I am that my mother and I came to live with her all those years ago, and how much she has shaped my life and the woman I have become. How I have *never* regretted staying with her after Mum died, not even for a single second. I tell her there is no other grandmother in this world as special or as wonderful or as loved as she is, and that the thing I am most proud of in life is being her granddaughter. I thank her for everything she has taught me, and tell her that she is, of course, by far the better cook out of the two of us. I also tell her I know she cheats at cards sometimes, but that her secret is safe with me.

She dies at 4.16 a.m., twenty minutes after they turn the machine off. I stay with her, holding her hand, until a nurse tactfully tells me that it's time for her body to be taken away. There's a room shortage; someone else is in need of the space and the machines. All around us, life goes on.

Sam is outside in the hallway. His head rests in his hands as he sits on the closest chair in a row of hard blue plastic seats. An empty coffee cup rests on the seat beside him. I had no idea he was even still here. My feet lead me to him. When my toes come into his view, he looks up, his eyes a question.

'She's gone,' I say flatly, and he exhales slowly.

'I'm so sorry, Ellie.' He stands up. 'Let me take you home.'

I stare out of the passenger window the entire way. Every time I think I'm all out of tears, my body produces new ones. As we come over the last hill, the sun is rising above the horizon, bathing Seclusion Bay in pale pink. Nan is gone, and I feel completely lost.

He pulls up and turns the engine off. Its comforting rumble is replaced by complete silence.

I unclip my seat belt and reach for the door handle. 'Thanks for driving me home.'

'Of course.' He opens his own door and swings his legs out. 'I'll make you a cup of tea, or would you rather something stronger?'

'Actually, I just want to be left alone.'

He stares at me over the roof of the car. 'I don't think that's a good idea.'

I close my door. 'It's what I need right now.'

'Ellie . . . '

'Bye, Sam.'

Everything looks exactly the same as it always does when I walk down the driveway and around the back of the house. There's no indication of what happened here last night. I don't understand how everything can look so normal.

'Ellie, wait.' Sam follows me. 'I think I should at—'

I whirl on him. 'Go home, Sam.'

'No. I'm not leaving you like this, not after what's happened.'

'You were happy to leave me a few hours ago.'

He winces. 'That's not fair. I wasn't leaving you. Everything was just overwhelming, and I needed to think. But none of that matters now.'

'It matters to me. I can't be on tenterhooks all the time. Worried about you leaving me again.' I'm so close to him, I can see the shadows underneath his eyes, the tiny bit of sleep gunk in the corner of the left one, near his lashes. His clothes are tousled from sitting on a hospital chair for hours on end, his eyes tormented from the memory of trying to restart my grandmother's heart with his hands. I have never loved him more than I do in that moment, but I'm telling him the truth. I am terrified, *terrified* of loving him and losing him again. I can't help how I feel, any more than he can. And right now, I feel alone. Numb. Abandoned. I know Nan didn't choose to leave me, but Sam did. Once, almost twice. I need to protect my own heart. 'You were right,' I tell him sadly. 'Love shouldn't be this hard.'

'I didn't mean that.'

'You did.'

I reach up and kiss him, hard, trying to imprint the memory of how this feels into my mind. It's a goodbye kiss, and he kisses me back as if he senses the same thing.

'Go home, Sam,' I say, stepping away from him. 'I've just lost the person I care the most about in this world. Right now, that's *all* I can think about. I don't have the time or the energy for us. Not now. You of all people should understand how I'm feeling. Respect my wishes, please.'

He nods slowly, reluctantly. 'OK. I'll go. For now. But the second you need me, you call and I'll be here.'

I turn away from him and head inside the house, sliding the door closed behind me and pulling the net curtains across. He stands there for a few moments, then lowers his head sadly and leaves. I hear his car start, out on the street, and listen as the sound of it driving away grows quieter before disappearing. I sink down onto the floor and hug my arms to my chest.

Sam

It's one of the hardest things I've ever had to do, walk away from her knowing that I've let her down right when she needed me the most. What kind of person does that to someone when they've been through a loss like she has? It's not who I am, but it's what she wants, she made that perfectly clear. So I leave, hating myself as I do.

I can make sure she isn't alone, though, so I call Chloe and tell her what's happened. She's devastated, and promises me that she will head around there as soon as we finish speaking. As an afterthought, she tells me she's had two decent offers on Grandad's house and will email them through.

Hours later, I stare at the two contracts on my computer without really seeing them. How can I make any kind of decision at the moment without knowing where I stand with Ellie?

Ellie

There is no funeral. No fuss. She was always adamant she didn't want one; it was even written into her will. Funerals, she said, were a waste of money, catering tea and scones for a bunch of people she hadn't seen in years, half of whom she probably didn't even like anyway or who had just come to be nosy. I'm not happy about it, but I do as she asked. It feels wrong not to celebrate her life in some way, though, so two weeks after she died, and two days after I collect her ashes from the funeral home, I organise an impromptu memorial at the local Irish pub. She liked going there for the occasional dinner, always had the Scotch fillet and chips, washed down with a Guinness. I order bowls of chips for the room, and a round of Guinness for everyone in her memory.

Gerry, the owner of the pub, who was fond of Nan, closes the doors and lets me have the place for a private function at no cost. He sets up a little table near the bar, where I put the container of ashes and a large framed photo of her taken three years ago at a summer BBQ at one of the neighbours'. In it, she is rosy-cheeked and laughing at something that someone has said. With a glass of sherry in her hand, and the sun setting behind her, she looks happy. It is my favourite photo of her.

I stand beside the little table and make small talk, listening to people's memories of Nan with tears in my eyes. Some of the stories I've heard before, some are new to me. I've prepared a little speech, but I wait longer than necessary to start, just in case anyone else is still to come.

Like Sam, even though he probably has no idea that it's happening. I haven't told him, and I made Chloe promise she wouldn't. I haven't even talked to him since the day after she died, though he has called and messaged quite a few times. The texts are brief, caring, along the lines of *Thinking of you, please can we talk*. The calls I let go to voicemail, because I honestly don't know what to say to him. I haven't listened to any of them. That night of Chloe's wedding feels like it happened a lifetime ago now. So much has happened. My world has changed.

Gerry rings the bell above the bar, indicating that it's time for my speech.

'I just want to thank you all for coming today,' I say, when everyone has a glass of frothy Guinness in their hand. 'I'm not going to stand here and do a eulogy, because Nan was quite clear that she didn't want a traditional service. Well, she didn't want any kind of service, but that didn't feel right, and there's not much she can do about it now, so . . . ' I shrug, 'here we are.'

361

Chloe smiles at me, which helps to steady my nerves. We're slowly rebuilding our friendship after she asked me to lie to Sam, and we'll get there, I know we will. It's just going to take a bit of time.

'Besides,' I continue, 'you all know everything there is to know about Nan anyway. Give her a stage and she'd make you her captive audience. She loved telling stories about her life, and of course embellishing them as well. I'm not at all convinced that we're related to English royalty, but she did insist.'

There's a murmur of laughter. I take a deep breath.

'Nan came into my life during a difficult time, after my parents had gone through a bitter divorce. After my mother died, I remember her telling me that everything was going to be OK, that I'd never be alone. Well, now I am, because unfortunately that's the one thing we have no control over. I know that if it had been up to Nan, she'd have preferred to go sitting in her favourite chair, watching the cricket on TV with a beer in her hand.'

'Oh yes.' A man nods. 'She did love the cricket.'

'I've been doing a lot of thinking since she died,' I say. 'About the kind of life she lived, and the kind of life I want to live. I know they say you shouldn't make any big decisions when you're grieving, but I also feel that with grief can come clarity. It makes you focus on what it is you want. With that in mind . . . ' I take another deep breath in and let it out slowly, 'I've made a decision. It's time for me to leave the bay. I want to thank you, all of you, for being part of Nan's life and mine.

You were all very special to her, and me, and no matter what happens, or where I end up, I'll never forget any of you. I wish you all love, luck and happiness.'

I raise my glass and everyone follows suit.

'To Audrey,' I say.

'To Audrey.'

I take a mouthful, and nearly spit it back out, hearing quite a few other people do the same. Choking it down, I put the glass on top of the bar. '*Fuck.* You can tip the rest of that down the sink,' I tell Gerry. 'It's disgusting.'

He chuckles, reaching for it. 'Aye, it's an acquired taste.'

I rub the surface of my tongue with my teeth, feeling like it's been coated with something. 'It's like drinking motor oil. How the hell did Nan drink that stuff? I'll have a glass of Sauvignon Blanc instead, please, when you've got a second.'

Someone tugs at my elbow. It's Chloe, and she's frowning.

'You're not serious, are you?'

I nod. 'I am.'

'Are you going back on the yachts?'

I shrug. 'Probably not. I think I'm too old for that lifestyle now. I don't really have a plan yet; all I know is that I want to see more of the world. Who knows, maybe I'll end up opening a cute little restaurant in rural France, or Italy.'

She stares at me, nonplussed. 'You're kidding, right? I mean, you will come back here some day, won't you?'

'Maybe.' Gerry passes me a glass of wine, and I take a sip. 'But I'm not going to commit to anything. I kind of like the idea of not knowing what's going to come next.'

'What about the café?'

'This morning I promoted Kelly to manager.' I smile at the girl, who is standing nearby, still looking like she's in shock and can't quite believe it's really happened.

'Kelly?' Chloe snorts. 'She's what, nineteen? What would she know about managing a business?'

'You'd be surprised. Between them, she and Maxine can run the place as well as I do. And I'll always be at the end of an email if they have any issues, not that I'm anticipating any. She's also going to rent Nan's house, at mate's rates, and look after Alfie for me.'

'Why am I just hearing about this now, at the same time as everyone else?'

'It was a pretty spur-of-the-moment decision.'

'You mean you knew I'd try and talk you out of it.'

'Honestly? Yes. I had to make this decision by myself.'

'What if you get homesick, or realise you've made a big mistake?'

'I won't. But I know this place will always be here if I need it.'

She stares at me sadly. 'You're really doing this?'

'I am.'

'Is Sam going with you?'

I shake my head, staring into my wine glass so I won't cry. 'No. Unfortunately that didn't work out.'

'Oh Ellie, I'm so sorry. Is it because of what the guys did?'

'That didn't help.'

'It wasn't your fault, though. Are you sure the two of you can't figure it out?'

'I'm not sure about anything, but I feel like this is the right thing for me to do.'

Tears well up in her eyes. 'I'm going to miss you.'

I give her a cuddle. 'I'll miss you too. But I'll keep in touch.'

She sniffs. 'You'd better.'

Sam

The sand is damp and cool underfoot. The sky and the surface of the water are a beautiful soft pale blue, the horizon to my left streaked with peach and yellow where the sun is starting to rise. A sharp wind blows in off the ocean. The sea is corrugated with waves, and the noise of them breaking is all the soundtrack I need. Conditions are perfect.

It's time.

I found my old wetsuit in the back of my wardrobe, but it was woefully small. I didn't realise just how much I've filled out since I left here; I couldn't even get it over my thighs. Grandad's old one fared slightly better, though he was narrower in the chest, so the zip only comes halfway up. Thank God no one else is around, because with my chest out on display, I look like Burt Reynolds.

Normally, this time of the year I'd have worn shorts, but it's been a long time since I've been out here, and I don't know it as well as I used to. I do know there is the odd rock in the bay. They poke their heads above water when the tide is out, but when it's in, like it is now, they're hidden from view and dangerous. The wetsuit isn't going to save me if a wave drops me on my head on one, but it will save a bit of skin if I scrape down the side.

I haven't heard from Ellie since the day I drove her home. Respecting her request for privacy while simultaneously worrying how she is 24/7 has been insanely difficult. She hasn't returned any of my calls or messages, so I have no idea where we stand, or even if there is a 'we' any more. I can't quite believe how quickly everything changed. A wedding and a new love story one day, death and heartbreak the next. Knowing that it was largely due to me is a bitter pill to swallow. Her loyalty was one of the things that attracted me to her in the first place, but in the end, it was also the thing that drove me away. She *was* put in the middle, in an impossible position, torn between friends. It was a choice I should never have expected her to make.

I can't change the past now; all I can do is apologise and spend the rest of my life trying to make up for it. And that's what I intend to do, if she'll let me. But in order to be the best man I can possibly be for her, first I need to remember who I am. I draw in a deep lungful of the brisk morning air. It energises me.

The water is colder than I remember, making me glad I went with the ill-fitting wetsuit rather than shorts. Grandad's carefully restored surfboard is tucked underneath my arm as

I stride out through the foamy breakers, unable to keep the smile off my face. It's my first time in an ocean in over ten years, and it's not until right at this moment, as the water swirls and fizzes around me, that I remember just how much I love it.

Once I'm waist deep, I slide the board in front of me and leap into the face of a wave, feeling the lip of it smack against the board as I pass through and down the other side. Water drenches my hair and my face as I paddle out to the line-up. When I reach it, I boost myself into a sitting position with a leg either side of the board, taking stock. Out here, there is no one except me and the water. Nature, raw and powerful. It's like coming home.

The sun bursts over the horizon as I choose my wave, taking my time, making sure my first ride in a long time is going to be a good one. I'll know it when I see it; I always have. Surfing is in my blood and my bones. Part of me belongs in the ocean, the rest belongs to Ellie.

It comes, my wave. Rippling and building across the surface of the ocean as if it has been searching the globe to find me. I turn and stroke, feeling the exact moment it picks up the back of the board. Then I'm on my feet, charging down the barrel, one hand buried in the face of the wave as it curls over me and I shoot for the sun. For an incredible moment, there's no sound. It's like the wave is motionless and so am I, suspended in time. Then it's over. Whooping and hollering, I shoot out of the feathered tip of the breaker as it crashes thunderously behind me.

I'm back.

Ellie

'Fancy seeing you here.'

I close my eyes and smile when I hear his voice behind me, because despite everything, my grief and the way things ended between us, the sound of his voice still makes my heart soar. I suspect it always will.

The difference between the Sam who first came back here almost two months ago and the man standing there when I turn around is remarkable. Gone are the shadows on his face and in his eyes. His posture is taller, looser, as if a weight has been lifted off him. He's wearing shorts and a T-shirt and his hair is . . . wet?

'Late shower?' I ask.

He smiles. 'Early swim. Well, surf, actually.'

My eyebrows shoot up. 'I didn't think you surfed any more.'

'I didn't think I did either, but I figured it was about time I got back out there.'

'How was it?'

'Honestly? Incredible.' He runs one hand through his hair. 'I can't believe I went without it for so long.'

'Neither can I.'

He looks down at something he's holding in his other hand. I realise immediately what it is and tighten my grip on the envelope in my own hand. We're here for the same reason.

'I think,' he says, 'it was just too painful. Surfing, I mean. It reminded me too much of my grandfather.' He lifts his chin and stares at me intensely. 'And it reminded me of you.'

'I can understand why you'd want to forget.'

He shakes his head. 'I never wanted to forget you, Ellie. But it was easier to pretend that part of my life was over for good. It was the only way I could let go of my anger and move on.'

'I'll always regret that I believed Logan.'

He shrugs. 'He's a pretty good liar.'

'Just so we're clear, it doesn't mean I didn't believe you too. It's not quite as black and white as that. I *wanted* to support you, but there was just no proof.'

'I know. If I wasn't such a hot-headed teenager and had stuck around, it wouldn't have taken me a decade to understand that you were just trying to be a good friend to everyone.'

I nod. 'Peacemaker. That was me.'

'Was?'

'I no longer care so much about trying to make sure everyone else is happy. Not after finding out that Logan and the guys were lying all along, and that Chloe cared more about her husband's reputation than the truth coming out.'

'Are you . . . ?'

370

'Still friends? Yeah, we are, though things are a little strained between us at the moment. A bit of space is going to do us good, but she's always going to be part of my life.'

'Space?'

I take a deep breath. 'I'm leaving town in a few days.'

'Oh. Right.'

'Now that Nan's gone, there's no real reason for me to stick around, and after everything that's happened lately, I feel like I need to remind myself that there's more out there. It probably sounds silly.'

'No. Actually, it makes perfect sense.' He pauses for a moment. 'The house is sold. I signed an offer a few days ago.'

'Congratulations.'

'Thanks,' he says flatly.

'How are you feeling? I mean, I know it's what you came here to do, but . . .'

'Mixed emotions,' he admits. 'It's just a house at the end of the day, but my grandparents were very happy there. I've kept a few little things, and the rest of it I've donated to a charity shop. The new owners are a family, two teenage sons. I just hope they have better luck in this town than I did.'

'I'm sorry your life was so miserable here,' I shoot back.

'That's not what I meant. I'll never regret coming here, because it brought me to you. It's the rest of it I could have done without.' He gestures to the envelope in my hands. 'So is that . . . ?'

I run my fingers over the smooth paper. 'I couldn't leave without saying goodbye.'

He frowns. 'Seriously? After everything that's happened

between us, you were going to say goodbye in a letter?'

'I suppose that's a shopping list *you're* holding, is it?' I retort.

He holds it up. 'This? No, it's not a shopping list. It's for you.'

'What does it say?'

'Why don't you read it and find out.'

'I'm not sure I want to.'

'Why, what do you think it might say?'

I ty to keep my voice steady, but it wobbles anyway. 'That you regret what happened between us.'

He shakes his head emphatically, holding the letter out towards me. 'Just read it, please.'

I tuck my own envelope in the back pocket of my shorts and take it from him reluctantly. He stands there, waiting.

'You want me to read this in front of you?' I say, feeling as if my heart is beating at a million beats per minute inside my chest. 'That isn't how this normally works.'

'Quit stalling, Ellie.'

'I'm not. I just—'

'Ellie.'

'Fine,' I sigh. 'God, you can be so demanding.'

I unfold the letter.

Dear Daisy the Giraffe, aka DG (Dolphin Girl), aka my Ellie,

I know I can live without you in my life, because I've done it, and while it's lacking (no one to let me know when I'm being a dick, for example), it is possible.

But here's the thing, I don't want to. I don't want to live without you any more. I don't want to miss seeing your smile

372

first thing in the morning when I wake up, or last thing at night when I go to sleep. I don't want to go a single day without hearing you say my name, whether it's with love or because I've done something to annoy you (heads up, I'll probably annoy you often, because I love how cute you are when you're angry. Also, think of all the fun we'll have making up afterwards ...).

Ellie, I'm all in. I want all of it. All of you.

We both know that life isn't all sunshine and rainbows. Love isn't perfect, or easy. Sometimes we'll argue, and sometimes we probably won't appreciate each other. The truth is, love can sometimes even feel a little bit like hate. (For the record, I could never hate you.) My point is, even if we can't stand each other's taste in music and you insist on making me watch a rom com when I'd rather watch something with Bruce Willis in (and yes, I remember your feelings about <u>Die Hard</u>, but we'll have to agree to disagree on that one), none of that matters, because all I know is that I want to spend the rest of my life feeling the way I feel when I'm with you.

I don't have all the answers, or know exactly how this will work. But I can promise you one thing. I will never walk away from you again. No matter how tough things get, or what kind of misunderstandings we might have. As long as we stick together, we can figure out anything.

Someone once told me that we're all like little water particles in a surf wave, bumping into each other on our journey, transferring energy to each other but travelling our own path.

I want to travel a path with you, if you'll have me.

Just say the word.

Sam

She finishes reading with tears streaming from her eyes, and even though I'm pretty sure they're happy tears, panic still seizes my gut, because what if I'm wrong? What if she's decided it's all too hard and she's better off without me? After all, I haven't heard from her in weeks; she might have decided I'm more trouble than I'm worth.

'Well?' I ask, desperately trying not to sound as needy as I feel, and failing.

Wordlessly she reaches into her back pocket and pulls out her own letter, holding it out to me. I take it from her, suddenly understanding how she felt when she said she was scared to read mine. What if *she* is the one with regrets?

Dear Sam,
I choose you.
Only you.

Always you.

I love you more than I ever thought it possible to love another person. It's the kind of love that can be exhausting sometimes, but it's a love I'll never give up on, not in a million years, because living without you would be like living without the sun. It's the kind of love that, if you're lucky enough to come across it in your lifetime, you do anything you can to hang onto it. Because you know how rare it is.

I want to do life with you by my side. Watch the sun rise and set from the shores of a hundred beaches. I want to laugh at your stupid jokes under the Northern Lights, raise my glass with you and Santa in that bar in Ireland (if I can find it again and he hasn't drunk himself to death). Play footsie with you under the table in a back-street eatery we discover off the beaten path in Thailand. Make you pose for embarrassing selfies with me on top of mountains and in front of historical monuments and in the crystal-clear water of a Caribbean island. I want to do so many things with you that I worry we won't have enough years left to do them all.

I'm leaving Saturday, and I want you to come with me. I want to spend the rest of my life loving you with everything that is me.

I just hope you still want the same.

Ellie

I drop the letter to the sand and swiftly close the gap between us, cupping her face in my hands and wiping her cheeks free from tears with my thumbs.

'Are you kidding me?' I say breathlessly. 'There's nothing I want more in the world.'

She half laughs, half sobs. 'You have no idea how happy I am to hear that.'

I have been lucky enough in my life to fall in love with two incredible women, for different reasons. And just as I loved Mei not realising that a part of me had never stopped loving Ellie, I can love Ellie now knowing that a part of my heart will always belong to Mei.

I kiss her with everything I have. All the love I feel for her, the fear I had that I might have lost her. And all the hope I have for the future. *Our* future.

My best friend and me.

Acknowledgements

Where to start? I'm so grateful to so many people. All my friends and family. Especially Mum, Dad, Kerrie, Rob and Ange. Each and every one of you contribute in some way to the books I write. Whether it's through your support and encouragement, buying my books, recommending my books, lending an ear when I'm having a crisis of confidence or answering my weird (and occasionally inappropriate) research questions. I have so many friends (online and in the real world) and family to thank that I'm scared if I list you all by name I might forget someone. So instead I'll just remind you that you know who you are, and I love you.

They say write what you know, and if there's anything I know well it's teenage angst, unrequited crushes and what it's like to have the very best of Best Friends. I've been blessed to have had many throughout the various stages of my life. Kelly Thompson, Bonnie Whitaker, Deb Martin, Brian Willers, Tash Morrissey, Bryce Donnellan, Gilda Galluzzo Seager, Emma Green, Emily Ciravolo, Rochelle Gibbs, Lorraine Tipene, Marika Pollard and

Sarah Brown, you guys spring to mind. Most of you I'm still in contact with, but unfortunately sometimes friendships don't last. Still, I'll always carry the memory of you and our adventures together with me like a comfort blanket for my soul. Writing this book about best friends, both as teenagers and then as adults, brought back so many memories of my times with you guys. Man, we had some fun. And while I hope my kids are as blessed as I was to have best friends like you, I hope to God they don't get up to any of the stuff we used to. I'm looking at you in particular, Deb.

Thanks as always to my wonderful and clever agent, Vicki Marsdon. For always cheering me on, keeping it real and reminding me that the best is yet to come.

Thanks to my editor, Becky, and the team at Piatkus UK for all your hard work, patience and your belief in me. Thanks to the team here at Hachette NZ, and to Rebecca at Paper Plus in Te Awamutu for always being excited about whatever I'm working on.

Thanks to my husband, Karl, and our gorgeous, sweet, kind and funny kids, Holly, Willow and Leo. You guys believe in me so much that I couldn't quit even if I wanted to. I'll never forget how excited you were when you googled me and I came up. Mum must be famous if she's on Google!

And of course, my eternal gratitude and thanks to you guys, the readers. When writing gets too lonely and I post into the void on social media and get all your excited, encouraging messages back, it reminds me why I do this. Thank you for all your messages and comments, your shares and posts. Whether you're one of the quiet ones, or the ones who are always telling me to hurry up and write the next book, thank you. You guys are the best.